When Hoopoes go to Heaven

GAILE PARKIN

CORVUS

First published in Great Britain in 2012 by Corvus,
an imprint of Atlantic Books Ltd.

This paperback edition published in Great Britain in 2012 by Corvus,
an imprint of Atlantic Books Ltd.

3 5 7 9 10 8 6 4

A CIP catalogue record for this book is available
from the British Library.

Paperback ISBN: 978 0 85789 411 3
OME ISBN: 978 0 85789 712 1
E-book ISBN: 978 0 85789 410 6

Printed in Italy by 🐝 Grafica Veneta

Corvus
An imprint of Atlantic Books Ltd
Ormond House
26–27 Boswell Street
London WC1N 3JZ

www.corvus-books.co.uk

In memory of Huwi,

brave warrior to the end.

ONE

THINGS THAT SEEMED REAL COULD SOMETIMES BE just pretend, and things that seemed just pretend could sometimes be real. It was hard to keep that in your mind all the time, especially when you were still small. But it was important to try, because if you didn't you could easily get confused. You could even get an accident, like the tiny bird he held in his small hands now. It had thought it was flying through sky, but it had flown into a sheet of glass instead, a windowpane that was showing it just a picture of the sky.

The bird was completely still. Its beak was open and its wide eyes didn't blink. He examined it carefully, searching with a gentle finger for any signs of damage under the soft yellow and black of its feathers. Finding none, he slid his back slowly down the outside wall of the house until he reached the ground where he could squat steadily without tipping over. Then he cradled the bird in his left hand, freeing his right to search in the pocket of his shorts for the precious brown bottle of rescue medicine. Without taking his eyes off the bird, he shifted his knees apart and placed the small bottle between his bare feet, holding it tight there so that his hand could unscrew its top, giving the rubber teat on it a squeeze before lifting it.

A quick glance at the glass dropper attached to the top reminded him that there wasn't much of the healing liquid left: he must remember to ask Auntie Rachel for some more next time he was at the other house.

Very carefully, he squeezed a drop into the little bird's open beak, watching it swallow before squeezing in another. Two drops should be enough. It was a young bird, not yet fully grown into its adult feathers, but unmistakably one of the weavers that built their nests near the dam further up the hill.

Replacing the top of the medicine bottle, he slipped it back into his pocket as he pushed himself up the wall until he was standing again. The bird blinked. Soon it would be ready to come back to itself after its sudden, painful shock.

Carrying it a little way away from the wall, he bent and placed it gently on the grass, talking to it softly as he settled down on the grass himself to keep an eye on it while he waited patiently for it to recover enough to fly back up the hill to its family. The movement of a butterfly flitting nearby caught his attention. It was one of his favourites: an African monarch, with wings somewhere between orange and brown, edged in black with bold white spots.

Monarch was another way of saying king; he knew that because there was a king here where they were living now on account of Baba's new job, and people were always saying that this king, Mswati III, was Africa's last absolute monarch. He wasn't entirely sure what an *absolute* monarch was, but when people said *absolutely*, what they meant was *definitely* or *completely*, so he guessed that there was simply no doubt about Mswati being the king.

On his family's very first day here in Swaziland, when they were still on the road in Baba's red Microbus with the trailer behind, on their way from Tanzania to their new home here near the foot of the Malagwane Hill, they had heard loud sirens screaming at them, and Baba had copied the cars in front and pulled off the tar road onto the dusty verge. First some motorbikes, then five, six, seven, eight big back shiny cars had sped past them with blue lights flashing. Later, people had told them that was the king, and if the king was ever on the road you had to get out of the way. Which pretty much showed that Mswati was absolutely the king and nobody must doubt it.

The little bird blinked again, and then again, turning its head from side to side as if to take in the garden around it.

To his own eyes, it was the most beautiful garden in the whole entire world – although, in truth, he knew that he would have found any garden at all beautiful after the bare earth of the compound in Kigali where they had lived last year on account of Baba's old job. He and his younger brothers would sometimes go from that compound to a house down the road where two Indian boys from their school lived. There was a garden there, but it was nothing like this one here on the Malagwane Hill. While his brothers had played football – or, even more boring, cricket – with Rajesh and Kamal, he had done his best to make friends with a crow that lived in that garden. There hadn't been that many other birds there, not like all the kinds here in Swaziland. But nearly every time that crow had come close, Mama-Rajesh had run out of the house to chase it away, telling him that birds had too many germs. There had also been a rat living in that garden, brown with beautiful dark eyes ringed in black just like Mama-Rajesh's. But he had never said.

Nobody bothered him in the garden here. How excited he had been to see it!

His family had gone from Kigali in Rwanda to Bukoba in Tanzania, Mama and Baba's home town on the shores of Lake Victoria, to spend Christmas with aunties, uncles and cousins before driving all the way to Dar es Salaam, where Baba needed to check on the family's house. Other people were living in their house on account of Baba being away from his job at the university there, so the Tungarazas had stayed with friends in Dar for the short time it had taken Baba to find this house for them in Swaziland.

When they had all arrived here late in January – nearly three months ago now – the garden had been green and lush, with flowers of all colours shining in it like jewels, and birds and butterflies flitting through it like glitter. *Eh*, it had looked so beautiful!

The bird sitting on the grass ruffled its feathers, gave a little shiver, and stretched its wings out slowly as if to check that nothing was broken. A sudden sound from behind the hedge startled it, and in an instant it was gone.

He smiled, watching its strong, quick flight for a moment before turning his attention to the sound. Hoping to hear it again, he crawled quietly but excitedly on his hands and knees towards the hedge of yesterday, today and tomorrow bushes with their flowers of purple, lilac and white.

When the scream first came, he was lying on his stomach, his neck twisted to the side, his right cheek flat against the grass. He paid the scream little attention and continued to listen instead for the sound that had flattened him to the ground, watching the base of the hedge for the slightest movement.

At last the sound came again from a little further back: a liquid *gloop-gloop-gloop*, like water being poured from a bottle with a narrow neck. And then the bird with the water-bottle call hopped from behind a stem, showing him a brief flash of white breast beneath its black hood and cinnamon wings before disappearing again amongst the undergrowth.

He smiled, ignoring the second scream, thrilled to have seen the shy bird for the first time ever.

'*Benedict!*'

It was Mama's voice now, and he could not – would not – ignore it. Scrambling to his feet, he dusted the grass and soil from his T-shirt and shorts as he hurried towards the house.

Mama stood on the bricked veranda, her plastic icing syringe in her right hand, her left hand on her hip. He felt bad: he had interrupted her work.

'*Eh!* Did you not hear your sisters?'

'Sorry, Mama, I was looking for something.' He could hear the girls whimpering inside now.

'And did you find it?'

He smiled proudly. 'Yes! A special kind of bird that you *never* see. *Never*. But I saw it, Mama! It was—'

'Benedict!' His eldest sister Grace appeared in the wide opening of the sliding glass doorway that led from the house onto the large veranda. The blue plastic sieve that she carried told him all that he needed to know.

In the bathroom, their sister Faith sniffed loudly as she hopped from foot to foot, her tearful eyes fixed on the bathtub where a tadpole less than two centimetres long wriggled tiredly in the shallow water.

Good. This one was still alive.

'I need the jar,' he said to Grace, who went to fetch the special one from the kitchen, the one with the red nail-polish X on its lid and another on its side so that it could never, ever be confused with any other empty jar in the kitchen cupboard. He half-filled it from the cold tap at the basin, then bent to scoop up the tadpole in the special blue plastic sieve that could never, ever be confused with either of the larger metal sieves that Mama used for making her cakes. As he tipped the tadpole from the sieve into the jar, Faith let out a little scream, and Grace let out another as he handed her the dripping sieve.

Eh! Girls? Uh-uh, he thought, tightening the lid on the jar.

He was a little taller now than Faith, whose solid, chubby body reminded him just slightly – and only sometimes – of a baby hippopotamus, while Grace, tall and long like a young giraffe, towered over him. They were always screaming for him to come and save them from something harmless that wriggled or scuttled or slithered. But he didn't mind, really. It made him feel big and important, and he didn't know what else could make him feel important when his age put him right in the middle of five siblings, or what else could make him feel big when he had two older sisters who more or less ignored him.

It had been different before, back when he, Grace and Moses were still living with their first mama and baba in Mwanza, and even when they had first started living with Mama and Baba in Dar. Grace had spent more time with him back then, back when she was still his only big sister. But ever since the two families had joined and Faith and Daniel had also come to stay, his two big sisters only had time for each other. Neither of them really bothered with him much, except at times like this.

Rescuing gave him a special part to play in the family: if anybody ever needed rescuing, Benedict was their man. Okay, he was their boy – he was only just ten – but he felt like a man when he was rescuing them. Sometimes he imagined himself in the special uniform of a rescuer, like a fireman or a paramedic, running towards his family in slow motion like on TV, saving them from a huge natural disaster or a war or an evil, man-eating monster.

He showed the tadpole to Mama.

'Well done, *shujaa wangu!*' she said, calling him her hero in Swahili, the language they spoke when they were at home in Tanzania.

He beamed. Mama gave him her smile that said she was proud of him but he mustn't bring what he had any closer.

She was sitting at the far end of the large dining table, putting the finishing touches to a cake for one of the ladies who worked with Baba at the ministry. That lady's brothers and sisters lived scattered throughout all four of Swaziland's regions, and every Easter they all got together. This Easter it was the turn of Baba's colleague to have them at her house in Mbabane, here in the Hhohho region.

Mama's cake for them looked like a big, round basket woven in strips of blue and green, filled with Easter eggs in a mix of brilliant colours.

'It's beautiful, Mama! Many more orders are going to come.'

Mama was piping bright patterns on to the eggs. '*Eh!* I hope so.'

'When they see it, Mama! When they taste it!'

The sigh that came out of Mama was almost as loud as the sigh of steam that Benedict could hear from Titi's iron in the kitchen. Putting down her icing syringe, Mama pulled at the neck of her T-shirt to reach for one of the tissues that she kept tucked into her underwear, then she took off her glasses and began to polish the lenses. 'When the first order came, that was what we said.' She shook her head as she spoke. 'We said people will see how beautiful my cakes are. We said people will taste how delicious they are, and the orders will come.' She put her glasses back on and picked up her syringe again. 'But that was a long time ago, Benedict. Three months! And this is only order number five.'

Putting his tadpole jar down on the table, Benedict pulled out one of the chairs and perched on the edge of it. 'It will get better, Mama. When we first came here and we were worried about making new friends, remember, Mama?'

'Uh-huh.' Mama piped some bright pink on to chocolate brown.

'You and Baba, you told us all just give it time. And we gave it time, and now we have friends. All of us, Mama, even me. If you just give it some time, your business will get customers.'

Mama stopped piping and looked up at him with a smile. Then she saw the tadpole jar on the table. '*Eh!* Benedict!'

Scrambling to his feet, he scooped up the jar. 'Sorry, Mama.'

She was telling him to put his shoes on before he dealt with the tadpole when her cell-phone rang. Adjusting her glasses, she looked at the small screen.

'Oh, please let this be a customer,' she said, half to herself and half to Benedict. It was what she always said these days when she didn't recognise the number. Shooing him away with her hand, she pressed the button to answer and put the phone to her ear, saying in her most professional voice, 'Good afternoon, Angel Tungaraza speaking.'

Briefly showing the tadpole to Titi as she ironed one of his sisters' school uniforms, Benedict left the house through the kitchen door, sitting on the step to slip his bare feet into his old pair of shoes that he kept out there. As he began to push his way through the trees and bushes on his way up the slope of the hill, he held the jar containing the tadpole in one hand and crossed the fingers of the other, hoping that the person who had phoned Mama was indeed a customer. He couldn't help feeling that it was his fault that her cake business wasn't doing so well here.

Okay, it wasn't *all* his fault; there were other reasons, too. Number one, Swaziland wasn't like Rwanda where there had been lots of business for Mama. Here there were quite a few shops that sold cakes, and Swazis were already used to buying their cakes from there. Number two, not so many people knew about Mama's cakes because she had to make them in secret. The law said that if you were married to somebody who had come from outside Swaziland to work here, you weren't allowed to work here yourself.

Reason number three was something Benedict already knew about from school. If you came here from another country in Africa, you were called a *shangaan* or a *kwerekwere*, and those weren't nice things to be because it meant that you were going to steal jobs from Swazis. Lots of people didn't want to order a cake from a *shangaan* or a *kwerekwere*; they wanted to give their money to Swazis instead.

But it was reason number four that ate at him. The house where they were living, which Baba had found for them when he had flown here for two weeks before going back home to Tanzania to bring the family in the red Microbus with the trailer behind; this house that Benedict loved so much on account of its garden full of birds and butterflies, its forest on the slope above and its dairy cows on the slope below; this house Baba had chosen especially for him. And this house was out of the way – very close to Mbabane, the capital city where Baba worked, but on the slopes of the Malagwane Hill that led down from the capital towards the Ezulwini Valley, and off the highway on a small road that buses or taxis never needed to take. So if you didn't have your own car or bicycle, or if you were too lazy for a long walk, it wasn't easy for you to get to the house to order a cake from Mama.

Baba had told the family that he had chosen the house because it was better not to live right in Mbabane, where there was a lot of crime because people didn't have jobs. But when nobody else was listening, Baba had told Benedict that he had chosen the house especially for him.

Benedict uncrossed the fingers that were hoping for a customer for Mama, and used that hand to balance himself against the big silver water-tank for the Tungarazas' house as he stepped over the pipe that connected it to the water-tank for the other house. Then he followed another pipe where it snaked up the hill through the undergrowth, all the way up to where the trees gave way to grasses and the ground flattened out onto a plateau.

The minute he emerged from the trees, the sounds of the traffic on the Malagwane Hill reached him: trucks heavy with logs from pine forest plantations shifting gears and applying brakes on the steep slope down into the valley; buses heavy with people straining to make it up the steep slope to the capital. People said that the hill was much safer now on account of the brand new highway that had two lanes for going up and another two for coming down. They said that before, when there used to be just one lane in each direction, there were so many accidents that the *Guinness Book of World Records* had called the Malagwane Hill the most dangerous stretch of road in the whole entire world. Mama said it was because drivers were impatient, but Baba said it was because drivers were drunk.

The ground near the edge of the plateau was wet and muddy. The small dam there that supplied water to the two houses was where the dairy cows came to drink when they were grazing on the pasture just the beyond the clump of trees, and Benedict could see that they had been drinking at this edge of the dam earlier that day: the mud that was now sucking at his shoes was patterned with hoof-prints and splattered with large rounds of fresh *kinyezi*.

Grace and Faith didn't know about the cows and their *kinyezi*, and Benedict wasn't going to tell. It was part of Titi's job of helping Mama with the house and the children to make sure that every drop of water they drank had been boiled for long enough to kill any germs, so nobody was going to get sick. But if his sisters ever found out that cows and cow-*kinyezi* had been in their bathwater, there would be a lot more screaming than Benedict could ever rescue the family from.

11

As he squatted at the edge of the water and emptied the tadpole out of the jar, he wondered how long it was going to take Grace and Faith to understand that a tadpole was a baby frog that hadn't yet lost its tail and grown its legs, and to realise that if a tadpole sometimes slipped into the pipe that led to the water-tank that led to the house, it had to mean that they were sharing their bathwater with frogs. *Eh*, the frogs made so much noise at night! Where did his sisters think the frogs lived?

On the plateau, the pipes leading to the two water-tanks were covered over by cement to protect them from the cows' hooves, until they met in a thicker pipe that travelled under the water towards the centre of the dam, where there was a pump for just in case. Just in case hadn't happened yet on account of good rains, but if it did happen, there was a narrow wooden bridge that led to the pump, and a person could walk to the end of that bridge and switch the pump on.

Benedict had wanted to walk to the end himself, but much to his shame, he hadn't been able to manage even a single step. There were gaps between the planks of wood, small gaps, gaps big enough for only a finger to slip through, but gaps that Benedict could imagine his whole body slipping through and being lost forever. *Eh!* He knew it was impossible, he knew that imagining such a thing made him seem such a very small boy, but still his stomach knotted itself in fear whenever he thought of trying again.

Right at the bottom of the hill, where the long driveway began at the dairy farm buildings before winding its way up towards the other house and the Tungarazas', there was a cattle-grid across the ground – smooth metal strips with gaps in between – that the cows were afraid to cross. Benedict didn't know if they worried that they might fall through the gaps, but it kept them from wandering off the property and into the road where they might get an accident. What he did know, without even trying, was that it would keep him on the property, too: while going over it in a vehicle held no fear for him, he wouldn't be able to cross it on foot.

Perhaps the gaps in the bridge to the middle of the dam were to keep the cows off it, too.

A low rumble of distant thunder made something move in the long grass far to the right of the dam, and he saw a skinny young man stand up. He must have been squatting there all the time, so quiet and still that Benedict hadn't noticed him. It was Petros, who helped with the cows and lived at the dairy below the other house. The Tungaraza children weren't supposed to talk to Petros because he smoked a lot – cigarettes with a funny smell that he made for himself – and people said that he wasn't quite right in his head.

Benedict had never spoken to Petros, but he liked him anyway. He liked the way Petros could be still enough to make himself invisible. He had once seen him standing next to the cowshed – only, even though he had been looking right at the cowshed, he hadn't seen him at all. Not until Petros had raised his hand to give a small wave of hello. Petros had a way of blending in to wherever he was so that nobody noticed him, just like a chameleon did, and that was something that Benedict sometimes tried to do himself. If you blended in, nobody noticed that you didn't belong.

Petros gave him a small wave now, and Benedict stood up from the water's edge to return it. Then Petros made a loud, whooping, whistling noise that brought his dog and a number of cows from the field beyond the trees. Benedict watched as the cows ambled slowly towards Petros's repeated call, their udders heavy with milk, speeding up only as a louder, closer clap of thunder rumbled through the darkening sky. When Petros was sure that the full count of cows was there, he gave Benedict another small wave before taking the cows to the far end of the clearing and leading them, with his dog, along their well-trodden path through the trees to the shed below the other house.

Benedict headed home himself, down his own path. Mama didn't want the children to be out when a storm was on its way, and Benedict knew that she was right to worry. Daniel and Moses, his two younger brothers, were in the same class at school, and a girl in their class had lost her mother and her baby sister to lightning just last month. The mother had been carrying her baby on her back when lightning had struck them, and now they were both late, and the girl from his brothers' class had never had a father, so now she'd gone to live in Siteki with her uncle.

Safely inside when it came, Benedict found the storm glorious. Deafening thunder rattled the tin roof of the house, making all of them stop what they were doing to cover their ears with their hands, and lightning stabbed at the sky's darkness, tearing it open with light. Rain pounded against the tightly-shut windows at the back of the house as though it was desperate to be let in to shelter from itself, and Mama and Titi, steaming up the kitchen with the evening's cooking, pushed a towel up against the small gap between the door and the floor to stop it from finding its way in underneath.

After the storm passed, the air felt cool and fresh – almost relieved – as if it had picked itself up after something really bad had happened to it, and was ready to start again.

They were all in their usual places after a delicious supper of stewed goat served with sweet potatoes and pumpkin leaves: the girls and the two younger boys on the two couches in front of the TV, Mama and Baba talking at the far end of the dining table, and Benedict between the children and the grown-ups, sitting on a big cushion on the floor under the lamp next to the bookshelf, his back up against the closed front door and a book open in his lap.

The bookshelf was another thing he loved about this house. It was something completely new. Baba was an educated somebody, he was Dr Pius Tungaraza, but any books he had were about his work so he kept them at his office; and Mama always said she wasn't an educated somebody who read books. Every second Saturday the children went to the public library in Mbabane, but borrowing and returning books was just not the same as having a bookshelf full of books to choose from at home. They weren't the Tungarazas' books – they belonged to the house like all the furniture and the pots and plates and sheets and towels – but Benedict could read them whenever he wanted. Amongst them was a whole entire set of encyclopaedias! Okay, not quite a whole entire set. Somebody had stolen XYZ so he could learn only as far as W. But still.

That night he was paging through the book about all the birds you could see in southern Africa, smiling to himself as

15

he saw the picture of the shy Burchell's coucal, the bird with
the water-bottle call that he had managed to see in the garden
that afternoon, so he was already smiling when he looked up
as Titi came in from cleaning up in the kitchen. She smiled
back at him before quietly taking her place next to Grace on
the couch. His attention distracted from the book, he tuned in
to what Mama and Baba were talking about.

'Only five cakes this whole time! *Five!*'

'I know, Angel, but—'

'It's my *business*, Pius. I'm a businesswoman, a professional
somebody. Baking cakes is what I do. It's how I contribute to
the family.'

'I know that, Angel.'

'But it's not just that I'm not contributing. What am I
supposed to be doing with all this time on my hands? It's not
like I have to do all the housework myself.'

'I know.'

'I'm bored, Pius! Bored!'

'Well—'

'*Eh!* Boredom is a terrible thing! Terrible.' She shook her
head. 'Uh-uh-uh.'

'Well...' Baba took a deep breath. 'Maybe you could... learn
something new?'

Benedict knew that Baba would suggest learning something
new. He had heard him suggesting it to lots of other people. If
somebody was unhappy, Baba suggested learning something
new. If somebody wasn't getting very far in life, Baba suggested learning something new. Learning something new was
Baba's answer to almost any problem.

'*Eh! Me?*' Mama put her hand to her chest. 'You know I'm

not an educated somebody, Pius. I'm not somebody who reads books.'

Benedict smiled, moving his eyes down to the bird book so that neither of them would notice that he was listening.

'Books are not the only way to learn, Angel.'

'What do you mean?'

'Well... haven't you taught other ladies how to bake cakes?'

'Yes.'

'And did they need a book to learn how?'

'No.'

'You see?'

'What? What are you saying? That I must learn something that doesn't take books? That I must learn how to milk cows? Because what else am I going to learn here on this farm?'

Baba was quiet for a long time, and Benedict knew that he was thinking. It was Mama who spoke next, and it sounded like she had been thinking, too.

'Maybe I could manage the downhill walk to the highway to catch a minibus taxi, then I could get to some kind of class in Mbabane. Those taxis are dangerous... overloaded... not looked after. But not *all* of them crash! But, *eh*, I don't know about the long uphill walk up the driveway to get home again...'

'*Eh!* Angel!' Baba sounded like he'd just had a very good idea.

'What?'

'Why didn't I think of this before?'

'What?'

'You could learn to drive!'

'*Eh?*'

'Yes! It's perfect!'

'*Eh!*'

'I mean, I have the Corolla that comes with the job, the Microbus just sits here in the garage during the week, and you just sit here at home without your business keeping you busy—'

'But am I not too old?'

'What are you talking about? Your cousin Geraldine learned to drive after her husband became late, and she's even older than you are.'

'That's true. I'm younger than Geraldine.'

'I really think it's the perfect solution, Angel. You won't be bored if you're learning a new skill!'

'But Pius, how would we pay for lessons? In case you've forgotten, we have five children to feed. *Five!* And my business is making such a small contribution now!'

'We'll find a way to be okay, Angel.' The sudden softness in Baba's voice made Benedict look up from his book, and he saw Baba reaching across the table for Mama's hand. 'We always do.'

Mama squeezed Baba's hand, then let go of it to pull at the neck of her T-shirt and reach for one of the tissues that she kept tucked into her underwear. She took off her glasses and wiped a tear from each eye.

'*Eh*, Pius! You've had such a wonderful idea.' She put her tissue back and squeezed Baba's hand again. 'Thank you! I'd love to try learning to drive!'

'It's settled then. What's the time?' Baba looked at his watch. '*Eh!* News!'

Baba got up, moved to one of the couches and began arguing with the children for the TV remote.

18

Benedict watched as Mama put her glasses back on. They looked at each other, and both of them smiled their widest smiles.

Later that night, Benedict lay fast asleep in the bedroom he shared with Daniel and Moses, the two of them in a double bunk, Benedict in a bed of his own. In his dream, he knelt on top of the silver water-tank behind the house, looking like he belonged there because his whole body was the exact same shiny silver colour. Holding Mama's icing syringe over a hole in the top of the tank, he pulled back the plunger so that the syringe filled with hundreds of little black tadpoles. Then, turning with the syringe towards the dam, he pushed the plunger in, shooting them all in a huge arc that landed them safely in the water. Lined up on the edge of the dam, the tadpoles' parents croaked their loud thanks, while round the base of the water-tank his sisters and some of the girls from school threw gold stars and glitter up at him, calling his name.

Then they started pushing at one another, and the water-tank began to rock, and the gold stars and glitter turned into a bright light in his face.

And then he was awake, and Titi was standing next to his bed with the torch, shaking his shoulder.

'*Benedict!*' she hissed.

'*Eh?*'

'*Chura,*' she said softly in Swahili, maybe because a language not your own doesn't come easily in the middle of the night, or maybe because her English lessons at the other house hadn't yet taught her the word.

'*Wapi?* Where?'

Crawling sleepily out of his bed, he followed her silently into the bedroom she shared with his sisters, which was the very worst place in the whole entire world for a frog to be. His sisters lay fast asleep, unaware of how close they were to screaming.

Titi led him to the window, where she pulled aside one of the curtains very slowly and quietly, and shone the torch directly at the glass.

Benedict couldn't help breathing in loudly in surprise and delight, and Titi had to nudge him to remind him to be quiet.

Stuck to the outside of the glass by the tiny sticky discs on its feet was a small tree frog about the length of one of Benedict's fingers.

'*Eh!*' His voice was barely a whisper.

'*Shh!*'

Almost silently, by the light of just the torch, they made their way into the lounge. To open the big glass sliding door leading onto the veranda would have made too much noise, so they turned the key quietly in the lock on the front door, just next to the bookshelf on whose top sat the small basket where Baba put his car keys whenever he came home. In there was the key to the security gate on the other side of the door. It made a loud click when Benedict unlocked it, and the two of them froze.

Just when they were sure that nobody had woken, the over-head light went on and Baba filled the entrance to the passageway.

'What's going on?' His voice was a harsh whisper.

Reluctant to meet his eyes, Benedict concentrated on Baba's

round middle, where a button on his pyjama top was straining to keep the two sides of it together.

'Sorry, Baba. There's a frog.' He kept his voice to a whisper.

'A frog? In here?' Baba scanned the floor.

'Outside, Uncle,' whispered Titi.

'Outside? But that is where a frog belongs!'

'A tree frog, Baba.'

'I see. And does a tree not belong outside, too?'

'It's on the window, Baba.'

'*Eh!* On the outside of the window?'

Titi and Benedict nodded.

'But what are you planning to do? Bring it inside?'

Benedict shook his head and opened his mouth to say no, but Baba went on.

'The logical thing to do, the *right* thing to do, is just to leave it alone. Surely!'

'It's the window of the girls' room, Baba.'

Benedict could see from Baba's face that he was now beginning to understand.

'I see. Can it get inside there?'

Benedict nodded. The windows were barred against possible intruders, but for the sake of extra safety the larger, lower windows remained shut at night, and just the smaller ones at the top were left open for air. While they were way too high for the average frog, a climbing tree frog could easily get in.

'It woke me, Uncle. *Dwah!* against the glass.'

'It could wake them, too.'

Rolling his eyes, Baba led the way out through the front door and round to the wide veranda, which was flooded in moonlight. He made as if to wait there, folding his arms around himself against the cool evening air, but Titi handed him the torch and waited there herself. She was somewhere in her early twenties – at least, that's what they all guessed – but Benedict knew that when it came to frogs, girls remained girls no matter how many birthdays they had.

Passing the boys' room quietly, Benedict and Baba moved towards the window of the girls' room that bore a stud like one of the shiny jewels at the neck of Mama's smooth satin dress.

The enormous orange eyes of the frog seemed hypnotised by the light of the torch. It barely struggled at all as Benedict detached it gently from the glass and held it in the palm of his hand, admiring the beauty of its delicate little body. Its colours looked like peanut sauce poured over spinach with raggedy strips of dark green spinach showing through.

He turned his hand to look at the creature from the back, and the instant the torchlight was no longer in its over-sized eyes, it seemed to remember itself. It leapt off his hand into the grass and was gone.

Back in his bed after Titi had made him wash his hands in the kitchen to avoid making a noise in the bathroom, Benedict thought about the beautiful little frog that had wanted to come in from the outside, in to where it didn't belong. Had it really been trying to get in, or had the moonlight made a pretend garden in the glass, a garden that the frog had thought it could hop through to get to somewhere else? Way past the stage of being a tadpole, it was still very small. Was it impatient to be big in the same way that Benedict was? Did tadpoles all come from their eggs at the same time, or was there always one male that came out sooner than the others, one that was always going to be responsible for all the others on account of being the eldest? Benedict didn't know, but he would look for some answers in one of the books on the bookshelf.

He thought about who he could tell about the frog. Not Mama or his sisters, for sure; and his brothers would listen with only half of their attention, longing to get on with kicking their ball around. Sifiso and Giveness at school, maybe. But they would be less interested in the frog itself and more interested in the part about trying to sneak out of the house in the middle of the night.

No, he was going to have to wait until he could tell Uncle Enock, at the other house.

TWO

GIVENESS WAS PEELING THE PAPER AWAY FROM HIS chocolate cupcake iced in bright green. '*Eish*,' he declared, 'I wish my aunt could bake like your mom!'

'Mm,' agreed Sifiso, whose mouth was full.

'She does lovely birthday cakes,' Benedict reminded them, 'and cakes for any kind of party you can imagine.'

The three sat alone in the shadow cast by one of the rows of classrooms. The cool air of early May meant it wasn't the warmest place to sit, but if Sifiso had been in the school's sunny yard on the other side of the classrooms, the children who spent their break there would have kicked a ball at him and laughed at his chubby uselessness in trying to kick it back, and they would have called him Thifitho on account of his lisp. And if Giveness had been there, he would have had to be sheltering himself under his umbrella on account of his skin being pink like Auntie Rachel at the other house, only he wasn't a *Mzungu* like Auntie Rachel, he was a Swazi and his skin was supposed to be brown like Benedict's, only God had made a mistake.

Benedict had been pretty sure that God never made mistakes, but he had checked it with Mama and Baba after supper one night.

24

'How can God make a mistake when He's all-powerful?' Mama had asked.

'Don't you make the mistake of confusing power with competence,' Baba had said, his finger wagging a warning at Mama. 'Powerful men are perfectly capable of making mistakes, and powerful nations—'

'We're not talking about men or nations, Pius. We're talking about God. And God does not make mistakes.'

Baba had looked at Benedict and raised his hands as if to say there was no arguing with Mama on that point, and then he had asked him why he was asking.

'Because when Giveness was born pink and he never turned brown, his mother said she didn't want to raise one of God's mistakes, and she gave him to her sister.'

'*Eh!*'

'Uh-uh-uh!'

'She went away to South Africa and she never came back.'

'Ooh, that was *her* mistake, Benedict. His mother's.'

'He's pink because his mother made a mistake?'

Baba had sighed deeply and looked at his watch, then he had said a lot of very big words about how sometimes things went wrong in science and biology and about how an accident wasn't the same thing as a mistake, and *eh!* it was time for news.

Benedict had thought about it all the way through news, stopping only to admire the footage of the king dressed up as Ngwenyama the lion with his huge mane of black ostrich feathers and his shawl of the long, hairy ends of cows' tails.

There were two ways of looking at it, he thought. Number one, God had made everything, including science and biology.

And if there could be accidents in science and biology, didn't that mean that God had made a mistake when he made them?

Number two, they sang in church that God made all things wise and wonderful. But Giveness's mother was neither wise nor wonderful. Did that mean that God had made a mistake when he made her, or did it mean that somebody else had made her? *Eh!* Benedict knew from Father's sermons at Mater Dolorosa exactly who that somebody else was! But God would never have let Satan make a person when it was His own job to do it. No. He was all-powerful.

So either way Benedict looked at it, God must have made some kind of mistake with Giveness. But not all mistakes were entirely bad. Okay, some children were mean to Giveness and he had to stay out of the sun, but he was kind to Benedict even though Benedict was a *kwerekwere*, and he was clever enough and patient enough to help Sifiso with his maths.

'Chocolate'th my betht,' said Sifiso, licking the paper casing to get at every last crumb.

'Mine's vanilla,' said Giveness, holding his pink arm next to Sifiso's brown.

All three of them giggled.

The lesson after break for their class was siSwati, which Sifiso preferred to call 'our language'. As a *kwerekwere* who wasn't going to be in Swaziland very long on account of Baba's contract being for just one year, Benedict was excused siSwati. Being excused meant he didn't have to write or pass any siSwati tests or exams, and when his class was doing siSwati he was supposed just to sit quietly and not disturb anybody. Miss Khumalo never expected him to be able to do more than join the chorus of greetings when she entered the classroom.

His brothers and sisters were happy enough to use the free lessons to go over some classwork or to read one of their books from the public library, but Benedict wanted to learn. If he didn't, how was he ever going to fit in? How was he going to belong?

He had tried following the lessons at first, but it was the fourth year of school and the fourth year of siSwati lessons for everybody else in the class, and most of them had in any case been speaking siSwati since they had first learned to speak. The textbook was just too difficult and Miss Khumalo spoke just too fast, so he hadn't been able to manage.

He had spoken to Baba, and Baba had come to see Mrs Dlamini, the principal, and together they had worked out a schedule of siSwati lessons in the first couple of grades that Benedict could attend when his own class was busy with siSwati. Mrs Dlamini had been happy enough to help, even though Baba hadn't brought her a plate of cupcakes as Mama had wanted him to.

The lessons for the younger children were easier to follow, though Benedict still struggled a bit sometimes on account of the textbooks being for children who already spoke siSwati at home, and on account of him being in different classes on different days so that nothing was really in sequence. But he was doing his best, which is what Mama said was all anybody could do, and the younger children were no longer laughing at him. Besides, he wasn't the only boy too big for their furniture: while some children didn't go to school at all, others had to wait until their parents could afford to pay or no longer needed them to work, so they were already big when they started.

After school, the Tungarazas and two of the children from the other house were on their way to the high school where Auntie Rachel would meet them, when two men walked past them carrying take-aways. The smells of hot chips and curry in their wake set Olga Mazibuko off, pulling at Grace who was holding her hand to make sure she walked safely on the road, and trying to get her closer to Mr Patel's little shop on the corner. None of the children had any money, and all of them knew that there would be a lovely tea waiting for them at home, but sometimes – if the shop wasn't busy, and if Mrs Patel saw them outside, and if Mr Patel wasn't there – they would be called in and given one or two chips each to nibble on.

But today Benedict wasn't interested in chips. His attention was drawn to a van parked on the other side of the road. Pale blue with white clouds painted on it, it had a sign in big dark-blue letters along its side reading *Ubuntu Funerals* and below that, in smaller green letters, *We bury the best*.

But it wasn't the van itself that Benedict was focusing on as he crossed the road carefully.

Caught up in the grid above the van's front bumper was what had been the most beautiful bird, about the size of a dove. In front of the van now, he squatted to examine it, admiring its body and head the colour of the cinnamon Mama sometimes put in her cakes, its high crest of cinnamon feathers tipped with black, and its wings patterned in black and white. The long, curved beak that it would have used for digging a meal of insects out of the ground was broken, the black of its eye completely still.

The little brown bottle of rescue medicine in Benedict's pocket would have been of no use at all.

'*Sawubona?*' said a voice somewhere above his head. 'Hello?'

He looked up. Peering round at him from behind the side of the van was a lady with a very confused expression on her face. Benedict stood up.

'*Yebo*. Hello,' he said with a smile, extending his hand. '*Ngingu* Benedict.'

They shook hands in the traditional grown-up way, shaking, then shifting their grip to clutch each other's thumb briefly before shaking again. Keeping her confused expression firmly in place, the lady examined him carefully.

'*Watalwaphi*, Benedict?'

'Tanzania.'

'Oh,' said the lady, as if coming from Tanzania explained everything, and she switched to English. 'And what are you doing to my van?'

'Look,' said Benedict, pointing at the bird and inviting her round from the side of the van to see. She was younger than Mama, with hips not quite as wide, dressed very smartly in a matching skirt and jacket.

'*Eish!*' Her hands rose to her face when she saw the bird, and she made tutting sounds with her tongue against the back of her teeth, just like the sound of a c in siSwati which you had to make by trying to pull a pretend seed out from between your top teeth with your tongue.

'It's a hoopoe,' he said.

'Is it late?'

'Mm.'

'*Eish!*' She clicked her tongue against the back of her teeth some more. 'Did I hit it?'

'You must have. It walks around on the ground looking for insects, so maybe something scared it and it started to fly off then it got an accident.'

'*Eish!*' It was a man's voice now, and they were joined by its tall owner, who carried two plastic containers of Mrs Patel's curry and rice, and two plastic spoons. 'When did we hit this?'

'I don't know. I didn't notice.'

'It's a hoopoe,' said Benedict.

'King Solomon's queen,' said the man.

'King Solomon's queen?'

'My grandfather used to talk about this bird. That crown that it wears,' the man pointed to the bird's crest with one of Mr Patel's plastic spoons, 'that was a gift from King Solomon.'

'*Eh!*'

'*Benedict!*' Grace was calling from the other side of the road, outside Mr Patel's shop.

'I have to go,' said Benedict, pausing for one last look at the bird. 'Will you bury it?' he asked.

'Bury a *bird*?' The lady's confused expression rushed back.

Benedict pointed to the van. 'Your sign says you bury the best.'

'That's true. But—'

'And this is King Solomon's queen.' Benedict knew that interrupting wasn't polite, but he could see that Grace and the other children were becoming impatient.

30

The tall man began to laugh. 'He's right, Zodwa! This bird is royalty! It deserves a good burial.'

Benedict called a goodbye as he crossed towards the others. '*Salani kahle!* Stay well!'

'*Hamba kahle!* Go well!' they called back, both of them laughing and shaking their heads as he gave them a wave from the other side of the road.

The children continued their walk to the high school, Olga Mazibuko quietly holding hands with Grace, who laughed with Faith about something that had happened that morning, and Fortune Mazibuko joining Moses and Daniel as they tussled for control of their football. Benedict hung back a little, thinking about the hoopoe. He had seen one or two in the garden, but he had never been so close to one. How beautiful it was! The brown of its body and the black and white of its wings were the same colours as an African monarch butterfly. A hoopoe was the queen of King Solomon! Imagine! That would be an interesting story to find somebody to tell.

He thought he might tell Auntie Rachel on the way home in her yellow Hi-Ace, but the two older Mazibuko children from the high school, Vusi and Innocence, wanted to sit up front so that they could try to persuade her to let them go to listen to a band at the weekend, and Grace and Faith wanted to sit close to the front so that they could listen to them trying.

So Benedict found himself seated near the back amongst the younger ones' chatter, thinking that as hard as it was to be one of five siblings, things could have been a lot worse. In addition to the four Mazibuko children in the yellow Hi-Ace, there were three more back at the other house who weren't yet old enough for school. Seven altogether. *Eh!*

But each one of the seven was lucky, on account of having been chosen by Auntie Rachel and Uncle Enock from all the other children whose first parents were late. Benedict's own first parents were late, the first parents he shared with his big sister Grace and his little brother Moses. Faith and Daniel's first parents were late, too. But unlike the Mazibuko children, none of the five Tungaraza children had ever had to wait to be chosen: their grandparents had become their new parents immediately.

The Mazibuko family lived in the other house on the farm, the bigger house just a little further down the hill from the one Baba was renting from them. Somebody at Baba's work who was family with somebody at Uncle Enock's work had told Baba about the empty house on the hill that a family had just moved out of, and that was how the Tungarazas had come to live in the same compound as the Mazibukos.

The garage for both houses was wide enough for two vehicles next to each other, and deep enough for one vehicle behind another, so Baba could park his white Corolla behind the red Microbus, and Uncle Enock's white bakkie could fit behind the yellow Hi-Ace, and all four could be sheltered from the rain.

Bakkie was a way of saying a small pick-up truck, and Swazis used the word even though it was part of South African English. Swaziland wasn't part of South Africa, it was a separate country with its own borders and its own culture and its own king. But South Africa surrounded it on the three sides that weren't Mozambique, and words could cross a border without any papers and without being called names or told to go home.

When Auntie Rachel pulled into the garage, Benedict was pleased to see that the white Corolla behind the red Microbus was an older one than Baba's, with dents and scrapes and a sign in black letters down its side saying *Quick Impact Academy of Driving*.

The first time he had seen that Corolla, Miss Hlophe had been climbing into it. The school day was over, and as Benedict had waited for his sisters to stop talking and laughing with their friends, Miss Hlophe had started the engine and reversed the Corolla right into the school's wire fence, hitting a wooden pole with a loud crack.

The door on the passenger side had opened quickly, and a man had shot out like a hare being chased by a cheetah and rushed to look at the back of the Corolla, cursing loudly.

Eh! Cursing in Swahili!

Putting his book bag down on the ground, Benedict had gone over to ask him if the damage was bad, and the man had already told him that it was a lot worse for the wooden pole than it was for the car before he had realised what language they were using. Then the man's face had lit up like a cake that was covered in birthday candles.

'*Unasema kiSwahili! Eh! Eh! Eh!*'

The man had shaken Benedict's hand in the same way that Mrs Dlamini rang the school bell, and the shake had gone all the way up Benedict's arm, making his jaw wobble and sending his left arm out from his body to steady him in exactly the way that Mrs Dlamini's left arm stood out from her body when she rang the school bell.

Where was Benedict from? Who were his family? Where did they live?

Then the man had stopped pumping Benedict's hand up and down, and he had given him one of his business cards and said Benedict's family should call him. When Benedict had seen on the card that he was Henry Vilakati, Director in Chief of the Quick Impact Academy of Driving, an idea had come to him, an idea of a way to help Mama. Not a way to help Mama's business, but a way to help Mama not to mind so much about not being busy with her business.

But by then Mrs Dlamini had come out of the office to look at the pole, and Miss Hlophe had begun telling her that the Corolla had no brakes, and Henry Vilakati was looking at them nervously.

'Mama doesn't know driving,' Benedict had said quickly, 'but, *eh*, there isn't really money for lessons.'

'*Hakuna matata*, my friend! No problem! I can do her a special, nè?'

Then Mrs Dlamini had used her stop-this-nonsense-right-now voice to speak to Henry Vilakati about the brakes on his Corolla and the money for a new pole, and Henry Vilakati had switched to siSwati and pointed at Miss Hlophe, and Benedict had moved away, slipping the card into his pocket for Mama.

That was some few weeks ago now, before Baba had had his idea that Mama should learn to drive, and long before Mama's lessons had begun.

Greeting Mama now as she was putting plates and paper serviettes on the dining table, Benedict went into the kitchen, knowing he would find Henry in there chatting to Titi. Henry knew Swahili on account of his mother having loved him enough to send him away to live with an uncle in Uganda when she couldn't afford to pay for his high schooling herself.

And Henry was wonderful because he always spoke to Benedict like he was big.

'Benedict! *Habari, rafiki yangu?* How are you, my friend?'

'*Nzuri*. I'm fine.' He returned Henry's strong up-and-down handshake, clenching his jaw and holding on to the counter-top for balance. 'How is Mama's driving coming along?'

'Too good, my friend, too good. Improving all the time. Now! Let us help Titi with filling these mugs.'

Over tea, Henry told them about old Mrs Gama, who had just passed her driving test after failing it ten times.

'*Ten?*' said Mama. '*Eh*, Henry! You didn't tell me I could fail many times before passing!'

'You are not Mrs Gama, Angel. First of all, you know the difference between left and right. *Eish!*' Rolling his eyes, Henry shook his head. 'I had to ask her granddaughter to spend time with her every day revising left and right. And she battled to hear me! She must be at least three-quarters deaf.'

'*Eh*, Henry! I hope you're not going to tell other people about *me* as a learner? You know it's not professional to gossip about the people who do business with you.'

Looking ashamed, Henry spoke very quickly. 'I do know, Angel. It's just that I'm so happy she's finally passed! It's not so much that I'm gossiping about her, it's more that I'm boasting about myself. Old Mrs Gama was my most difficult student up to so far.'

'Is she older than Mama?' asked Grace, and Mama gave her one of her looks that said she must be very careful about what she said next. 'I mean, how much younger is Mama?'

'Oh, your mama is a child compared!' declared Henry. 'Titi is just a baby!' He beamed at Titi, who looked down quickly at her slice of pineapple before smiling shyly. 'Her hair is as white as the snow on top of Mount Kilimanjaro. It's her grand-daughter who encouraged her to learn. Told her it's never too late to be modern.'

'That is true.' Mama helped herself to another piece of pawpaw. 'But tell me, Henry. Is her family going to celebrate? For Mrs Gama to get a driving licence at her age is a very big achievement.'

'In fact, they're all gathering for a party after church on Sunday. They've invited me to join them.'

Benedict had been just about to take a bite of banana, but he paused, almost holding his breath. Under the table, the hand that wasn't holding the banana crossed its fingers.

'Of course!' said Mama. 'How could they not invite you? You're the man who taught her to drive! *Her* achievement is *your* achievement!'

Henry laughed, slipping some more mango into his mouth. Mama continued.

'*Her* celebration is *your* celebration!'

Henry chewed. 'I suppose.'

'Of course! Have you not just told us how happy you are that she's finally passed because people can think that a slow learner means that your impact as an instructor is slow?' He nodded. 'And now that you've been successful with her, at her advanced age, everybody will know that Henry Vilakati is the driving instructor who does not fail, no matter how difficult the learner. Everybody will know that if they need a miracle in the matter of driving instruction, Henry Vilakati is the man to go to. That is truly something for Henry Vilakati to celebrate!'

Henry laughed, shaking his head, and Titi looked at him as

if he really was a miracle-worker. Everybody except Benedict concentrated on their fruit and tea. Benedict could hardly breathe.

Then Mama began again. 'Old Mrs Gama has become a very fine advertisement for your business, Henry. And yet you gossiped about her in a way that was unprofessional.'

Looking ashamed, he opened his mouth to speak, but Mama wouldn't let him.

'Perhaps you could make it up to her in some way? Find a way to thank her?'

Henry was quiet while he thought.

Benedict knew from Mama that men preferred ideas that they had arrived at themselves, but he could wait no longer for Henry to arrive at this one. '*Eh!* Why don't you take a cake to her party?'

Henry looked at him, his eyebrows shooting up. '*Eish!* My friend! That idea is too good!'

'One of Auntie's cakes!' said Titi, and Henry gave her a very big smile indeed. Almost as big as the smile Benedict got from Mama.

The creamy banana was delicious in his mouth.

The cake was needed for Sunday, so Mama began baking it as soon as Henry left. He had wanted to choose something simple, but Mama had helped him to see that a simple cake wasn't at all right for a man who could do miracles.

Seated at the dining table with the other children for homework, Benedict had listened to them planning the cake on one of the couches. Baba said there was never no homework, even when teachers didn't give it. If you were a Tungaraza, you knew that your homework every day was to go over your class-work and make sure that you knew it.

The cake was going to look like the old, lime-green Beetle that the late Mr Gama had left to his brother, only old Mrs Gama was using it on account of the late Mr Gama's brother being blind. The cake-board was going to be iced in grey to look like a road, with a ridge of marzipan at the side looking like the edge of a pavement, and a white stripe in front of and behind the Beetle to show that Mrs Gama had finally managed parallel parking. Lying on the road next to the Beetle would be a large white square of sugar-paste with a red L on it, torn in two. It was going to be a very fine cake indeed, the kind of cake that might bring many more customers to Mama.

When he had finished his homework, Benedict went outside into the garden, which had the kind of tidiness about it that Samson always left behind him on the days that he came, a bit like the look Benedict and his brothers always had after Baba had cut their hair with the hair-clipper. The grass was shorter – cleared, at the side of the house, of the fallen leaves from the large lucky-bean tree – tidier near the yes-terday, today and tomorrow bushes, and neater where it met the bed of arum lilies, strelitzias and red hot pokers at the garden's edge. Benedict had never imagined that trees and plants and flowers all had their own name, but there was a book about them in the bookshelf, and all the ones in the garden were in there, with pictures.

Beyond the flower bed the ground fell away sharply, held in place on the steep slope down to the garage by a wild mass of banana and pawpaw trees. But there was never any fruit for the people in either of the two houses, on account of the monkeys always getting to it first.

In the clumps of wild trees where the garden ended at the side of the house beyond the lucky-bean tree, Benedict could see flickers of movement. Birds were waiting for him to go or to settle into stillness so that they could feel safe enough to come down and explore what Samson's gardening had turned up. A few butterflies flitted amongst the flowers. But he wasn't in the mood for sitting quietly in the garden and watching.

Making his way down all the steps to the garage, he hoped that he would see Uncle Enock's bakkie there. It was a Friday, and sometimes on a Friday Uncle Enock managed to get away a bit early. But the garage held only the red Microbus and the yellow Hi-Ace.

Wiping his feet on the mat, he knocked at the open front door of the other house, and Auntie Rachel called for him to come in. She was trying to tame the hair of one of the three littlest children into a pattern of small bunches, but the girl was squirming, wanting to get down on the floor to play with the other two little ones.

'Hi, Benedict. *Ag*, how many times do I have to tell you, you don't have to knock?'

'Mama says it's polite.'

'*Ja*.' Auntie Rachel gave a small shrug.

'Is Uncle Enock coming early today?'

She gave up on the child's hair and let her join in the others' play. 'It's month-end Friday, hey.'

Benedict felt disappointed. Uncle Enock spent every day taking care of sick animals and saving their lives, but the last

Friday afternoon of every month was different because that was when he worked at the dog orphanage. The dog orphanage got very full on account of people changing their minds about wanting a dog, and on account of other people letting their dogs have too many puppies, so every month they had to make more space. Dogs that had been there for a long time without being chosen had to go to sleep for ever, and it was Uncle Enock who helped them to go.

It was a job that made Uncle Enock sad. He would come home saying how many more tails were wagging in Dog Heaven now, and he would want to be left alone.

Benedict wasn't sure that he liked the idea of a separate Heaven for dogs. Say you loved your dog and then you both got an accident and went to Heaven, but your dog had to go to a separate Heaven. Wouldn't being without your dog feel more like being in Hell? What if the Heaven for dogs was next door, and you had to speak to your dog through a fence and you could never hold him? *Eh!* God had made people and animals, all creatures great and small, and He had put them all together here on Earth. Why would He put them in separate Heavens afterwards? It didn't make sense.

It sounded much more like something people would do, not God. Auntie Rachel had told him about an old law in South Africa that said people had to live separately according to what colour their skin was. That law said that when Auntie Rachel had come home from being away learning her teaching diploma and she had found Uncle Enock doing his practicals on her parents' farm, they weren't allowed to fall in love.

They had tried falling in love in secret, but Auntie Rachel's parents were afraid the law would put them in jail, so after

Uncle Enock qualified they came to get married here in Swaziland where Uncle Enock's parents were from and where there wasn't that law, and then Auntie Rachel's parents bought this small farm for them.

'*Ag*, sit, Benedict. I'm going to have some tea. Would you like a glass of milk?'

'Yes, please.' He loved the fresh, creamy milk from the farm. In the house up the hill they had semi-skimmed milk from the supermarket on account of Baba watching his cholesterol and Mama watching her hips, and it just wasn't as nice.

Auntie Rachel called for Lungi, and when Lungi didn't come, she got up and went to look for her. The house was once the same sort of size as the Tungarazas' house up the hill, but the Mazibukos had added on a big extra room at the side where the children could play and watch TV, and a whole new upstairs with more bedrooms. Benedict sat on a chair near the door, marvelling as always at the full bookshelves lining the walls of the lounge. Some of the shelves went all the way up to the ceiling, and others were shorter, like the one in the house up the hill.

On top of the shorter shelves stood some framed photographs of Auntie Rachel's family and Uncle Enock's, which always made Benedict think of the photograph hanging on the wall of the lounge up the hill. It showed the first baba he shared with Grace and Moses, and their first baba's sister, the first mama of Faith and Daniel.

In between the Mazibukos' photographs were some special stones and rocks called crystals, which Auntie Rachel believed in. She was supposed to believe in the God of the Jewish people, but Swaziland didn't have a place where a Jewish somebody could go to pray. Mama said Auntie Rachel was out of practice, but Baba said she had rocks in her head.

She came back in now with Benedict's milk, saying that Lungi was just making her tea.

'Auntie Rachel, you know hoopoes?'

'Ja?'

'I heard they're called King Solomon's queen.'

'Ja, I've heard that. Their crest is supposed to be a crown he gave one of them to thank it for giving him some advice.'

Benedict sipped the delicious, creamy milk. 'Do you know what advice it gave?'

Leaning forward with a tissue and dabbing at the milk at the corners of his upper lip, she gave him a serious look. 'Okay, you have to understand that it's a story from a very long time ago, long before people learned to respect women.' He nodded, knowing from Mama that respecting ladies was important. 'Apparently the hoopoe advised the king that women mustn't be honoured, they must be tamed and controlled.'

'Eh!'

'Exactly!'

Lungi came in with a mug of tea on a tray, carefully stepping over the three young children playing on the floor. She and Benedict exchanged greetings in siSwati before she went back to the kitchen. Watching her go, Benedict smiled. Lungi always wore black, which a Swazi lady had to do for two whole years after losing her husband, but tucked into the waistband of her skirt at the back there was always a brightly coloured duster on a stick that looked like the bushy tail of a squirrel all dressed up for a party. She didn't need to have a duster handy, it was Mavis who cleaned while Lungi cooked. But still.

Auntie Rachel took a sip of her tea. 'You lot are clever, hey? You learning siSwati, Titi learning English. How's she doing, by the way?'

Titi was coming for English lessons with Auntie Rachel in exchange for a bit of childminding. Benedict was fond of Titi. She had been taking care of him since before he had come to live with Mama and Baba four years ago.

'She's doing well,' he said. 'She speaks English with Mama every evening while they're cooking supper.'

'*Ag* shame, she's trying hard, hey?' Auntie Rachel sipped more of her tea. 'You know, that story about the hoopoe has always bothered me. I mean, King Solomon wouldn't have made the hoopoe a queen unless it was a female, so why did a female give him advice like that? Unless it was saying only female *people* needed to be tamed and controlled.'

Benedict gave it some thought as he finished his milk. 'Maybe. Wasn't the female hoopoe *already* tame? I mean, it spoke with King Solomon and it let him put a crown on its head. You couldn't do that with a wild hoopoe in the garden.'

'*Ja*, maybe you're right.'

Then Mavis came in to say the bath was ready for the small children, and she knelt on the floor to gather up their toys and tidy them away into a plastic crate. Benedict thought Mavis looked almost small enough to be one of the bigger Mazibuko children, and he often wondered how old she was. But he never asked. He knew from Mama it wasn't nice to ask about a lady's age.

When Auntie Rachel stood up to help Mavis to get the little ones upstairs, Benedict said thank you for the milk and left. There was no point in waiting around for Uncle Enock, who wouldn't feel like talking to him after his time at the dog orphanage.

Further down the hill, Petros was leading the cows from the milking shed towards the one where they would sleep, his dog by his side. He gave Benedict a small wave, and Benedict returned it before heading back up the hill.

THREE

THE SLOPE OF THE STEEP HILL TO WHICH THE FARM clung lay in almost total darkness. A little further up, not a single light shone in the other house where the *kwerekwere* family slept, while some distance further down, the hostel for the dairy workers was lit only by a sliver of moon. In the main house, everybody was asleep – or, if they lay awake, they did so without switching on a light.

It was only in the small servants' room behind the main house that a light burned, the naked bulb suspended from the ceiling over the narrow space between the bed in which Lungi snored softly and the one in which Mavis sat, her hands expertly rapid with her crochet hook and a large ball of soft, pale blue wool. When the baby-jacket was done, she would place it with the other pieces that lay folded neatly in the plastic bag on top of the wardrobe – a child's jersey striped in yellow and red, a lady's jacket in black, three hats in different single colours – ready to take to the friend who would sell them for her at the market in Mbabane. The money would go with the rest, in the cleaned-out Cobra floor-polish tin under her bed.

Cleaning for the Mazibuko family was certainly a good job

to have. Madam paid Mavis the same kind of wage that any cleaner in Mbabane might be paid, and she also got this room to live in and three meals a day, left over after the family had eaten. The family was big, but Lungi cooked a lot of food, and there was always plenty left.

Mavis earned enough money, she didn't need to crochet for extra. No. She crocheted because she needed something to do whenever sleep fled from her in the night, leaving her suddenly wide-eyed and restless. When that happened, she would tiptoe from her bed to the door of the room, slide her hand between the wall and the big wardrobe, and press the light switch slowly, careful not to let it make a sound that might wake Lungi. Then, retrieving from under her bed the old pillow-case that was her crochet bag, she would get back into bed.

Tonight, as she worked, her thoughts went to the other house, and in particular to the maid there. Titi would right now be asleep not just inside the house, but inside one of the bedrooms with the family. *Eish!* Madam had offered – Mavis had heard her with her own ears – to clear out all the things that were stored in the other servants' room behind the main house, the one just the other side of the shower and toilet that Mavis and Lungi shared, the one that Samson didn't need because he came to work in the garden just two days a week. But Titi's madam had said no, Titi would sleep inside, she was part of their family.

Their family had lived in many places and they always took Titi with them, so Titi had already seen the world. She had finished her primary schooling, just like Mavis had, and now she was coming to Madam for even more learning. Mavis tried to make sure that she was dusting or polishing nearby whenever Madam was teaching Titi, but it wasn't always easy because the smaller children needed watching then and Lungi was sometimes too busy watching a pot.

Madam had taught Titi the word *minor*, which meant not grown up, like all the children in the house. That was what a woman was here, she needed a man to be in charge of her or to sign things for her. Titi had told Madam it was different in her own country, there she was allowed to own cows if she wanted, and also land. But Mavis wasn't so sure that Titi was telling the truth. If Titi could own cows and land at home, why was she here with her madam's family, doing all the cooking and cleaning all by herself? Titi couldn't be cleaning nice-nice, there was too much work: the *kwerekwere* family was big, almost as big as the one here, meanwhile this family had both Mavis to clean for them and Lungi to cook for them.

Boys made more mess than girls, every maid in the whole of Swaziland knew that. Here there were only two boys, but at the other house there were three. The two younger ones were always here, playing in the garden with Fortune then tracking mud and dirt into the house. *Eish!* Mavis shook her head as her fingers worked. She had asked Madam to speak to them about it, and Madam had, but still they tracked in mud and dirt.

The eldest *kwerekwere* boy was different, he always wiped his feet on the mat before he came inside. There was often soil on his clothes, but that was Titi's problem, not Mavis's, and it was a big problem because the other house didn't have a machine for washing and Titi had to use her hands. Mavis had had jobs before where she had to wash with her hands, and it wasn't until she got this job here and learnt to use a machine that she fully realised how much time and how much work it had always taken to do a family's wash by hand. Here there were two machines, the new one in the kitchen that opened with a round door at the front, and the old one outside the back door in the sheltered area where she could hang the washing when it rained and where Samson kept his mower and his other gardening tools. That machine opened at the top, and she had to fill it with a hose attached to the outside tap. Titi had one like that back in her country, not one like the nice new one inside.

The eldest boy from the other house was quiet and serious, like the eldest boy in Madam's house. Vusi wanted his own bedroom, he didn't want to share with Fortune and Fortune's noise and mess. He wanted a desk in place of Fortune's bed so he could be serious about his schooling. Madam and Doctor had told him maybe next year he could have the downstairs room that was for visitors, because next year would be his last year of school and he was going to work hard for his exams and do well so that he could make something of his life. Meanwhile, he was supposed to be a good example for Fortune, and meanwhile Mavis still cleaned Vusi's nice, tidy part of the room and still picked up all the mess in Fortune's part so that she could find the floor to clean.

Vusi was the same age as Petros, who would be asleep now in the dairy-workers' hostel at the bottom of the hill, unless there was a cow that was sick. Then he would be curled up with the sick cow inside the shed, with that dog of his that slept in the shed anyway because the other workers didn't want it inside their hostel, and he would wait there until Doctor came in the morning to check on the cow. Doctor had offered him schooling but he had said no, he just wanted his job with the cows.

Mavis stilled her hands and rested them on her blanket. Flattening her back against the wall, she closed her eyes tight. She shouldn't have let her thoughts wander all the way down to the bottom of the hill. She shouldn't have let them go to Petros. She should have made them stay inside the main house with Vusi, Vusi who was nothing like her own boy would have been.

Eish, thoughts about her own boy were sometimes too hard. Sometimes they twisted her stomach tight, in the same way that her own hands used to twist washing before there was a machine to spin the water out. And sometimes the thoughts spun round and round inside her head until they squeezed water from her eyes.

Sighing quietly so as not to wake Lungi, she opened her eyes and assessed the baby-jacket. In just a few minutes it would be done. She would start another immediately. Meanwhile, she needed something to help her to still her mind before it started to spin.

Slipping silently out of her bed, she went to the wardrobe, quietly opening the side where there were shelves rather than hanging space. The top two shelves belonged to Lungi, who was taller, and Mavis needed to sit on the end of her own bed to get at her own two lower shelves. At the very back of the upper of the two, further back than her deodorant and her comb, safely stored behind her underwear and her thick winter jersey so that they couldn't accidentally drop and spill, were the two small bottles that Madam had given her, both of them dark brown.

The one called Rescue was for if she was panicking or if she'd had a fright or a shock. She didn't need that one, not tonight. No. She would just use the other one, the one that was called Lavender, which was for if she was worrying and finding it hard to go to sleep.

Lying back across her blanket, she held that bottle firmly in her left hand as she stretched her right arm back, just managing to reach the edge of her pillow and pull it towards her. Then, sitting up again, she put two careful drops from the Lavender bottle on a corner of the pillow-case. It was oil, but that didn't matter: in the cupboard next to the inside washing machine she had a special spray to use before washing that was good with oil like this. But it didn't work so well with dirty oil, like if Doctor had done something to his bakkie and then wiped his hands on his clothes. That kind of oil needed some of Lungi's corn flour and then some Sunlight liquid.

Back in her bed, she was about to begin work on the baby-jacket again, when she saw that one of the threads from her blanket was coming loose. It was her own special blanket from home, Lungi had nothing like it on her bed. Her mother had made it for her from squares crocheted in bright colours, each square outlined in black. It was old now – almost seventeen years – and Mavis had repaired it over and over, sometimes replacing whole squares. Now a bit of black was unravelling, but she would leave it till tomorrow to fix. Her black wool was under her bed in a supermarket bag that would make a crinkly noise when she opened it, and she didn't want to wake Lungi.

Until the oil on her pillow-case did its work, she would finish this baby-jacket, and start on the next.

FOUR

Auntie Rachel hadn't yet come to fetch them from under the thorn tree outside the high-school gate, and Benedict was starting to long for the tea that would be waiting for him at home. He had wasted the sandwich that Titi had made for his lunch by accidentally dropping it in the sandy schoolyard, and his slice of cake hadn't been enough to fill him. As he waited, he found himself imagining that he was going home to a plate of delicious, warm *ugali*. It wouldn't quite be ready yet: Titi or Mama would have boiled the pot of water, and they would have stirred in the maize meal, put the lid on the pot and left it on a low heat to cook. Now they would be stirring a simmering sauce of tomatoes and onions, sampling it to see how delicious it was going to taste with the *ugali*.

In Swaziland *ugali* was called *lipalish*, and maize cobs were called mealies. There was a lady selling mealies at the school gate now. They had been boiled still wrapped in their green leafy covering, and Benedict knew that if he bought one and unwrapped it, a little puff of steam would rise off it and the plump seeds would be warm and tasty when he chewed them off the cob, even though the mealie had been out of the pot for a long time in air that said that winter was on its way. But Benedict didn't have any money to buy a mealie.

Another lady was selling bunny-chow, which was a quarter of a loaf of bread with its inside scooped out and replaced with curry. In Mr Patel's shop they sold banana bunny, which was bunny-chow with a banana sliced in half lengthways sticking up out of the curry like a rabbit's ears. Sometimes Mr Patel came to check on the bunny-chow sellers outside the school, and sometimes he shouted at them and chased them away. Mama said it was on account of his own curry business being just down the road, but Baba said Mr Patel just wanted to be sure it was only food that they were selling.

Benedict had taken Mama to meet Mrs Patel, and Mrs Patel had agreed, as one professional somebody helping another, to try selling Mama's cupcakes in the shop. But it hadn't worked out. Mama had gone back there hoping to get her empty plate and a regular order, but instead she had got stale cupcakes that smelled of curry and that were only good for Benedict to crumble in the garden for the birds.

'There are no any customers here for sweet,' Mrs Patel had told Mama sadly, handing back the still almost full plate. 'They are coming here for spicy, isn't it? For salty. Fried. Sorry, nè?'

Mama had said it was okay, then she had put on one of her smiles and asked Mrs Patel how her family was. Mrs Patel had stared hard at the counter-top before reaching for a paper serviette and pressing it to her eyes with trembling fingers. Benedict had known, without Mama even needing to give him any kind of look at all, that Mama and Mrs Patel wanted to be confidential, and that it wouldn't have been enough for him just to look instead at the pictures of gods on the walls inside Mr Patel's shop. He had waited patiently outside until Mama had come out with her plate of stale cupcakes, and he hadn't asked because he knew that when something was confidential, Mama would never tell.

Outside the school now, he thought he might not say no to one of those cupcakes, no matter how stale they were or how much they tasted of curry. Today he hadn't even been able to get any chips as a gift from Mrs Patel, on account of Mr Patel being there supervising new glass being put in the shop window. It was the second time Benedict had seen him do that, and once before he had seen him scrubbing at rude words that somebody had sprayed there.

Everybody loved Mrs Patel's curry, but not everybody was nice to Mr Patel. Sometimes, if the wind was strong and coming from the side, it would blow at Mr Patel's hairstyle so that long bits would hang down on one side and the top of his head would be bald. Benedict thought it looked funny, but nobody really seemed to mind, and it couldn't be why people weren't nice to him. He wasn't a *kwerekwere*. Nobody could be a *kwerekwere* without being an African from another African country.

Mrs Patel had told Mama that the Patels' ancestors had lived in Swaziland since before the British and the Afrikaans people called Boers had finished fighting about who owned the land, and long before the Swazis had said no, this land is ours. Both of them were the children of the children of indentured labourers. Benedict wasn't exactly sure what *indentured* meant, but old Auntie Geraldine in Bukoba had dentures. Mrs Patel had two teeth missing at the side at the top, so if she had dentures they weren't very good. Mr Patel never seemed to smile, so it was hard to tell.

Back in the days of belonging to Britain, Mr Patel's ancestor had helped to build the railway line between Mombasa on the coast of Kenya and Kampala in Uganda, and when he was free he had travelled south to set up a shop for the people who had come to look for gold.

Mrs Patel's ancestor had come to work on the sugar plantations where the Zulu people lived. The British had had to bring people from India to do the work on account of the Zulus refusing. Then Mrs Patel's ancestor had become a trader, and at last the two families had met in the same place, which was one day going to be Swaziland.

So the Patels weren't really from anywhere else, not any more. But Benedict understood that if you looked or sounded – or felt – different, it was sometimes hard to feel welcome even when you belonged. Anyway, what kept happening to Mr Patel's shop might not be about belonging or not. Mama said maybe it was about somebody else wanting Mr Patel's shop, but Baba said maybe it was about Mr Patel interfering in other people's business. Benedict had certainly seen him interfering in the business of the ladies who sold food outside the high school.

Most of the children from the high school who walked home had gone now, but quite a few of the ones who were fetched in cars were still waiting, so Benedict knew that there must be a roadblock somewhere. The army liked to do roadblocks. They stopped all the cars and looked in the boots and the cubbyholes for guns, and made people prove that they hadn't come without papers from Mozambique. Mozambique had a border with Swaziland, and the Tungarazas had driven through it in the red Microbus on their way here from Tanzania.

Benedict couldn't help smiling whenever he remembered that journey. Baba had asked him to help with navigating, and he had sat up front with Baba the whole way while his brothers and sisters had played or slept in the back with Mama and Titi. Mama preferred to sit in the back anyway, on account of her skirts being too tight for her to get in comfortably at the front, so usually the children took turns to sit in the front seat. On that trip, though, they never had a turn, even though they had tried.

'*Please*, Baba!'

'Can you read a map?'

'Uh-uh.'

'Can you stay awake?'

'Yes.'

'Then how is it that I've watched you in my mirror going to sleep after only half an hour?'

'It's not *fair*, Baba!'

'Fairness is not going to keep me awake at the wheel with a sleeping child next to me. Fairness is not going to tell me which road I need to be on and where I need to turn. Fairness is not going to tell me how far away the next town is so that I know when I need to buy fuel. Is fairness what you really want, or would you prefer it if we actually arrived at our destination?'

And so Benedict had sat up front having Baba all to himself.

He had felt so proud, Baba believing he was big enough to help. He knew that Baba felt sad about his son – Benedict's first baba – being late, and Benedict always felt he should try hard to be grown up like his first baba had been. That way maybe Baba would be a little less sad. But it was hard to be grown up about everything when you were still small.

Baba must have thought him very small on an earlier journey they had made, right at the beginning of the year. The first part, from Mama and Baba's home town of Bukoba on the western shores of Lake Victoria, to Mwanza on the lake's southern shores, Baba kept having to pull over and stop so that Benedict could get out to be sick.

'What is wrong with that boy?' he had heard Baba saying while he retched into the bushes at the side of the road. 'He's never suffered from travel sickness before!'

'I don't know, Pius. Something he ate just isn't sitting well in his stomach.'

'*Eh*, I hope this is not an example that Moses and Daniel are going to follow!'

He had done his very best not to be a bad example to his younger brothers, but try as he might there was always one more time he had to ask Baba to stop. He knew he was making everything that much worse for everybody: nobody was feeling very comfortable anyway, heading towards Mwanza where the first parents he shared with Grace and Moses had both become late.

That was certainly part of what was upsetting Benedict. But more than anything, it was about Titi.

Titi had spent Christmas in Mwanza with her family and friends, having crossed the lake from Bukoba on the ferry, and they were heading there to pick her up on their way to Dar es Salaam. But what if she didn't want to come? What if she wanted to stay with her own family instead? What if they had to go to their new home in Swaziland without her? The worry of it all swirled nastily in Benedict's stomach and forced its way up his throat.

Titi was there, where she was supposed to be, in a pretty new dress, with her suitcase packed and a very big smile on her face, and Benedict had wept like a little child to see her. But on the way from Mwanza to Dar, the relief he felt did battle with the heaving that his stomach had grown used to, and it wasn't until Titi herself had held him as the nothing that was left inside him bent him double at the roadside, and she had wiped his face and held him to her in the Microbus, it wasn't until then that he had been okay again.

The journey from Dar to Swaziland had been completely different. Up front next to Baba, he had followed their route on the map and chatted to Baba as much as he could, knowing that when he just couldn't keep himself from dozing off, Mama would lean forward from the seat behind and keep Baba awake.

There had been no possibility of dozing until they were well into Mozambique, as the final stretch of the coastal road down from Dar had been sandy and difficult, and then on the flat boat that had taken them and the Microbus across the mouth of the Ruvuma River, they had all held their breath, sure that the Microbus would slide off, taking all of them with it. Then from the river – which was the border between Tanzania and Mozambique – there had been another stretch of difficult, sandy road until the town of Moçimboa da Praia where they had stopped for sodas and cupcakes.

The memory of those cupcakes made Benedict even hungrier now, and he turned his attention away from the ladies outside the high school who were packing what food they had left into large plastic tubs which they hoisted onto their heads before moving off. Inside the school, the students who were on cleaning duty were finishing off, locking the windows against any afternoon rain.

A girl emerging from one of the classrooms caught his attention. She was carrying an exercise book away from her body, holding it flat and looking at it carefully. It was the kind of thing Benedict did when he was taking a spider outside, but this girl couldn't possibly be taking a spider outside, on account of her being a girl. He watched her carefully as she made her way past the other classrooms, past the bare ground at the front of the school, moving slowly towards a clump of grass on the other side of the fence from where he was waiting under the tree. There she bent and tipped something off the exercise book before turning round and going back to the classroom.

Unless Benedict was mistaken, what she had tipped on to the clump of grass was in fact a spider. *Eh!* Girls did not save spiders!

He watched the girl as she went back into the classroom, then a few seconds later he saw the head of a broom coming quickly out of the classroom a couple of times, shooting a puff of dust along the floor ahead of it. He waited for her to finish

cleaning and come out with her schoolbag, but before she did
he heard the children on this side of the fence cheering and
some cars hooting, and at last Auntie Rachel was there in the
yellow Hi-Ace.

He wanted to think about the girl on the way home, but
Auntie Rachel was busy apologising for being late, asking
everybody if they were okay and assuring the Tungarazas that
Mama wasn't worrying about them because Auntie Rachel had
used her cell-phone to call her from the roadblock. And then
they went past the roadblock, which was only stopping the
cars on the other side of the road, and Auntie Rachel told them
about the soldier who had been surprised that there wasn't a
gun in the Hi-Ace's cubbyhole, and kept asking her over and
over where her weapon was.

Auntie Rachel didn't have a gun, she was like Mama and
Baba, she didn't like them, even though she'd grown up with
guns on her parents' farm in South Africa. Uncle Enock had a
gun, but Auntie Rachel made him keep it in the safe at his
work, on account of guns being dangerous around children.
Uncle Enock had to have a gun in case a cow or a horse was
too sick to be made better, but he didn't like to use it. Benedict
wondered if Uncle Enock thought there was a separate Heaven
for cows and horses, or if he thought they went to the same
Heaven as dogs.

As they passed the roadblock, one of the soldiers winked at
Auntie Rachel and gave her a cheeky smile, and the girls in the
Hi-Ace giggled.

'Ja,' said Auntie Rachel. 'Take me home to meet all the
wives you have already, hey.'

Then a man at the side of the road tried to flag down the

Hi-Ace, and Benedict joined all the others in shouting, 'We're not a bloody taxi!' and then laughing. *Bloody* wasn't a nice word and the Tungarazas weren't supposed to say it. But still.

After homework that afternoon, while the girls took turns doing each other's hair in their bedroom, and the younger boys watched cartoons on TV, Benedict lay flat on his stomach on the grass near the flower bed, watching a creature as long as one of Baba's hands basking in the late-afternoon warmth of one of the steps down to the garage. It was either a lizard or a skink; he wasn't sure. He observed it carefully, trying to remember all its details so he wouldn't be confused when he looked it up in the book later.

Lizards could sometimes be a bit flat, but this one had a rather thick body that was striped along its length: dark brown on top, then a lighter brown on its side, then a black stripe just above its white belly. He was trying to decide whether to remember its throat as yellow or orange, when it shot off the step and disappeared amongst the banana trees, frightened by the sudden noise of a vehicle heading up towards the garage.

It was the Ubuntu Funerals van! *Eh!* For a moment Benedict was unsure what to do. Was he in some kind of trouble? Was somebody at the other house late? Should he go down and greet the people?

Or maybe he should stay exactly where he was, flat on the grass behind the flowers, unmoving and unseen, like Petros.

The van disappeared into the garage, and then the lady and the tall man he had spoken to before emerged and walked towards the other house. The man was carrying something that looked a bit like the box Benedict's new pair of shoes had come in. *Eh*, of course! Auntie Rachel and Uncle Enock were having a birthday party for the dairy manager after the milking that evening. The Ubuntu Funerals people were simply coming early for the party and bringing a gift.

Benedict dusted himself down and went inside to look up the lizard. Mama was just finishing off the cake for the party. She had suggested a cake shaped like a silver-grey milking bucket lying on its side with white milk spilling out of it, but Auntie Rachel had said no, that made her think of kicking a bucket, which was a way of saying becoming late, and that wasn't right for a man who was turning forty, which was old in Swaziland.

Mama had told her about old Mrs Gama who was much older than the dairy manager, and Auntie Rachel had said that the people who were already old before, those people had been able to get older like old Mrs Gama had, but nowadays most people were young on account of the average person not managing to have a thirtieth birthday.

It was a big celebration for the dairy manager because nobody in his family was as old as he was, so the cake had to be happy and not about kicking a bucket. So Mama had made the side view of the underbelly of a cow with a fat pink udder with four teats. On the cake-board she had used her plastic icing syringe to make forty stars of white icing in four rows of ten, looking like drops of milk from each of the teats. Now she was busy fixing a white birthday-candle into each drop of milk.

As Benedict looked for the section on reptiles in the book, he thought about the Ubuntu Funerals van. It wasn't very nice to bring a funeral van to a party, especially a party for somebody who shouldn't have a cake about kicking a bucket. He knew from Baba what *ubuntu* was. It was a word there wasn't a word for in English or Swahili, it just had to be called ubuntu otherwise you had to use lots of other words instead: words that talked about how human beings were all connected, and about how people needed other people in order to become the best people they could be, and about how working together with other people made people human.

When he discovered that it was a skink, not a lizard, he wondered if skinks had their own kind of ubuntu. Was it important to a skink that it should be the best possible skink that it could be? Did skinks support and help one another? Did they feel connected to all other skinks? Or maybe they felt connected to all of God's creatures. He was wondering if there was a word for an ubuntu that was about connecting people to all other animals instead of just to other people, when somebody knocked on the open front door and a lady's voice called, '*Sawubona?*'

'*Karibu!*' called Mama in Swahili, before correcting herself in siSwati. '*Eh*, sorry! *Ngena!*'

The funeral people stepped into the lounge, the man still holding the box.

'Hello, Benedict,' said the lady. 'Hello children!' She waved to the boys on the couch in front of the TV, and then went towards the other end of the dining table where Mama was standing up and wiping her hands on a cloth.

The man nodded a greeting at Benedict, whose eyes were big with surprise.

'And you must be Benedict's mother.' The lady extended her hand and Mama shook it, looking confused. 'I'm Zodwa

Shabangu, and this is my colleague Jabulani Ndwandwe.'

Mama shook his hand, too. 'I'm happy to meet you. Are you... Are you Benedict's teachers?'

'No, no, we're the people from Ubuntu Funerals,' said Zodwa, handing Mama a business card. 'I'm the director. Mrs Patel told us where to find you.'

Mama looked at the card. Benedict could tell that she was very confused, but it was all happening too quickly for him to explain.

'*Eh!*' Mama looked up from the card, fear spreading suddenly across her face. The beautiful brown of her skin began to turn grey, and when her voice came, it was a whisper. 'Is my husband late?'

Her body seemed to sink, and Jabulani rushed forward to hold her up, putting the box on the table. Zodwa pulled out a chair, and they helped her to sit.

'Mama, no!' cried Benedict.

'Nobody is late, my dear.' Zodwa's voice was kind but firm. 'Everybody is fine.'

'*Sisi*, we've just come to see Benedict,' Jabulani said softly, kneeling beside Mama's chair and stroking her arm.

Mama breathed out loudly. She looked up at Benedict.

'I'm sorry, Mama,' he said, feeling tears beginning to prick in his eyes. 'I'm sorry.'

'What is it that you've done?' she asked him.

Zodwa put an arm around Benedict. 'No, no, he's done nothing wrong. Didn't he tell you about meeting us last week?'

'He told me nothing.' Mama's eyes were accusing; his own flooded with tears.

Mama told Moses and Daniel to turn off the TV and sent them to play outside, then she sent Benedict to wake Titi up from her afternoon nap and have her make tea for everybody. When he had done that, he went into the bedroom and curled up on his bed, covering his head with his pillow so that if his brothers came in they wouldn't see that he was crying. His tears were about upsetting Mama, but the fact that they had come meant that he had let himself down, too.

Mama had told him that if somebody had tears inside, those tears needed to be cried out, and it didn't matter if the some-body who cried them out was a boy, a girl, a man or a lady; anybody was allowed to be sad. But Baba had told him that he was supposed to be strong on account of being the eldest boy.

It didn't matter that he was still young, or that he some-times felt that he was still small. It didn't matter that Grace and Faith were older than him. They were girls. He was the eldest boy, and the eldest boy had responsibilities. He was supposed to take care of his sisters, he was supposed to be a good example to his younger brothers, and he was supposed to look after the whole entire family if Baba ever became late.

Under the pillow, he sniffed loudly.

Eh! Say the funeral people had come to say that Baba *was* late! Imagine! And here he was in the bedroom, weeping like a baby! *Eh!*

He sat up and wiped his eyes with the edge of his T-shirt, taking a few deep breaths to calm himself. Then he went into the bathroom to splash water on his face, recognising as he did so that his tears had been selfish. Mama had thought that Baba was late! *Eh!* What a fright she must have had!

And it was all his fault.

In the lounge, Jabulani was tucking in to a large slice of chocolate cake iced in the same pink that Mama had used for the udder, while Zodwa was looking through the album of photographs of Mama's cakes and sipping from a mug of tea made the Tanzanian way with boiled milk and plenty of sugar and cardamom.

'I'm sorry, Mama.'

Mama opened her arms wide, and he went to her on the couch, squashing up against her large, soft body and burying his face in the clean, cocoa-butter smell of her neck. He stayed there only a few seconds, knowing that he was a bit too big now for her to feel comfortable with him on her lap. Slipping down next to her on the couch, her right arm still holding him, he apologised again.

She pulled him closer and planted a kiss on his forehead.

'We're sorry too, nè?' Zodwa leaned forward, putting her mug of tea down on the coffee table and patting his leg. '*Eish!* We felt so bad!'

'Sorry, nè?' said Jabulani.

'Your mother's right, though. A cup tea and a slice of cake can make everything better. Have you had?'

Mama sent him into the kitchen, where Titi was scrubbing the milk saucepan in the sink.

'Are you okay?' she asked him, leaving the saucepan and drying her hands on a cloth.

He knew she had seen his tears when he had woken her. He said he was fine, but she hugged him anyway, and then she insisted that he have the cup of tea that was waiting for her on the draining board with a saucer on top of it to keep it warm.

'Don't keep them waiting,' she whispered, cutting him a thick slice of cake. 'They have something for you.'

'For me?' Benedict remembered the small box. '*Eh!*'

But when he went back into the lounge with his tea and cake, the box wasn't where it had been on the dining table, and it wasn't on the coffee table or either of the couches. He ate and drank quietly while the grown-ups talked.

'My husband Ubuntu,' Zodwa was saying between mouthfuls of cake, 'he's the one who started the business. Then when Ubuntu himself was late in an accident, *eish*, I don't know how it is in your country, my dear, but here a woman can't inherit a business, she's a child in the eyes of the law. Some things may be beginning to change now, slow-slow, but at the time of Ubuntu's accident there was no way.'

'I've heard of such things.'

'The business went to his younger brother. Thanks God he's an academic, doesn't want to be dealing with the late. So he lets me do what I want with the business and he takes a percentage.'

'That is very good,' said Mama, finishing her cake before the others. Benedict knew that her slice had been smaller on account of her watching her hips.

'It's a good business to be in,' said Jabulani. 'Second only to security.'

Benedict knew about the security business: Sifiso's father worked in it. Every morning, Sifiso's father dropped him at school in the Buffalo Soldiers van after he'd been out early collecting Buffalo Soldiers from their night shifts and dropping others off for day shift. He had started as a guard protecting people's homes at night, and then he had got a promotion to

66

supervisor, which made Sifiso's mother happier because she didn't have to worry about him getting shot any more. Getting shot was something that Benedict didn't like to think about, so he hadn't told Sifiso that his own first baba had got shot even without being a security guard; he had simply been somebody coming home and finding robbers in his house.

'*Eish*, but it's competitive! People are trying to start up their own funeral businesses all the time.'

'A younger business can be less professional,' said Mama.

'Mm.' Zodwa had just taken a sip of tea. She swallowed. 'Up to so far, we've survived by being experienced professionals. But we need to find a way to differentiate ourselves in the market. We need an edge.'

'What's a nedge?' asked Benedict.

'Edge, nè? Edge,' said Zodwa. 'It's what makes you stand out as different so that customers come to *your* business rather than the business next door. Sometimes its called your unique selling point.'

'*Eh!* Now you are talking like my husband!'

'He's also done a certificate in business management?'

'He's done so many things! He's a consultant here at the Ministry for Trade and Industry. His job is to find ways to increase Swazi exports throughout the world, more especially to research ways of encouraging other African countries to prefer Swazi goods rather than importing things from afar.' Mama flapped her hands around in the air. 'Something complicated like that. I'm not an educated somebody myself.'

Benedict finished his tea, and as soon as he put his mug down on the coffee table next to his empty plate, Jabulani leaned towards him and spoke softly while Mama and Zodwa talked.

'I have something for you.'

'*Eh!*'

'Your mother made me put it outside. Come.'

Benedict followed him out through the front door and round to the veranda, where the box sat on top of the stack of plastic chairs against the wall that they never used for sitting on out there on account of Mama not wanting to be in the garden because of snakes.

Jabulani gave the box to Benedict, and he took it carefully. It was made of a light-coloured wood, and worked into its lid was a beautiful carving of a hoopoe. Breathing in sharply, he looked up at Jabulani.

'Is it...?'

'Yes. It's your King Solomon's queen. I made the casket myself.'

'*Eh!* It's so beautiful!' Benedict turned it round in his hands, examining it from every angle. 'Does it open?'

'No, I glued it shut. She broke into pieces when I pulled her off the van's grille, so I went for closed casket. Sorry, nè? I kept her in a plastic bag in the fridge till I'd finished making it.'

Benedict didn't know what to say. Nobody had ever done anything like this for him before. There was so much work in the carving!

'Shall we bury her now, or do you want to invite your friends and family?'

Benedict thought about it. Giveness and Sifiso wouldn't understand, and nobody in his family would be interested in a funeral for a bird. Baba might even shake his head and look at him with disappointment. Uncle Enock, maybe. But Uncle Enock might say something about the hoopoe flapping its wings in Bird Heaven now, and Benedict didn't want to think about himself maybe one day ending up in a separate Heaven without any beautiful birds to look at.

'Let's do it now,' he said, glad to have Jabulani with him.

They chose to bury the bird under the lucky-bean tree at the side of the house on account of the hoopoe being lucky to be buried in such a beautiful casket, and on account of a lucky-bean tree also being called a sacred coral tree. Somewhere sacred was a proper place for a queen. And when the tree's flowers came they would be red, which was the colour of royalty in Swaziland. It was also a good place for the burial because queens wore jewellery, and lucky-bean seeds were often threaded together to make necklaces. Jabulani said the bark of the tree was good for treating aching joints, which the hoopoe might be experiencing, being all in pieces. And the tree was next to the hedge of yesterday, today and tomorrow bushes that would help the bird to be remembered for eternity.

Taking turns with the small spade Benedict kept outside the back door for his chore of clearing any *kinyezi* the monkeys did on the grass, they worked together to dig a hole, place the casket in it, and pat the soil into a small mound on top.

Then Jabulani stood to the side as Benedict knelt, crossing himself and saying a silent prayer. He asked God to bless the hoopoe and to look after her in Heaven even though she had given King Solomon some bad advice about not respecting ladies, and to bless Jabulani for making such a beautiful casket. And then he asked God to do everything He could to help an edge to come to Ubuntu Funerals.

Mama didn't need an edge for her business, she already

had one: she was confidential. A customer could tell Mama anything they wanted, and Mama would never tell. But Mama's business needed customers, and while he was on his knees, Benedict took the opportunity to ask God for some of those.

He stood and brushed the soil from his knees. 'Thank you, Jabulani.'

'Not to mention.'

'The casket is so beautiful I almost didn't want to bury it.'

'I liked making that! *Eish*, it was a nice change from the ones we make every day!'

They made their way past the family's washing lines and round the back of the house, past the window of the bathroom that belonged to Mama and Baba's bedroom, and past the window of the bathroom for Titi and the children. Outside the kitchen, next to the gas tank for Mama's special oven that they had brought with them on the trailer behind the red Microbus, was the outside sink made of concrete where Titi did their washing. There they washed the soil off their hands, and Titi gave them a towel to use, handing it to them carefully because her hands smelled of the onions she was chopping.

'Jabulani!' Zodwa's voice came from inside the house.

They went in through the kitchen, finding Zodwa standing at the dining table with her purse, counting out some emalangeni notes which Mama took, folded, and tucked through her neckline into her underwear.

'It'll be ready next week Friday, as we've agreed,' said Mama, patting the Cake Order Form that lay on the table.

'Good. I'm so pleased I was able to give you some business

after we scared you so badly. Come, Jabulani, ours is not to linger, nè?'

As he watched Mama walking with them down the steps to the garage, Benedict held the Cake Order Form to his chest.

Eh! God could answer a prayer quickly sometimes.

FIVE

O N SATURDAY MORNING, BABA TOOK BENEDICT AND his brothers and sisters to the public library in Mbabane. Mama and Titi never went there; Baba usually dropped them at the supermarket at either The Plaza or The Mall so that they could do the family's shopping for the week. Baba didn't mind if Mama shopped at the supermarket, on account of prices there being the same for everybody, but if they were going to a market where you could argue for a lower price, Baba wanted to do that himself because Mama was too kind. Mama said she was being fair to the seller, but Baba said she was being unfair to his budget.

Today they had dropped Titi at the supermarket, and Mama and Henry would be collecting her from there. Mama was having a driving lesson in the Saturday morning traffic of the capital city for the first time ever, and she had been too nervous to eat her breakfast.

'What are you expecting?' Baba had asked her. 'New York rush hour?'

'Of course not, Pius, we're in Africa. You've seen how bad the traffic gets in Dar.'

'Dar es Salaam is the biggest city in East Africa, Angel.

There are somewhere round two million people living there – twice as many as live in the whole of Swaziland. And not everybody in Swaziland drives a vehicle. *Eh*, here people are lucky if they have a wheelbarrow to push!'

'Please eat, Mama,' Benedict had said. He knew from Baba that they were lucky to get breakfast and that most of the people they shared the continent with didn't. Most were lucky to get just one meal a day.

'Please, Auntie,' Titi had tried. 'At least have more tea.'

'I can't.' Mama had pushed her empty mug away and put a hand to her stomach.

'*Eh*, Mama!' Grace had said. 'Being nervous could help you to reduce.'

Mama had given Grace one of her looks that said she must be very careful what she said next. Then Daniel and Moses had asked if they could share Mama's bread and she had let them, and Baba had thrown his hands in the air and muttered something about Mama not blaming anybody but herself if she fainted behind the wheel and killed somebody.

At the library, Benedict volunteered to stand in line at the counter with all the books they were returning, because he wanted to ask the librarian for some information on King Solomon. There hadn't been much in the encyclopaedias at home, little more than the story that Benedict already knew from the Bible. Two ladies had said that a baby was theirs, and they had gone to King Solomon so that he could say who the real mother was, but he had said he would cut the baby in two so that they could share. The lady who had said no, he mustn't cut the baby in two, he must rather let the other lady have the whole baby, that lady was really the baby's mother. The story showed that King Solomon was wise.

The librarian recommended a storybook called *King Solomon's Mines*. It hadn't been taken out and it hadn't been stolen, so that was what he chose. He showed it to Baba, even though he knew that Baba wasn't interested in storybooks; Baba was busy looking at the books that people had written about their own lives.

A voice close behind them said, '*Sanbonani!* Hello,' and they both swung round.

'Dr Mazibuko!'

'Uncle Enock!'

'And how are my tenants this morning?'

'Fine,' said Baba. 'And how are you?'

'Tip top.'

'We don't normally see you here.'

'It's not my natural habitat!' He winked Benedict, who smiled back at him. 'I'm just from the bank. I saw the Microbus outside and I came in to check if you were here.'

'*Shh!*' A *Mzungu* woman sitting with a newspaper looked at them angrily over her shoulder.

Uncle Enock said *eish!* very quietly and the three of them moved closer to the open door. His voice was a whisper when he continued.

'Benedict's duck may be well enough to come home today. I'm on my way to check on her. Do you want to come with me, Benedict?'

It was the most wonderful news! Benedict had rescued the duck from the dam some time back, sure that she was on her way to being late. Uncle Enock had said he would try to save her, though he had warned him that there wasn't very much hope.

'Please, Baba!'

'*Shh!*'

'Of course. Here, give me your book, I'll take it home for you.'

Uncle Enock's bakkie was big and powerful, just like Uncle Enock himself. Benedict strapped himself in, and as they set off together he checked how much traffic there was in Mbabane for Mama to be coping with. It was nothing like it could get back in Dar, though it was a little crowded and confused at the circle near the market where the United Nations had sponsored a wall with a picture painted on it. It was a picture about a bad disease, and it showed the planet Earth with Africa on it, and the flag of Swaziland and a person and a mask both crying. There was a skinny, skinny person wearing a white robe, with black letters on it saying *hospital bed, diarrhea, weight loss, TB, sores, death*, and behind the skinny person there was a casket and a gravestone that said RIP. It was a scary picture, and Benedict didn't like to look at it.

They didn't talk much to each other on the way out of Mbabane, on account of Uncle Enock talking to the other vehicles and shouting at many of them.

'Now what are you trying to do?' he asked a dark blue Mazda. 'Oh, I see.' His voice rose to a shout. 'Why don't you bloody indicate?'

'No, no, no,' he said to a minibus taxi. 'This is *my* lane, don't you dare! Hey! Hey! Hey!' He slammed his hand down on the hooter as the taxi squeezed in front of them anyway.

'Come on, try a little harder,' he said kindly to the old

bakkie in front of them that was struggling to get up to the crest of the Malagwane Hill on the outskirts of the city. 'You're way too old to be carrying so many people on your back.'

Benedict asked him if he always spoke to vehicles in English, and Uncle Enock laughed and said he was sure that vehicles wouldn't understand siSwati, and since he himself spoke no Japanese or German, English was probably best.

Over the crest of the hill they went, and the road sloped down steeply, twisting and turning. Just near the turn-off to the Baha'i centre they stopped to buy some new chicken-houses from a boy who was selling them at the roadside. Quite a few chickens lived down near the dairy, sleeping in round houses woven from dried grass just like the ones Uncle Enock was buying. They laid their eggs in there, too. Auntie Rachel ate a lot of eggs on account of not eating any meat.

Mama had been afraid that Benedict might want to become a vegetarian, especially after meeting Auntie Rachel, who had seen too many animals killed for food on her parents' farm. But Benedict had told her no, if he did that, when his time came to get confirmed in the church, he wouldn't be able to join Mama, Baba and his sisters in having parts of Jesus. And yes, there were animals that didn't eat meat, animals like cows and giraffes, but there were also plenty of animals like lions that ate meat, and birds that ate fish.

'People are animals, too, Mama,' he had assured her, 'and people are supposed to be omnibus.' She had given him one of her looks that said she wasn't quite sure if what he had said was a good thing or a bad thing, but she had said she was happy.

Uncle Enock wasn't a vegetarian. Being a vegetarian was

un-Swazi, and something un-Swazi was a very bad thing for a Swazi to do.

When they turned off the busy new highway onto the old road through the Ezulwini Valley, the Valley of Heaven, there were fewer cars to shout at and Benedict felt that it was okay to talk.

'Uncle Enock, you know King Martin Luther Junior?'

'Er... you mean Martin Luther King Junior?'

'Mm. I found him in the encyclopaedias when I was looking for King Solomon.'

Uncle Enock shouted at a bus to stay on its own bloody side of the road. It was coming towards them at an angle: the wheels were heading in the right direction, but the body seemed to be trying to cross over to the far side of Uncle Enock's lane. When they had passed it safely, Benedict continued.

'It said he tried to get respect for black people in America.'

'Respect and rights, nè?'

'Mm. That law in South Africa, that law that said you and Auntie Rachel weren't allowed to fall in love. Did they have it in America too?'

'It wasn't quite the same law, but the effect was the same. I'm not sure you went to jail for loving somebody different, but a mob might have killed you.'

'*Eh!*'

'If your indicator doesn't work, stick your bloody arm out of the window!' The Toyota in front of them was dead still; it was waiting to turn right onto the road to the Calabash Restaurant, where rich people ate. Baba had eaten there once with the minister, but their cakes weren't as nice as Mama's.

'Did they have a law like that anywhere else?'

'*Eish*, ask Rachel and her mom what happened to their Jewish ancestors in Germany!'

Auntie Rachel's mother, Mrs Levine, had been with her in the yellow Hi-Ace after school on Friday with her suitcase in the back, straight from the airport in Matsapha. The Mazibuko children had been happy – though surprised – to see their *Gogo* Levine. She was friendly enough, though the tight, straight line of her mouth told Benedict that something was making her angry. He really didn't feel like asking her about her ancestors.

Uncle Enock went on. 'But you know, I doubt you should be using past tense about these things. You've done past tense at school, nè?'

'Mm.'

'People are not everywhere respected. People are not everywhere free. What? What? You're a luxury tourist bus and you can't afford brake-lights?'

The bus in front of them was pulling off the road near the big hotels so that tourists could look at the things for sale at the long line of wooden roadside stalls. Sellers hurried towards the bus, hoping to lead the tourists to their own stall and persuade them to buy their own hand-made baskets, clay pots and carvings of wood or stone, or their own selection of brightly coloured cloths. Mama had bought some of the cloths to wear as *kangas* tied around her waist, which she said was a much more comfortable and sensible way to dress at home than a smart, tight skirt.

'Do you mean like a *shangaan* or a *kwerekwere* not being respected here?' Benedict asked.

'*Eish*, thanks God you're here and not South Africa! That side a mob can kill a *kwerekwere*!'

'*Eh!*'

'Here we'll just be rude to you or send you home.' He slammed his foot on the brake. 'Are you bloody blind? How can you just turn in front of me like that?' He swerved to overtake the tractor that had joined their road from a side road and was now barely moving on account of the driver being busy with his cell-phone. 'No, as Swazis we're too peaceful. Our last king, this king's daddy, on his memorial it's written *I have no enemy*. But there's ever a problem for outsiders, nè? Everywhere. What would you call me if I came as a Swazi to live in Tanzania?'

'Welcome,' said Benedict, and Uncle Enock laughed, even though Benedict hadn't said anything funny.

'But it's been okay for you at school, nè?'

'Mm, except when they thought Baba was the Pipi Doctor.'

Uncle Enock looked at him and began to laugh again.

Benedict had read about the Pipi Doctor in the *Times of Swaziland* that Baba brought home from work for Mama every day. That doctor had come from Tanzania to Manzini, the big commercial town down at the end of the highway, and everybody called him the Pipi Doctor because he was doing special operations on men to make their pipi bigger. Some days the newspaper said that men wanted him to go home and ladies wanted him to stay, but other days it said that ladies wanted him to go home and men wanted him to stay. Now ministers in parliament were going to decide for everybody if he should stay or go.

At school all the children knew that the Tungarazas were

from Tanzania, but only some of them knew that Baba was *Dr* Tungaraza. Those children had done what Baba called adding two to two and getting six instead of four, which is a way of saying they had looked at the evidence and then guessed wrong.

Eventually Mrs Dlamini had spoken to the whole school and explained to everybody that you could be called Dr Somebody if you had read a lot of books and been to school for a long time, or you could be called Dr Somebody if you knew how to help sick people and to do operations, so Dr Tungaraza wasn't even the same kind of doctor as the Tanzanian doctor in Manzini. She never said Pipi Doctor, but everybody had known and some of the older ones had giggled. But after that they had stopped asking Benedict about his pipi.

Uncle Enock was finding it difficult to stop laughing. He would say he was sorry and try to keep quiet, but then he would start up again. His laughter was like a cold that somebody else could catch, and soon Benedict began to laugh with him.

He managed not to laugh when he saw Execution Rock, the high, rocky mountaintop that long-ago criminals got pushed off. It was also called Nyonyane, meaning little bird, on account of the criminals looking like little birds on their way down from the top. But when Uncle Enock was too busy laughing to shout at the minibus taxi that overtook them at high speed when another was coming towards them, Benedict began to laugh again.

Crossing the bridge over the Lusushwana River, they both took in great gulps of air, filling their lungs to calm themselves, and Uncle Enock asked for one of the tissues from the cubbyhole to wipe his eyes. Benedict handed him one then used the end of his T-shirt himself.

He was calm enough to be respectful when they passed the Royal Kraal of the late King Sobhuza II, who was the father of Mswati III, the current king. Some of the late king's wives had lived there, but only twenty-six of them; the other forty-four had lived in other places. King Sobhuza II had been a bit like King Solomon, who the encyclopaedia said had had seven hundred wives.

Benedict couldn't imagine having more than one mama. Okay, he had had a first mama, and then he had got a new mama, but they hadn't both been his mamas at the same time and in the same house. Say you lived in the Royal Kraal with twenty-six mamas. How would you ever be able to read a book without a mama calling you to do something? And say each mama had children. How many brothers and sisters would you have? How would you ever get time to be alone with butterflies and birds and all the other creatures God had made? Imagine!

Before they got as far as the big fruit and vegetable market at Mahlanya, they had to slow right down, on account of cattle being in the road. Bearing long, curved horns as far apart at the tips as Uncle Enock's shoulders, some black, some chocolate, some the colour of peanut sauce, they ambled slowly, not seeming to be going anywhere in particular. One or two cars hooted at them impatiently, but Uncle Enock let them be.

Then they saw a tiny boy, smaller than Moses or Daniel, running barefoot down towards them from round the slight bend in the road just before the market. Though winter had already begun, the boy was naked except for a tattered old pair of brown shorts. He carried in one hand as he ran a long branch from a willow tree, all its leaves pulled off, while in the other hand he clutched a mealie with blackened seeds that had been roasted over a fire.

Before he reached the cattle, the boy began shouting and waving his willow-branch in the air, and the huge creatures listened to him and began to move slowly off the road. As the cars began to move again, the boy bit into his mealie.

'*Eish*, the cops aren't going to be happy,' Uncle Enock said.

And they weren't. Vehicles were only just beginning to get going again as they rounded the bend, so the police waiting there with their radar machine weren't going to get any money out of any of them. Baba said the radar machine didn't work properly: everybody Baba knew who had got caught had exactly the same speed written on their ticket, which couldn't be possible on account of statistics. Anyway, somebody at Baba's work had a cousin in the police who could make a ticket go away for a lot less than half of what the ticket cost.

Two of the police at the side of the road were buying mealies from a man who was roasting them at the edge of the market. Benedict hoped that the man had given the mealie to the small boy herding the cattle rather than making him buy it. It wasn't right for a man with a mealie-roasting business to take money for food from a child who didn't have shoes.

They turned off the old road, Uncle Enock shouting at a pineapple-laden bakkie that was supposed to stop for them but didn't, and a short distance further, just before the small settlement called Malkerns where pineapples were put into cans, they pulled up outside Uncle Enock's work.

Inside, an old woman waited with a nervous, skinny dog,

while a man sat with a lamb lying across his lap like a rag. The receptionist told Uncle Enock that Dr Mamba was at the back. Benedict wasn't sure that Dr Mamba was a good name for a vet. A mamba was a kind of snake: there was a green mamba and a black mamba. Both had a head the shape of a casket, and both could kill a person or any other animal very quickly.

At the back, Dr Mamba was giving an injection to a goat that lay shivering in a wheelbarrow, while a young man watched anxiously. Benedict left the two doctors to talk and ran to the holiday home for pets at the end of the property.

The long building making a T with the rear wall had dogs on one side and cats on the other. Lining the side wall that faced the section for dogs was another row of dog accommodation, while lining the side wall facing the cats was accommodation for the manager of the holiday home and space for him to prepare the animals' food.

Benedict began in the dog section, where each animal had its own little house to sleep in at the back in a covered area protected from the rain, and a patch of grass to play on at the front. Most of them had brought their favourite blanket from home and one or two of their toys to play with. Benedict knew without having to think about it that he would bring his cushion and the bookshelf full of books.

The first dog, an old black Labrador, came to the chicken-wire at the front of its cage wagging its tail, and licked his hand. The two small brown-and-white dogs next door jumped high in the air like Maasai men, straight up and down, barking at him like he was a robber and everybody must wake up and call the police. All the other dogs joined in, even the tiny one that was a ball of fluffy white curls with a purple bow on its head.

In the section opposite, a huge brown and black creature barked with a very deep voice, curling back its lips and showing Benedict its enormous teeth. He moved round to where the cats were.

Dogs and cats didn't like each other much; he knew that. Not unless they had been raised together and they had grown up understanding and respecting each other. Then they could be good friends; they could lie down together like the lion and the lamb in the Bible. But while they didn't trust each other, it was best for them to holiday separately.

The accommodation in the cat section was different, on account of cats liking to climb. As well as a house to sleep in and a section sheltered from the rain, each cat had part of a tree to play on. Draped over a thick branch in the first cage was a sleepy creature that looked like something Moses or Daniel might have painted. Splodges of orange, brown, black and white seemed to be fighting with one another all over its body.

Auntie Rachel had taught him the word *splodge*. When he had finished his first ever glass of farm milk at the other house, she had leaned forward with a tissue and said, 'Here. You've got two splodges of milk,' and she had dabbed at either side of his upper lip. Auntie Rachel used the word a lot, but Benedict had never used it himself, not even in his mind. Not until now, when the patches of colour on that cat couldn't be thought of as anything other than splodges.

Next door, two black cats, one skinny and the other rather fat, rubbed up against the mesh, pushing each other out of the way to get near him. Squatting down, he put the palm of his hand flat against the wire, feeling the vibration of their purrs. Then he pushed a finger through to give one of them a gentle scratch. Twisting round, it licked at his finger with its sand-paper tongue.

There were several more cats: a white one that didn't even want to look at him, a sleepy pair with grey-and-white stripes, and a noisy orange one with an angry-looking face. Then there were two empty cages before the last one that had a piece of board up against the mesh at its side, blocking the view into it from any cats that might have been in the neighbouring cage.

Benedict went to look.

Sitting in a shallow tray of water on the grass was his duck! *Eh!* He had expected her to be inside, in the clinic!

Squatting down, he greeted her in a gentle voice, unsure whether she would know him or be frightened of him. But she simply continued to sit in the water.

He looked at her carefully. As far as he could see, there were no patches missing from the black feathers with flecks of white on her wings and tail, and her grey beak seemed to be fine. *Eh!* She looked so much better than she had when he had rescued her, exhausted and almost drowned, from the dam and run with her all the way down the hill to Uncle Enock, panic pounding in his chest and tears streaming down his face.

'You found her!' said Uncle Enock now, squatting down next to him.

'Is she better?'

'Just need to check her leg,' he said, standing up and

opening the gate at the front of the cage. Inside, his big hands lifted her up out of the tray of water and put her gently on the ground. Standing, she shook her tail from side to side and took a few steps on her big orange feet.

'Tip top,' he said to Benedict. 'Go and ask Dr Mamba for one of the small cages, and we'll take her home.'

'Um... Uncle Enock...'

'*Yebo*. Yes. What?'

'Maybe we shouldn't take her home.'

'What are you talking about?'

'I mean, maybe she doesn't want to go back there. On account of bad memories.'

Mwanza, where Benedict had spent his first six years, had bad memories on account of his first parents getting late there. Okay, there were happy memories, too: memories of him, Grace and Moses doing nice things with their first mama and baba, and also with Titi. But now it was much better for them to be away from that place.

'*Eish*.' Uncle Enock scratched his head. 'You think a duck has memories?'

'Of course!' Benedict was surprised, but then he reminded himself that this was Uncle Enock's first duck patient. 'How can ducks do migration if they can't remember where the other side of the world is?'

'*Eish!*'

'I'm thinking... the bird book says this kind of duck likes to be in running water with rocks in the day and then she goes to something like the dam in the evening to sleep for the night. So maybe we could take her to a river now, and then she can decide for herself if she wants to go back to the dam later.'

Uncle Enock laughed and shook his head. 'Fetch a cage from Dr Mamba,' he said.

They freed her from the cage next to the Lusushwana River where it ran parallel to the road over a scattering of large rocks. It was where ladies came to wash their clothes and where people said mermen sometimes put spells on them.

'The mermen won't put a spell on her, will they?' Benedict asked as they waited for her to waddle towards the edge of the water.

'*Eish*. You know, I think a merman can only put a spell on you if you believe in him. Can a duck believe in a merman?'

The duck was at the water's edge now. She hopped in and swam in circles, then began to quack.

'I suppose. I mean, half of a merman is a man, and she's quacking at us now so she knows people are real and not just pretend. And you saved her life, so of course she believes in you. And the other half of a merman is a fish. How can a duck not believe in a fish?'

'Er...' Uncle Enock picked up the empty cage. 'Maybe... Maybe mermen save their spells for ladies, nè? Maybe they leave ducks alone.'

'I hope.'

At lunch, Benedict didn't have the chance to tell anybody about his duck, on account of everybody being too busy laughing at Mama's and Titi's stories.

Mama had found her first driving lesson in Mbabane as easy as cutting a slice of cake, with a lot less traffic than she had feared, and with Henry sprinkling praise on her like sugar on a doughnut. Near the end of the lesson, Mama had stopped at a red traffic light where the street she was on intersected with a street sloping down a hill. Who had been waiting at the lights on that other street, heading up the hill, but old Mrs Gama in her lime-green Beetle!

The light for old Mrs Gama's car was red so that the vehicles coming down the hill, for which there was a green flashing arrow, could turn right to go to The Plaza, where Mama and Henry were heading to fetch Titi. But old Mrs Gama wasn't concentrating, and her Beetle was slowly sliding backwards down the hill. She didn't hear the vehicle behind her hooting, and she didn't notice Mama flashing her headlights at her.

Henry had been so embarrassed he had wanted to be small enough to hide himself in the cubbyhole of the Quick Impact Corolla. It was only when the lights for old Mrs Gama turned green and the big four-wheel drive vehicle behind her moved forward, pushing the Beetle ahead of it, that she put the car into gear and accelerated across the intersection.

When they had arrived at The Plaza and Mama had gone in to the supermarket to find Titi and pay for the groceries, Titi had been white!

She had just picked up a ten-kilogram bag of *ugali* from a shelf, when Mavis, who was on a day off from cleaning at the other house, greeted her. They stood and chatted in the aisle for a few minutes while other shoppers moved around them, and then the bag of *ugali* began to grow heavy for Titi. Without looking – on account of being busy talking with Mavis – she put the bag into her trolley, which was behind her. Only it wasn't behind her any longer, on account of somebody having moved it out of the way. The bag had dropped to the ground and burst open, sending a big white cloud of maize meal into the air around her.

She had been so embarrassed she had wanted to make herself as small as the smallest child at the other house so that Mavis could take her by the hand and lead her away. The manager of the shop hadn't been angry, on account of it being an accident and accidents being things that happened. He had sent a man to sweep it up, but Titi wasn't somebody who was used to having people clean for her, and nor was Mavis, so both of them had tried to help. And in helping, Titi had got even more of it all over her.

Mama had asked the manager for some old newspaper, and while she was spreading it over Henry's back seat so that Titi couldn't leave a powdery white mess all over it, Henry had walked around Titi laughing loudly and pointing, which had made other people look. That had made Titi want to be small enough to fit into the cubbyhole of the Quick Impact Corolla, and Mama had had to remind Henry that just a few minutes earlier he had felt embarrassed enough to want to hide in there himself. That had made Titi feel a little bit better about the unkind way Henry had behaved, and they had managed to laugh together all the way down the hill.

After lunch, Baba took Moses and Daniel with him to watch football at Somhlolo stadium, where he was meeting a man from work who was also bringing his boys. Benedict kept trying to like football, but he just couldn't, even though he knew that Baba was disappointed. His first baba had loved it.

The girls went down to the other house, where Innocence

Mazibuko's friend was coming to visit with an older sister who was going to teach them lipstick. Mama had a lipstick. It was only for best, when she went out in one of her smart dresses. But that hadn't happened for a long time now.

It hadn't always been like this, his older sisters together, his younger brothers together, and Benedict all by himself in between. When it had been just him, Grace and Moses at their first parents' house in Mwanza, they had all been friends together. Grace used to spend hours reading to them, and Moses had been happy to do with Benedict whatever Benedict felt like doing. When their first mama had got so sick that she needed to be in the hospital, and their first baba had taken the three of them and Titi to live with their grandparents in Dar, they had become even closer. At first they would even sit right up close to one another, their bodies touching so tight that not even a single layer of the thin, greying sheet their Mama lay on in the hospital back in Mwanza could fit between them.

But two years later Faith and Daniel had come to live with them, and after that everything had changed. Moses had found that he preferred to play with Daniel, who was closer to his age, and Grace had decided that her new sister was much more fun than books or spending time with Benedict.

Baba had started working late at the university then, taking on extra projects for extra money on account of the family being so much bigger now, and Mama had begun to spend much more time on her cake business. Even Titi was busier, with five children to take care of and clean up after instead of just three.

It was then that Benedict had begun to take an interest in

other animals, animals other than the people who no longer had time for him. He had begun with the dog in the garden of the house behind Mama's and Baba's. The dog's collar was attached by a chain to a pole at the side of the house so that it couldn't run away if anybody left the gate open, and the chain was long enough to let it attack any robbers who came to the front door or the back door, and to let it lie in the shade at the front or the back depending.

When Benedict had first noticed it, noticed it as one of God's creatures rather than just a background shape in a neighbouring garden, he had wanted to reach out and touch it. But when he had put his whole arm through the fence and stretched it as far as he could, and when the dog had come as far as the chain would let it and stretched its neck as far as it could, there had still been a gap the length of a storybook between the tips of Benedict's fingers and the tip of the dog's tongue. It was only when Titi had called him to come in and wash his hands for supper that he had realised that he and the dog had spent a whole entire afternoon reaching towards each other, and during that whole time he hadn't felt bored or lonely, not even once.

After that he would spend hours sitting on his side of the fence chatting to the dog and being interested in anything that the dog showed him: a bird, a lizard, a bee. Their best was when all the pigeons that belonged to somebody across the city flew home from wherever they had been taken in their box and set free. As the birds flocked overhead, the dog would jump and twist against its chain, barking like a hyena drunk on fermented marulas, and Benedict would join in, jumping and shouting excitedly. Then Mama would appear in their back

yard with her mixing spoon or her icing syringe and ask
Benedict if he was okay.

He was more okay than he had been in a long while, but he
didn't say.

Today he decided to go up the hill to the dam, so that Mama
and Titi could have the house to themselves to carry on laughing about their morning. There was no point in going down to
see Auntie Rachel because she was busy with her mother's
visit, so he took his new library book up to the dam with him,
and in the shade of a water-berry tree he settled down, cross-
legged, to read.

The book started with Introduction, where a man called
Allan Quartermain said the story in the book was true. The
English was difficult, on account of the book being from long
ago; English was also difficult back when they wrote the Bible.
Benedict wished that Mr Quartermain knew Swahili. The
library in Mbabane had a storybook in English that Grace had
already read to him in Swahili: *Safari za Gulliver*, about a man
called Gulliver who, unlike Benedict, hadn't had to struggle
to feel big. But in Swaziland people spoke only siSwati and
English, and there was no hope of finding a Swahili version of
Mr Quartermain's story here.

He looked at the back of the book to see what the story was
about; maybe it wasn't going to be worth all the difficult
English. It said there that it was about three men following a
treasure map and going on an adventure to find the mines of
King Solomon that were full of diamonds and gold.

Flipping through the pages to see if there were any pictures that might make the English easier, he came across the treasure map that the men had followed. *Eh!* That meant that anybody could follow it and find the mines! He studied the map carefully. There was a cross showing compass points, but they weren't marked. Really! What kind of map didn't say where north was? And it didn't even say the country! But the names of two rivers were given: Kalukawe and Lukanga. He could look those up in the atlas at home. Two big circles were labelled Sheba's Breasts; maybe those were mountains. A kraal was indicated, and also a koppie, which was a word in South African English for a hill. Did the South African word mean that the 'treasure cave' at the end of 'Solomon's Road' was right next door to Swaziland, in South Africa? Imagine!

Something pressed up against Benedict's back.

Eh!

He jumped up and swung round, dropping the book.

A dog circled round him, sniffing at his clothes. Golden brown with black ears and a black patch around each eye, she didn't really look like any kind of dog in particular.

'Krishna!' A voice called angrily from the field behind the clump of trees. 'Krishna!'

'It's okay,' Benedict called, 'I don't mind!' He squatted down and petted the dog. 'Hello, Krishna.'

Petros emerged from the trees. 'Sorry, nè?'

'It's okay.' He smiled shyly up at Petros, still petting the dog that was sniffing him excitedly. 'I'm Benedict.'

'Petros.'

'I think she can smell other dogs on me. I was at Uncle Enock's work today.'

Smiling, Petros bent to pick up Benedict's book. 'Sorry, nè?'

93

'It's okay.' Benedict stood up.

Petros turned the book over and over in his hands. 'What does it say?'

'This?' He took the book from Petros. 'I've just started, but I think it's too difficult for me.' He told him what it said on the back.

Petros listened carefully, shaking his head. 'The gold, it is not in the mines,' he said. Then he patted his chest. 'The gold, it is with me.'

He laughed, his laughter soon turning into coughing. He patted his chest harder.

'Are you okay?'

Petros nodded through his coughs, struggling for breath. Benedict waited patiently, focusing on the dog.

At last Petros could speak. '*Eish!* Sorry, nè? Auntie, he have *muti* for me. Come, Krishna.'

'*Hamba kahle!* Go well,' Benedict called after him as he made his way with his dog towards the path that would lead him down to the other house.

Not wanting to try again with his book just yet, Benedict sat again and looked at the water, where a dragonfly skimmed across the surface. Petros had smelled mostly of his funny cigarettes, but underneath that was the smell of cows. It was hard to tell how old he was, but he must be younger than Titi. Could he still be a teenager? Maybe. He lived on the farm, but not in the house with Auntie Rachel and Uncle Enock. *Eh*, he was so skinny! Did he have parents somewhere? Benedict didn't know. But at least Auntie Rachel was taking care of him with medicine for his cough.

What had he meant about the gold being with him? He

certainly didn't dress – or smell – like a rich somebody. Was that what people were talking about when they said he wasn't quite right in his head? Did it mean he was wrong about things? Was he simply wrong about the gold? Or maybe the gold was just pretend.

Who could Benedict ask? Definitely not Mama or Baba, on account of the Tungaraza children not being supposed to talk to Petros. Maybe Uncle Enock.

A sudden gust of wind shook the colony of weavers' nests in the trees near the dam. It was winter now, so the nests were empty and there were no eggs or baby birds in danger of falling out. Each nest had been built by a male and then decorated on the inside and made comfortable by a female. Weavers were clever with their nests, building them at the very ends of thin branches where snakes couldn't get to them, and putting the entrance at the bottom of the nest to make it more difficult for a snake to get in if it ever got as far as the end of the branch. That was the weaver version of the window bars and security gates on people's houses in Swaziland.

Benedict thought about his duck, hoping she was okay and being left alone by any merman that might be in the river. It was too early for her to come to sleep at the dam – if she even wanted to – so he decided to go back home for some tea.

As he left his old shoes outside the back door, he realised that the house was very quiet. Good. But the kitchen made him sad, on account of there being no smell of cake just out of the oven, no sight of Mama's icing syringe drying along with mixing bowls on the draining board, and no sieve full of weevils from the flour waiting for him to take them outside for the birds.

In the lounge, Mama lay asleep on one of the couches. Scattered on the floor around her were a number of crumpled tissues.

Eh! Had Mama been crying? Tears stung the back of his own eyes.

Tiptoeing closer, he saw an open magazine on the coffee table. Without making a sound, he scooped it up and moved away with it to the dining table. Mama had been looking at the story about a very special wedding where they used to live on account of Baba's last job, and the beautiful cake that Mama had baked for it. Looking at the photographs had made Mama sad, and Benedict knew that she was sad because her business was so slow now.

Feeling bad, he closed the magazine and put it with Mama's two other magazines on top of the bookshelf, next to the basket where Baba kept the keys to the red Microbus and the Corolla from his work. He slipped it underneath the other two magazines, hoping that Mama might forget. On top of it was the magazine with pictures of road signs that Mama had used for getting ready to learn how to drive, and on top of that was the magazine that a friend had sent her from Ghana in West Africa. Was it safe for that to be on top, or was there anything in it that could make her sad?

He moved with it to the dining table, and sat down to flip through it. It had stories about artists and craftspeople in Ghana, with lots of photographs. One of the stories was about a group of ladies who were printing designs on cloth that other ladies could use to make dresses. It looked a bit like the kind of cloth for the dresses at the special wedding in Mama's other magazine. *Eh!* This magazine could upset her, too.

He was about to close it when another story caught his attention. It had photographs of people making the most beautiful caskets. The story said that if a person was a car salesman before he became late, he could have a casket that was carved into the shape of a Mercedes Benz. And if he was a musician, he could be buried in a casket that looked like a guitar. Or a fisherman could have a casket shaped like a fish. All the caskets were painted so that the Mercedes, the guitar and the fish looked real.

They were even more special than the beautiful one that Jabulani had made for Benedict's hoopoe.

Jabulani would love them!

Eh!

Benedict opened his mouth and breathed in quickly.

Maybe caskets like these were the edge for Ubuntu Funerals that he had asked for in his prayer at the hoopoe's grave. In that same prayer, he had asked for customers for Mama's business. Maybe if Mama showed these caskets to Jabulani and Zodwa, they would be so grateful for the edge that they'd send each and every one of their customers to Mama for cakes.

Eh!

He went to the couch with the magazine and shook Mama's shoulder.

'Mama!' he whispered excitedly. 'Mama! I've found an edge!'

SIX

SITTING ON THE COLD EDGE OF THE STEP OUTSIDE her room, Mavis pulled her blanket more tightly around her, tucking her knees closer to her body and rocking gently while she waited for Madam's drops to do their work inside her body. Whatever it was that had wrenched her from her sleep tonight had left her sweaty and shaky and needing air.

As usual, the buildings on the hillside lay in darkness. But Mavis knew that if she were to walk round to the other side of the main house, the side where Madam and Doctor's bedroom opened onto the garden, she might see a tiny red light glowing at the window of the downstairs bedroom that was for visitors.

Visitors weren't allowed to smoke inside the house. Madam said it wasn't healthy around the children and Doctor said it was a bad example. Mavis knew from jobs she'd had before that cigarettes made a smell and a mess. Tiny flecks of ash fell everywhere, and an ashtray was a very unpleasant thing to clean. And, *eish*, the smell on the clothes as her hands had washed them!

Mavis tutted loudly on the edge of the step, sure that Lungi – fast asleep on the other side of the door – would not hear her. Sure, too, that in the morning she would find herself cleaning the dark smudge off a dishcloth that smelled of smoke. *Gogo* Levine had not been staying long, but already she had a routine. During the chaos of the children's breakfast at the big table in the kitchen that seemed almost as big as the whole house at one of Mavis's old jobs, *Gogo* Levine would quietly take Mavis's dishcloth – damp from washing the morning teacups – and go to her room, where she would wipe from the outside windowsill any mess from stubbing out her cigarettes at the open window in the night. Then she would put the cloth back next to the sink as if she thought that Mavis was a bad cleaner who wouldn't see the dirt on it or smell that it wasn't clean.

But Mavis would never say anything to Madam. What would that be for? *Gogo* Levine was Madam's mother.

Madam had too much luck, she was able to be a mother meanwhile she had delivered no child. Mavis would never be a mother herself, and she would never meet a man like Doctor who wouldn't mind. Doctor had been out in the world, he had schooled in South Africa, he didn't mind that Madam wasn't a Swazi and she couldn't deliver. Mavis would certainly never meet a man as rich as Doctor. *Eish*, he had too many cows!

But her mind was going to dangerous places. If she thought about cows she might think about Petros, and if she thought about Petros just after she had thought about never being a mother, then she would have to think about how Petros was so like her own boy would have been, and that would be too hard.

Rising from the step, she pulled her blanket around her. The little gaps in each crocheted square made it not the best blanket for wrapping up in against the cold night air, but her mother had made it for her, and that was what made it warm. This year there would be a good sum of money to take home to her mother: the Cobra floor-polish tin under her bed was filling up nice-nice.

She felt calmer now, but she had woken up sweaty, and it wouldn't be nice to go back to her bed without first having a wash. The door to their bathroom creaked a little, but it never woke Lungi. *Eish*, she envied Lungi her sleep! The room on the other side of the bathroom was used for storing things, so Mavis didn't need to worry about waking a gardener or any other worker sleeping in there. She was glad that the bathroom was for her and Lungi only. She wouldn't want to share it with a man who might not keep it clean – though Lungi wouldn't have minded if Samson lived in. On the days when Samson came to work, if Madam was out, Lungi sometimes asked Mavis to make sure that none of the children came near the outside room.

Lungi was already a widow, though she was young, just twenty-six. Mavis was five years older, but she looked younger because she was small next to Lungi. When Lungi had lost her husband an uncle of his had wanted to take her, but Lungi's family had pretended that she was sick, and when that didn't work they gave back the cows that his family had paid for her. They didn't have to give back the *lobola*, it wasn't like Lungi hadn't been able to conceive – she had just never had the chance because her husband was always away at his job in the mine in South Africa, and then he was late when part of the mine fell down on him. Anyway, the uncle accepted the cows in Lungi's place, and now Lungi was free.

The neon light in the bathroom was so bright after the darkness, Mavis had to close her eyes for a few seconds. When she opened them, she saw that one side of her shoulder-length relaxed hair was standing straight up, pushed there by lying on her side as she slept. She was always asleep before Lungi in the first part of the night and it was always Lungi who woke her in the morning. But most nights something else woke her in between. It had been happening for years – almost seventeen years – and she had had plenty of time to grow used to it. It really didn't matter at all, especially now that she had found a way to use her time awake to earn some extra money to support her mother. She would get back to her crocheting as soon as she had washed.

The bathroom had hot and cold water, but only one at a time. That made a shower a very difficult thing to have, so neither Mavis nor Lungi used it. Instead, a big, red plastic tub lived on the floor of the shower, and with the plastic curtain drawn so that the water didn't splash, they would fill it with first one and then the other, like a bath. Mavis was just small enough to sit right inside the tub, but it was much easier to wash standing up in it. Tonight, though, she would have just a small wash at the basin.

The main house had the same problem of not having hot and cold at the same time. Doctor said it was to do with the geysers and the water-tanks from the dam, and there was nothing to do to fix it, so when they had added the new upstairs for the children's bedrooms, they didn't waste money putting a shower in the upstairs bathroom. Mavis was glad of that: nobody ever used the downstairs shower, but the small tiles in the floor of it took a long time to clean nice-nice. The one-at-a-time water wasn't a problem, they must just always put cold before hot in the baths so a child could never climb in to a bath of water so hot it could hurt them.

It was the same at the *kwerekwere* house. Titi told her that sometimes an insect or something would come into the bath with the cold water and then the girls would be afraid. Probably there weren't insects in their own country; the eldest boy certainly looked at them like he had never seen them before. Mavis had once watched him in the garden from an upstairs window, squatting down and staring for a very long time at something that was crawling in the grass.

Patting herself dry with her towel, she thought about how different that boy was, for his age. He was like Vusi, serious and wanting to learn. He always came to the house with questions that needed answering, meanwhile his brothers came to play with Fortune and his sisters came to play with Innocence. Titi said he liked to read books and to be quiet by himself outside. Petros also liked to be by himself outside.

Eish!

Now she was thinking about him again.

Sighing deeply, she pulled her nightgown back on over her head, wrapped her blanket around her again, and sat down on the closed lid of the toilet. Maybe she should stop trying to keep him out of her head. Maybe she should just let him walk around in there and then maybe he would go out of it again.

Petros was a good boy. He was mature, responsible, already earning his own money. He didn't need anybody. But in the late afternoons when she heard the cows beginning to make their way down past the house towards the milking shed, if she didn't have a child clinging to her or one in the bath or a mess to tidy or clean, and if nobody was watching, she would take some leftover food from the fridge – something nice that he might not cook for himself – and she would go out to meet him on his way home with the cows. He would take the food and thank her politely, then he would chat for just a minute or two, always watching the cows, always making sure that his dog didn't jump at her.

Such a good boy!

She always felt disappointed when the cows came past with somebody else instead of Petros. Then she would pretend to be picking some vegetables in Madam's garden, and she would act like the supermarket bag with Petros's food in it was for the cabbage or the carrots or the onions that she was choosing. The food was for Petros, she didn't want to give it to anybody else.

When she had talked to him recently he had coughed and coughed, and after he had continued on his way with the cows, Mavis had seen that his spit on the ground was red with blood. She had told Madam, and Madam had taken him to a doctor for some pills, so he was going to be better soon. But just to make sure, Mavis had taken the small jar of Vicks from the house and given it to Petros to rub on his chest. Here, he had asked her, patting his chest with one hand as he took the jar with the other. Yes, there, she had told him, longing to rub it there for him, longing for him to be her own boy so that she could do that for him. But her hand had made a circle in the air instead, and he had thanked her politely and continued down the hill with his dog and the cows.

She had watched him go, knowing he had no mother to go to, no family anywhere, and hoping that he would turn and come back up the hill to her, holding out the jar and saying to her, here, show me, please, take care of me. But he hadn't turned, not even to wave, and on Saturday she had bought a new jar of Vicks at the supermarket, putting it in the cupboard before anybody had noticed that the other one was gone.

Petros's cough would go much sooner if he didn't smoke. Really, he was too young to smoke! If he was her boy, she would tell him to stop. *Eish*, the smoke and the cows and his dog made him smell very bad. She so wanted to wash his clothes for him! She never had, but if she ever did, while she was doing it she would want him to lie in a bath of nice warm water; she would make it smell lovely with one of Madam's special oils.

Did he have a nice thick blanket to keep him warm at night? She would love to crochet one for him like the one her mother had made for her. But when she had been clearing up at the end of the birthday party that Madam and Doctor had made for the dairy manager, she had heard the dairy manager telling Doctor about Petros. Give him something, the dairy manager had said, and he gives it away to somebody who needs it more. The two men had laughed about him giving things away like a rich man who already had everything he needed. But Mavis hadn't wanted to laugh, her heart had swelled with pride.

Such a nice boy!

But if she made a special blanket for him, she wouldn't want him giving it away to somebody else.

Wrapping her own blanket more tightly around her, she left the bathroom. She would get back into her bed and crochet until sleep came back to her.

SEVEN

THERE WERE TWO REASONS WHY THE LAST FRIDAY in June was an exciting day for Benedict, and he thought about both of them as he bolted down his bread and tea at breakfast.

The first was that it was his and Sifiso's day to get a turn presenting their project in class. They had chosen bilharzia, dividing the topic in two so that Benedict could do the life cycle and Sifiso could talk about how not to get it and how to know you might have it. Bilharzia could make grown-ups too exhausted to work and it could make children find learning their subjects at school very difficult, so it was a very bad disease. It couldn't really make you late, but still.

After helping Sifiso to find a way to do his part without any words that would make him lisp, Benedict had spent many hours working on a big poster that showed bilharzia's life cycle. Mrs Patel had given him a large cardboard box that she no longer needed, and he had flattened it out to make a piece of board as big as himself.

He had drawn some pictures on the back of some used paper that Baba had brought home from the office, and then cut out what he had drawn and glued the pieces to the board.

On either side there was a person and in the middle there were some snails, people and snails being the two co-hosts of the story of bilharzia.

The person on the left was a man standing next to a river and using it as a toilet, with a dotted line arcing from below his waist into the water. Next to him was a group of little worms, with an arrow showing that the worms were inside the man and he had bilharzia. There were lots of little worm eggs in what he had sprayed into the water, with an arrow showing the eggs getting inside the snails that were in the water. Underneath the snails was a picture of the eggs hatching into worms, and an arrow showing that it happened inside the snails; then there were lots of little worms swimming towards the other person, a child who was swimming in the water. Then next to the child was a picture of lots of little worms, and an arrow showing that they were inside the child now and he had bilharzia.

It was a story that interested Benedict on account of people not being able to give the disease to each other: a person could only give it to a snail, and another person could only get it from a snail. It was like malaria, which a mosquito got from one person and then gave to somebody else.

Despite trying his best, he hadn't been able to find any information about bilharzia that said if the snail got sick. Was a snail just fine when the eggs from a person hatched into worms inside it? People got really tired when the worms were inside them laying their eggs. Did the snails get tired too? And if a snail was too tired to swim, could it drown? People could avoid getting bilharzia by staying out of water that had snails in it. But how could a snail avoid getting it? Water was its home. It couldn't just leave if somebody used the water as a toilet.

If a snail ever gave a presentation about bilharzia, what would it say? Maybe Uncle Enock would have an idea.

The second reason for Benedict's excitement was that Mama would soon be showing Zodwa the beautiful Ghanaian caskets in her magazine and suggesting them as an edge for Ubuntu Funerals.

Zodwa had arranged to collect her cake that morning, and it waited for her now on the coffee table as the family ate their breakfast at the dining table. It looked like a very large, very thick version of Swaziland's 20-cent coin with its wavy outline. Mama had baked two round vanilla sponges, one bright green, the other purple, and she had sandwiched them together with a layer of red icing. Benedict had suggested the colours himself, choosing them because they were the colours of the *ligwalagwala*, the purple-crested lourie that was Swaziland's national bird. It was a truly beautiful bird with a shiny green head and neck, purple crest and wings, and a bright red eye that matched the flash of red under its wings when it flew.

Mama had cut away at the perfect round edge to make the coin's wavy outline, nibbling at the bits she had cut away as she worked. She had covered the whole cake with a smooth, light grey sugar-paste, and then set to work on another rolled-out piece of the same sugar-paste to make the design for on the top. Placing a real coin next to her on the table with the side facing down that said Swaziland and had a picture of King Mswati, she had looked very carefully at the other side and asked Benedict for some help, on account of that side having a picture of an elephant's head.

Elephants were important in Swaziland, the king's mother being called Indlovukati, The Great She Elephant. Benedict liked that the king was a lion and his mother was an elephant; people really shouldn't think of themselves as separate from all the other animals. There was a picture of Indlovukati's head as a lady on the 1 lilangeni coin, and on the 20 cents there was the head of an elephant.

Benedict had helped Mama to draw a simpler, less detailed version of the picture on the coin, and together they had cut it out of the sugar-paste and stuck it on to the top of the cake. Then Mama had cut out sugar-paste numbers that said 20, and letters that said *years* instead of *cents*. That was because the ladies of Zodwa's *inhlangano*, their savings society, had been meeting for twenty years, and the special meeting to celebrate the twenty years was going to be at Zodwa's house that weekend.

Zodwa had told Mama that the twelve ladies in the *inhlangano* met once a month to support one another, and every month each one of them put the same amount of money into the group's savings. Then they took turns for everybody's money to come to one of them so that once a year each of them got a turn to get a big sum of money. It was a way of ladies helping one another when the banks didn't take them seriously.

The last step in getting the cake ready had been the most exciting, on account of Mama getting the chance to use something new for the first time ever. Auntie Rachel had told Mama about a shop over the border in Nelspruit that sold everything you could possibly need for making and decorating cakes. Imagine! And there was a lady in Mbabane who made regular trips to a clinic in Nelspruit, taking ladies and girls who had got into trouble and needed to go to South Africa where there wasn't a law against helping them. Auntie Rachel often gave that lady some money and a list for buying vegetarian things, so she knew that Mama could give her some money and a list for buying cake things.

Using one of the children's paintbrushes, Mama had dusted very lightly over the whole cake with her brand new Dusting Powder (Silver). *Eh!* Now the cake looked just like a shiny new coin!

Benedict knew that Mama didn't like a cake to have just one colour, but silver was a very special colour for a cake to have, unlike white, which was Mama's worst single colour. And besides, there were three more colours inside the silver. Zodwa and her *inhlangano* ladies were going to love it!

Sifiso was nervous during their presentation. Knowing that he would be, he had written some notes on a piece of paper, but holding it made his shaking more obvious.

Standing next to him at the front, Benedict watched the class. Giveness was listening carefully, even though he had heard the presentation already during break while they had practised it. But Giveness seemed to be holding his breath.

Some of the boys near the back were listening carefully, too. Benedict knew he could quiz them on what Sifiso was saying and they would get zero because they were only waiting to hear a lisp that they could laugh at. They were going to be disappointed. Some of the girls were paying attention, and one or two even seemed to be writing down some of what Sifiso was saying.

Then it was Benedict's turn. He propped his poster on top of Miss Khumalo's table, and with Sifiso holding one side of it and Giveness the other, he pointed with his ruler to each stage of the life cycle as he explained it. When he indicated the dotted line arcing from the man into the water he heard somebody near the back whisper the word *pipi*, then some others laughed. And all the girls made faces when he talked about the worms inside the man and inside the child.

Sifiso had dropped a bit of red icing from his purple cupcake onto the board during break, so the eggs hatching inside the snail were a bit greasy, but nobody seemed to notice.

When he finished, everybody clapped for both of them. *Eh!* Benedict felt himself smiling all the way up to home time.

On the way to the high school, he took his poster into Mr Patel's shop to show Mrs Patel what he had done with her old cardboard box. She was busy serving customers, spooning bright orange curry into plastic containers and filling paper bags with chips and big, fat sausages called Russians.

Indian people weren't like Christian people who had just one God who had to do everything for everybody. No. They had lots of gods, each with their own work. Some of them even had lots of arms and hands so that they could do lots of work at the same time.

Of all the gods on Mr Patel's walls, Benedict liked Ganesh the best. Ganesh was a man with the head of an elephant, and his job was to move away the things that were standing in your way of getting something done. He had his big, strong trunk and four arms to help him to move things, so there wasn't really anything he couldn't manage. Benedict wondered if the king's mother, the Great She Elephant Indlovukati, was as strong as Ganesh. Perhaps they knew each other, or were even family.

While he waited for Mrs Patel, Benedict looked carefully at the picture of the god called Krishna. He could see at once why Petros had chosen that name for his golden-brown dog. Dressed in a softly draped gold trouser and a matching sleeveless jacket, Krishna wore white beads around his ankles and a long necklace of pink and white flowers as he held up a golden flute, just about to play it. He had only two arms, and unlike the other gods on Mr Patel's walls, his skin was blue. *Eh*, his face was so beautiful! Beneath a golden headdress decorated with a feather from a peacock's tail, his eyes were ringed with black – just like Petros's dog – his lips the colour of Mama's when she wore her lipstick for going out. A cow rested at his feet.

How Mama would love all those colours!

When Mrs Patel was ready to look, she was just like the girls in Benedict's class: she didn't like the worms on his poster. She thought it was best for the worms not to be in the shop with her food, but she thanked him for showing her and gave him three chips, telling him he should continue to be a good boy at school.

'Don't be doing any nonsense,' she told him.

Benedict began to nod then changed his nod to a shake on account of nonsense not being something to nod about.

'Nonsense is deadly bad.' Mrs Patel wiped grease from the counter-top with a cloth as Benedict changed his shake to a nod. 'Nonsense can make your father send you away, isn't it?'

Benedict didn't know what to do with his head now, but he was sure that keeping it still might make him look like he wasn't listening, and it would be rude not to listen to some-body who had just given him some chips as a gift. He felt that what his head was doing must make him look like one of the Indian men who used to work with Baba at his old job in Kigali. That man's head had bobbed this way and that on his neck, never quite showing whether he thought what some-body was saying was right or wrong.

Mrs Patel continued. 'That can break a mother's heart, isn't it? *Break* it!' As she slapped the damp cloth down on the counter, her eyes began to blink very quickly. Reaching for a paper serviette with one hand, she nodded towards his poster and waved the back of her other hand towards the door. 'Go, go.'

Outside, Benedict gave the three chips to his brothers and Olga Mazibuko, and the children continued on their walk. Right now, Mrs Patel was probably using that paper serviette to wipe her eyes, just as she had done when he had been there with Mama. But that had been right before Mrs Patel and Mama had become confidential, so he knew it wouldn't have been right to ask anything or say anything. Anyway, Mrs Patel would probably have said it was just onions, which he knew from Titi could make a person's eyes red and very wet.

He thought carefully about what Mrs Patel had said. He didn't really know what doing nonsense meant, but he didn't want Baba sending him away for doing it, and he didn't want Mama's heart to break because he'd been sent away for doing it. He would have to be careful not to do it, not even by mistake.

The yellow Hi-Ace was already at the high school when they got there, but it was locked and Auntie Rachel was nowhere to be seen, so they waited in the shade of the thorn tree. When the high-school children came out, Vusi Mazibuko told them that Auntie Rachel and his sister Innocence were in the office with Mr Magagula, on account of Innocence being in trouble. He wasn't sure why, but Elias Gamedze and Obed Fakudze from her class were in there with her.

They waited for a long time. The ladies selling mealies and bunny-chow left, classrooms were cleaned, windows were closed, teachers went home, and still Auntie Rachel and Innocence didn't come.

Then Daniel and Moses needed the toilet, and Vusi told Benedict where to take them. Leaving his poster and their schoolbags with Grace, he led his brothers in through the school gate and round to the block of toilets at the far end of the school.

While he waited for them outside the toilets, a classroom door opened and a girl came out, the same girl who had saved the spider. Hauling her schoolbag onto her back, she headed quickly towards the school gate. Benedict was still thinking about whether or not he should try to catch up with her and talk to her about spiders, when a teacher came out of the same classroom, putting on his jacket. He seemed angry when he caught sight of Benedict.

'What are you doing here?' he asked in a big, booming voice.

Benedict suddenly felt very small. He lowered his eyes respectfully. 'I brought my brothers to the toilet, sir.'

Moses and Daniel emerged.

'Hah!' said the teacher, straightening his tie and buttoning his jacket. 'These toilets are for big boys only, nè?'

Looking down, all three boys nodded.

'I don't want to see you here again.'

They all shook their heads.

'Very good.' Turning on his heel, the teacher walked away.

Benedict hoped that the spider-girl would be at the gate and he could show her his bilharzia poster, but she was nowhere to be seen. At last Auntie Rachel came out of the office with Innocence. She gave Innocence a tissue from her handbag and wrapped her in a very big hug. Behind them Elias Gamedze emerged with his father, Elias looking frightened, Mr Gamedze furious.

'*Eish*, there'll be a beating tonight,' said Vusi.

Benedict was shocked. 'Auntie Rachel?'

'*Ngeke!* Never! Gamedze.'

Obed Fakudze didn't come out, but sounds of shouting came from Mr Magagula's office.

Her arm around Innocence, Auntie Rachel hurried towards the yellow Hi-Ace, handing her keys to Vusi so he could open for them.

'Sorry, sorry, sorry!' she said, and as everybody got in she made calls to Mrs Levine and Mama on her cell-phone to say they were going to be home a bit late.

On the way down the hill, nobody spoke. Auntie Rachel didn't seem angry, but Innocence was upset and sniffed loudly. Benedict was finding it difficult to know what everybody was thinking, but on the whole he felt it would probably be best not to say that his and Sifiso's presentation had gone well.

It wasn't until a man tried to flag them down and Innocence shouted, 'We're not a bloody taxi!' that everybody laughed and began to chatter. And it wasn't until the yellow Hi-Ace pulled into the garage and the Quick Impact Corolla was there that Benedict remembered the Ubuntu Funerals van being there a few days earlier, and that made him remember his idea for their edge.

'*Eh*, I'm sorry,' said Mama, greeting him at the front door and taking his poster from him. 'Uh-uh. Jabulani already knew about those caskets from Ghana. He loves them but a tradition like that cannot work here. Zodwa says it's a *kwerekwere* tradition, it's un-Swazi.' She shrugged her shoulders. 'And besides, people here cannot afford.'

Benedict felt disappointed. He had so wanted his idea to be good! He had wanted it to be a nice thank-you gift for Jabulani, for spending all that time on the casket for his hoopoe. He had wanted it to make Jabulani and Zodwa dance with happiness and send lots of customers to Mama as a reward for all the customers the edge was going to bring them.

But now he would still have to find another way to help Mama.

'My friend!' Henry came out of the kitchen with a mug of tea in each hand. They greeted each other warmly, though the mugs of tea meant they weren't able to shake. Henry stepped aside to let Benedict pass. 'Titi has more, nè?'

In the kitchen, Titi was still filling mugs with spicy, milky tea from the milk saucepan.

'*Eh*, you came late today!'

'Mm. Because of Innocence.'

'Innocence?' Titi put the empty saucepan in the sink and began filling it with water. 'Innocence at the other house?'

'Mm. She got into trouble. With two boys.'

'*Eh!*' Titi's eyes were big. '*Two?*'

'Mm.' Benedict picked up two of the mugs, looking forward to the warm, milky spiciness.

Titi's eyebrows seemed to be struggling to meet across the top of her nose. 'What's going to happen?'

'I don't know.' He shrugged as best he could with the mugs of tea in his hands. 'Maybe she can go with that lady to Nelspruit.'

'*Eh!*' Her eyes still big, Titi covered her mouth with a hand.

'Come, come, come!' Henry was in the kitchen now, picking up two more mugs. 'Let us tuck in to the tasty plate of fruit that Titi has prepared for us so beautifully!' He winked at Titi, who dropped her hand from her mouth and smiled shyly as she turned off the tap.

Benedict was glad that Henry was there. He needed somebody to speak to him like he was big and not the little boy the teacher at the high school had spoken to. The tea and the fruit would soon make him put away the disappointment about his idea not being good, and when he told everybody about the success of his and Sifiso's bilharzia presentation, his smile would quickly come back.

After supper that evening, Benedict sat on his cushion under the lamp and looked for Sheba in the encyclopaedias, hoping to find out whose breasts they were on Mr Quartermain's map. Neither the Kalukawe River nor the Lukanga River had been in the atlas, but maybe their names had changed, like Allister Miller Street in Mbabane changing its name to Gwamile Street on account of it no longer being more important to remember a *Mzungu* from the time of Swaziland's gold rush than to remember King Mswati III's great grandmother. Even his own country had changed its name, from Tanganyika back in the old days to Tanzania now.

The encyclopaedia said that Sheba was a queen back in the days of the Bible, and she brought King Solomon lots of gold as a gift. It also said that some people called Rabbinicals knew that King Solomon invited Sheba to visit him by sending a bird to her with a letter tied to its leg. The bird was a hoopoe.

Eh!

Benedict could feel his heart beginning to skip with excitement.

Then it said that people in Ethiopia knew that Sheba and King Solomon had been in love and their children and their children's children had ruled Ethiopia until 1974.

Benedict was confused. There was a lot about King Solomon under Sheba, but he didn't remember reading about Sheba under King Solomon. He paged forward until he found Solomon again. There, at the end, it said *See also Sheba, Queen of.* Back at the end of Sheba, he found *See also Solomon, King,* and *See also Selassie, Haile.*

He was paging back to Selassie, Haile when Mama's cellphone rang, interrupting the background murmur of her conversation with Baba at the dining table. Baba shouted for the TV to be turned down.

Benedict couldn't concentrate on Haile Selassie being Emperor of Ethiopia, on account of Mama's voice sounding strange.

'*Eh?*... What?... Uh-uh-uh!... Mm-mm... *Eh!*... No!... Uh-uh... Of course... Yes... Mm... Immediately... Yes.'

Putting her phone down on the table, Mama took off her

glasses and buried her face in her hands for a few seconds while Baba asked her over and over what was wrong. Benedict wondered if he should get up from his cushion and go to her.

She looked up and put her glasses back on. 'Benedict,' she said, in a voice that made him feel suddenly cold, 'come here, please.'

Instantly he knew he had done something wrong. But what? He cast his mind back desperately over the day. But there was nothing. Unless… Could that teacher have complained about small boys using the high school toilets?

'And Titi,' said Mama more loudly above the noise of the TV that the other children were turning up because it wasn't them in trouble.

Titi rose from the couch and looked at Benedict with big eyes full of questions. He gave her the tiniest shrug, and together they went and sat nervously at the dining table.

Mama looked at them, shaking her head. 'I'm so disappointed in you,' she said, and immediately tears began to prick at the back of Benedict's eyes.

Mama looked at Baba.

'Yes,' he said, uncertainly.

'Gossip,' said Mama, 'is a very bad thing.'

Gossip?

'Yes,' said Baba again.

'And to gossip about a child! *Eh!*'

'*Eh!*' Baba agreed.

'More especially, *that* kind of gossip.' Mama took off her glasses, reached down through her neckline for a tissue, and began to polish the lenses, shaking her head sadly.

Benedict and Titi gave each other a quick look that said neither of them knew what they had said about which child. Baba looked just as confused.

'Angel, perhaps if you—'

'Pius, these two have been gossiping.' Mama put her glasses back on. 'They've been telling everybody that two boys have impregnated Innocence Mazibuko!'

What?

'No, Mama!'

'No? Then why did Mavis at the other house shout at Innocence for getting pregnant at less than fourteen years just like she had done herself? Innocence went to Rachel in tears, and Rachel found out from Mavis that Titi had told her and Lungi, and it was Benedict who told Titi.'

Baba made tutting noises against the back of his teeth.

Benedict was very confused. 'I never said she was pregnant.'

'Yes!' said Titi. 'You said she would go to Nelspruit with that lady.'

'Only because she's in trouble,' said Benedict. 'She got into trouble at school with Elias Gamedze and Obed Fakudze. Her brother Vusi said she was in trouble. When girls are in trouble that lady takes them to Nelspruit.'

'*Eh!*' Titi covered her mouth with both hands.

'*Eh!*' Mama covered her mouth with her tissue.

'*Eh!*' Baba got up and went to sit on the couch, even though it wasn't yet news.

Mama explained to Benedict about different kinds of trouble, and about being in trouble being a way of saying pregnant. He asked her if his first mama had been in trouble with him, but Mama said no, there was another way of saying pregnant and that was being blessed, and it just depended. He wasn't quite sure what it depended on, but he nodded when Mama asked him if he understood. He was just so relieved that he had misunderstood rather than gossiping, which he knew to be a bad thing.

Titi had gossiped, though. She knew it was wrong, and she said she was sorry over and over again.

The two of them had to go down the hill with the torch and say sorry to Innocence and Auntie Rachel. While they were still on the steps there was a loud racket as some monkeys scrambled across the tin roof of the house, scurried across the garden and plunged into the bank of banana trees. But they were both too busy choosing their words to pay attention, and they barely noticed the month-end sounds of the dairy workers drinking their wages further down the hill.

Just outside the Mazibukos' front door, they found Auntie Rachel's mother, Mrs Levine, sitting on a deckchair, a cigarette in one hand and a glass in the other.

'Hi, there,' she said. 'You two are in trouble, hey?'

Benedict and Titi nodded, not really wanting to talk to her but thinking it would be rude not to. All they wanted to do was go inside and get it over with.

'Me too,' said Mrs Levine, taking a large sip from her glass and setting the ice-cubes in it clinking.

'*Eh!*' said Titi, nudging Benedict with her elbow.

'You're in trouble?' he asked, knowing that Titi was wondering if Mrs Levine might mean the kind of trouble Titi had thought Innocence was in. She was a smallish woman with white hair cut short like a boy's, but her middle was rather large.

'Mm-hm.' She pulled on her cigarette, making the end glow red.

'What did you do?' The question was out of Benedict's mouth before he realised how rude it sounded. He made mistakes like that when he was nervous.

'Christ, what *didn't* I do?' Mrs Levine rolled her eyes, took a big gulp of her drink and swallowed hard. '*Ag*, but we don't have all night, hey? You better go in.'

Saying *Christ* wasn't nice, but Benedict didn't say. Maybe it was okay if a Jewish somebody said it.

They knocked before going in.

At first, Innocence, Auntie Rachel and Uncle Enock were angry, but when they heard how Benedict had made his mistake, they smiled and said it was okay and he should wipe away his tears. Innocence told them that Elias Gamedze and Obed Fakudze had brought a bottle of brandy to school and asked her to hide it in her schoolbag. She'd forgotten that it was there, and when she'd opened her bag to get a book, Miss Dube had seen it.

When Titi went with Uncle Enock and Innocence to have a conversation with Mavis and Lungi in the kitchen, Auntie Rachel gave Benedict a glass of milk, and he apologised again.

'*Ag*, no, it's over,' she said. 'Forgotten. Forgiven.' She leaned forward with a tissue and wiped a splodge of milk from either side of his upper lip.

'Auntie Rachel?'

'*Ja?*'

'Have you ever been blessed?'

'Blessed? What, you mean by a priest?'

'Uh-uh. With a baby.'

She smiled. 'No, that never happened for Enock and me. But so what, hey? This house is full of blessings anyway!'

'Mm.'

Sounds of raised voices came from the kitchen, and as he glanced towards the doorway he noticed a new piece of rock on top of the bookshelf between the Mazibukos' family photographs. It looked like a slice of stone, as thick as a slice of bread, held upright in a small plastic stand. Putting down his empty glass, he went to have a look at it.

'Is this new?'

'*Ja.*' Auntie Rachel came to stand next to him. 'It's nice, hey?'

'Mm.' He liked the concentric rings in pale greys and browns. 'It looks like a slice out of a log.'

'That's exactly what it is.'

Benedict touched it gently, carefully. It was smooth and cold. 'But it's stone!'

'*Ja*, it used to be a tree, centuries ago in Madagascar. But it's so old it's turned to stone.'

'*Eh!*'

'Petrified wood. And before you misunderstand, it doesn't mean the tree got scared, hey? It just means it turned to stone.'

'*Eh!*' Benedict ran his fingers over its smoothness. 'Can it happen to a person?'

'No man, you'd have to be ancient.'

'Though people can have a heart of stone,' said Uncle Enock, coming in and sitting down.

'*Eh!*' Benedict put his hand to his chest.

'Don't confuse him, Enock.' Auntie Rachel took Benedict's

122

hand away from his chest and pulled him down to sit with her. 'No, the chances of a person ever turning to stone are about the same as him turning to gold.'

Benedict twisted his neck to look up at her. 'King Midas turned people to gold!'

'That's just a story, hey?'

Suddenly, Benedict remembered. 'Petros says he's got gold.'

'Our Petros?'

'Mm.'

'*Eish*, don't listen to his stories, Benedict.' Uncle Enock shook his head. 'There's no gold here, not any more. The gold rush here is ancient history, over before 1900.' Then he seemed to have an idea. '*Ag*, he probably means Swazi Gold, it's the *dagga* that grows here. You know *dagga*, nè? They smoke it.'

'*Ja*, don't listen to Petros.' Auntie Rachel gave him a squeeze. 'He's sick, hey? He's quite far gone now and it's in his head. Probably the beginnings of dementia.'

Mavis and Lungi came quietly into the room, followed by Titi.

'Sorry, nè?' Mavis and Lungi chorused softly, their heads bowed.

'Even me,' said Titi.

Mrs Levine and her chair were gone when they left the house. Uncle Enock insisted on walking the short distance up the hill with them to make sure that they got home safely, and as they walked the quiet of the night was interrupted by loud laughter from the drinking party further down, where the dairy workers lived.

'Uncle Enock, you know Mrs Levine?'

'*Yebo.*'

'Did she do something wrong?'

'*Eish.*' Uncle Enock came to a halt, sighing deeply. 'She doesn't want to realise that she's not on *her* farm. She can't go telling my workers what to do like that!'

'Sorry, Uncle,' said Titi.

Benedict tried to comfort him. 'It'll be okay. She'll go back to her own farm soon.'

A sound like a buffalo would make came out of Uncle Enock's nose. 'She's not *going* back! She's left her husband!'

'*Eh!*' said Titi.

'*Eh!*' said Benedict.

'*Eish,* what am I thinking? These are grown-up things.' Uncle Enock started walking again. 'Forget I said, nè? Please.'

The three of them moved up the steps towards the Tungarazas' in silence. They were almost at the top when something moved on the grass nearby.

All three of them froze.

Then Uncle Enock and Benedict shone their torches onto the grass.

A vervet monkey was staggering unsteadily, a can of Lion Lager hanging loosely from one hand. Then another monkey hurled itself at the first, knocking it over and making off with the can.

'*Eish!*'

They held their torch-beams steady. The monkey did not get up.

Benedict wanted to help it, to give it some of Auntie Rachel's rescue medicine and maybe a blanket. But Uncle Enock said no, the monkey just needed to sleep it off, like the dairy workers would when they finally fell over from drink, and then the monkey would wake up needing lots of fluids.

Before he went to bed, Benedict sliced an orange into quarters and went out with the torch to check on the monkey. It lay exactly where it had fallen, the top half of its pale grey body side-down on the grass, its bottom half belly-up, showing a pair of balls the bright turquoise that Mama sometimes chose to colour a cake. Its small black face, framed by a ring of white fur, was perfectly still, its eyes only halfway shut. Its chest barely moved with its breathing.

Benedict placed the juicy orange quarters on the grass where it would see them the minute it woke up needing fluids.

EIGHT

HENRY SAID THAT MAMA WASN'T QUITE READY FOR her driving test, though she'd been learning for three months. Mama said it was because when she got her licence Henry would stop having an easy opportunity to see Titi, but Baba said it was because when Mama got her licence Henry would stop getting his fee out of Baba. But still, Mama agreed to have an extra lesson to tidy up her parking one Sunday afternoon, even though Sunday was supposed to be for family. Baba was going to be away anyway. He would be leaving straight after church to drive to Johannesburg for a conference that was starting on Monday.

Baba had been away before, usually for just one or two nights when he went to other parts of Swaziland to look at projects that needed helping or encouraging, but this time Benedict was going to be the man of the house for a whole entire week. Each evening of the week before Baba left, Benedict reported to him all the things he had done that day that could make Baba feel confident that he was leaving the family in good hands.

'Titi found a spider in the girls' room, Baba. I took it outside before they even saw it.'

'Baba, I think the monkeys must have had a party in the garden today. I don't know what fruit they'd been eating, but, *eh!* I cleared up all their *kinyezi* so the grass is clean for Samson's mower tomorrow.'

'I helped Daniel and Moses with going over their classwork this afternoon, Baba, then I did English practice with Titi. She likes it when Auntie Rachel can see she's been practising.'

'Baba, Mama looked sad about her business this afternoon, so I picked a flower for her from the garden and it made her smile.'

On the Friday afternoon, it was Mama's business that made her smile. She had a customer.

Mrs Zikalala sat on one of the couches and Mama on the other as they sipped the tea that Titi had brought them. From his cushion next to the bookshelf, his library book open in his lap, Benedict had a side view of their visitor. Tall and slim, she wore a dress and elaborate matching headdress patterned in green and golden yellow, just like the belly of an African green pigeon with its fluffy yellow leggings. The fabric was beautiful, but a little old and faded. In patches, the white plastic of her sandals still bore some remnants of shiny gold. She ate her slice of cake greedily, in a way that would make Baba tell one of the children to stop behaving like a refugee who had survived on nothing but leaves for weeks.

'My neighbour works with your husband, Mrs Tungaraza—'

'Angel. Please.'

'What?'

'Angel. That's my name.'

'Yes. Anyway, she had her whole family there for Easter, and when I looked over the wall, I saw the cake. *Eish!* That was the day I said to Mr Zikalala, Mr Zikalala, we are getting that cake-maker for Queenie, nobody is going to look over their wall and see a cake made by an inferior cake-maker here.'

Mama patted at her hair, and even though her back was to Benedict, he knew that she was smiling. 'And what—'

'She's our only daughter, our only *child*, Mrs Tungaraza—'

'Ange—'

'Ours is not to reason why, nè? Ours is but to accept the one gift that God has given us, and ours as parents is to make sure our child gets the best.'

'Of cou—'

'Yes. You do the same for yours, I'm sure, even though they are many. The girls. Just the two that were in here when I came?' Mama nodded. 'Still too young, nè? And of course our king will never marry a *kwe*—, er, a foreigner.'

'*Eh!*' Mama sat up straight. 'Your daughter is marrying King Mswati?'

Benedict was suddenly so excited that he completely forgot that he was pretending to read his library book and it slammed shut in his lap. But the sound of it coincided with Mama clapping her hands together, and nobody turned to look at him. *Eh!* A wedding cake for the king! This was going to make Mama's cakes famous throughout the whole entire world! Nobody was going to mind that Mama was a *kwerekwere* who shouldn't have a business here. She was the king's cake-maker!

Eh! Maybe the king would invite her to go and bake in his kitchen at the palace! Okay, he had many palaces. The main one was at Lozitha, but he preferred to live in the Nkoyoyo one, on the hill just the other side of Mbabane. Any king's home really was a palace, even when a king pretended it wasn't that special and called it a royal residence instead. Mama didn't trust just any oven. She would insist on moving her own oven to the palace, the gas one that had travelled with them from Tanzania in the trailer behind Baba's Microbus. It wouldn't matter that one of its knobs had fallen off with all the jiggling and jangling on the bad roads and Baba had had to replace it with a metal nut that worked just fine but didn't match. It would be the king's cake-maker's oven!

'Mrs Tungaraza,' Mrs Zikalala was saying, 'my daughter will marry King Mswati one day. That is my hope. He will give her a much better life than Mr Zikalala and I can give her. But that is not why I came.'

Mama slumped back on the couch. Feeling her disappointment on top of his own, Benedict sighed as softly as he could and opened his book again at no particular page.

'I said to Mr Zikalala, Mr Zikalala, this is the year. This is the year.'

'I see. And, er... perhaps you would like a cake for your daughter's birthday? Queenie, is it?'

'Queenie. Yes. But not for her birthday.' She smiled proudly, sitting up a little straighter. 'Queenie has passed her test.'

'Er... A test at school?'

Mrs Zikalala shook her head as she swallowed some tea. '*Eh!* Her driving test?'

'More important, Mrs Tungaraza. The most important test a girl can ever pass. I took her across the border to South Africa. We don't do it here.' She shook her head, clicking her tongue against the back of her teeth. '*Eish*, we are too modern here. Meanwhile we have our lovely Somhlolo stadium. That doesn't have to be just for men and their soccer, we could test our girls there too. But no, I had to travel with Queenie across the border.' Again she clicked her tongue against the back of her teeth. 'The stadium that side was inferior, Mrs Tungaraza. Not even full! And thanks God I took a grass mat from here for Queenie to lie on. The girls on either side of her had mats that were inferior. And when you're not in Swaziland the ladies who do the checking are of course not Swazis, but when you have no choice but to rely on Zulus to test your daughter, what can you do?'

'Mrs Zikalala, I'm not sure that I—'

'Some of us are mobilising for facilities to get our girls tested here.'

'But what—'

'*Eish*, what am I thinking?' Taking an envelope from her handbag, she removed a piece of paper from it and handed it to Mama. 'Here's her certificate, Mrs Tungaraza.' Her smile was very wide. 'My daughter is a virgin!'

While Mrs Zikalala beamed with pride, Mama turned around and gave Benedict one of her looks that said he must do what she said without even thinking of asking why, and she told him to go outside with his book.

He went out through the back door, taking *King Solomon's Mines* with him. He kept renewing it at the library, feeling that he really should read it even though it was just too difficult. He had decided to try his best to get through it before Baba got back from his conference; that would make Baba feel proud of him. Watching him renew it over and over at the library was surely making Baba think he was still small.

He knew that Mama had sent him out because her customer was about to tell her something confidential that nobody else must hear. Sometimes she and Baba sent him out when they wanted to talk about something that was too grown up for him, but that wasn't the case now. He knew about Virgins, he'd seen them on TV, though not in real life: they never came to any airport he'd been to. Glad that Queenie Zikalala had passed the test to get a job serving meals on an aeroplane – at least up until the time she married the king – he was proud that the girl's mother knew Mama was the best person to come to for a cake to celebrate it. But Mrs Zikalala didn't look like the kind of person Mama could persuade to order a cake that was expensive.

Unsure exactly where he felt like going, Benedict perched on the step outside the kitchen door, thinking that he might need to put on his shoes. Bits of what Mrs Zikalala was saying to Mama drifted through the kitchen. 'Wide open, Mrs Tungaraza, wide apart.' His sisters had gone down to the other house to see Innocence, and his brothers were playing there with Fortune. 'Of course there's an audience in the stadium, Mrs Tungaraza, everybody must see, they must know.' The afternoon was overcast and windy, so he didn't feel like sitting in the garden or going up to the dam. No, he wasn't going to need his shoes. He stood up from the step. Perhaps it was one of those Friday afternoons when Uncle Enock could get away from the clinic early.

But Uncle Enock's bakkie wasn't in the garage. Auntie Rachel was sitting on the lounge carpet, helping the youngest Mazibukos to build something out of Lego. Standing up and putting an arm round Benedict, she moved to the couch to sit with him.

'Auntie Rachel, have you read this?' He showed her his book.

'*Ag* no, man, Benedict, don't tell me that's what you're reading!'

'You know it?'

'*Ja*, we did it at school. Centuries ago!'

'I've been trying to read it but it's too hard for me.'

'*Ja*.' She flipped through a few pages. 'This would be too hard even for Vusi.' Hearing that it was too difficult for such a big boy made Benedict feel better. 'You'll never manage this. I can tell you the story if you like.'

'Really?'

'Sure, there's not much to it. A real boys' adventure. These three white guys go in search of gold and diamonds – oh, and they're also looking for the brother of one of them who's gone missing. On the way they kill some black people, including a black woman who's a witch. I seem to remember there's only one other woman in the story, a nurse who's also black. One of the white guys likes her, but it's not allowed. Something about it not being natural for the sun and the darkness to get together. Can you believe it? Anyway, the white guys have a lot of manly adventures, and eventually they come back with the treasure and the missing brother. And that's it. The end.'

'They followed a map to the treasure,' said Benedict, taking the book from her and finding the right page.

Auntie Rachel looked at the map. 'Hey, I remember this! We used to do this!' She turned the book so that the map was upside down. 'What's it look like?'

Benedict examined it carefully. It looked like the map,

only upside down. He shrugged his shoulders. 'The map?'

'*Ag* no, man. Forget it's a map.'

Benedict tried again. After a few seconds he saw it. '*Eh!* It's a face! These are the eyes,' he pointed to the circles labelled *Sheba's Breasts*, 'and this is the smile.' His finger traced the semi-circle labelled *koppie*.

Auntie Rachel laughed. 'We used to see two breasts here,' she indicated Sheba's breasts, 'and this little triangle of mountains down here was... *Ag*, never mind, you too young for this!'

'Is it in South Africa, Auntie Rachel?'

She gave him an odd look. 'What?'

'The mine. King Solomon's mine.'

'*Ag*, it's not real, hey? It's a made-up story.'

'No, but it says here *koppie* and *kraal*. Those are words from South Africa.'

'And it says here *Sheba's Breasts*.' She tapped at the map. 'Sheba's Breasts are just down the road, but there's no treasure cave here! It's a made-up story.'

Benedict couldn't believe what he was hearing. 'Sheba's Breasts are down the road?'

'*Ja*, didn't you know?' Benedict shook his head. 'Just after the Malagwane Hill, down there on the right.'

'*Eh!*'

'*Ag*, don't come with your *eh*, Benedict, it's not real! Don't you think a thousand men have gone looking for King Solomon's mines since this book? And why do you think Rider Haggard wrote it? Thousands had already gone looking.'

'But a Portuguese somebody found it!' Benedict tapped at the book. 'He's the one who drew the map. Baba says

133

Portuguese people used to live next door to Swaziland in Mozambique—'

'*Ja*, they colonised it. And *ja*, some of them came here in the gold rush hoping to get rich. But no one has ever found the treasure in that book and no one ever will, because it doesn't exist!'

'But—'

'No buts!' Auntie Rachel stood up, pulling him up with her. 'Come down the hill with me and see if the chickens need feeding, then we'll have some milk. Okay?'

Calling to Mavis to keep an eye on the little ones, she led him out through the side door, next to the big added-on room where Grace and Faith were listening to music with Innocence, and through the garden where Moses and Daniel were playing a running and chasing game with Fortune. Benedict wasn't sure Auntie Rachel was right about the treasure being just a made-up story. Things that seemed just pretend could sometimes be real.

They fed the chickens together, Auntie Rachel laughing as she threw handfuls of seed close to Benedict's bare feet, and Benedict squealing and giggling as he danced around the chickens, trying to avoid being pecked by their beaks and tickled by their feathers. Then when one of the dairy workers came to her with a problem, Auntie Rachel sent Benedict back up to the house by himself to ask Lungi to give him a glass of milk.

Walking up the driveway and waving to his brothers and Fortune as he passed the garden, he wondered what the dairy worker's problem was. He hoped it wasn't something about Petros being sick and needing more medicine. It wasn't nice to be sick, he knew that himself. He didn't know what dementia was, but it must be something to do with a person's throat or chest. Petros had had his cough for so long! Auntie Rachel's medicine didn't seem to be helping him much.

Or maybe the dairy worker wanted to complain about Mrs Levine telling him what to do, even though it wasn't her farm.

He found Mrs Levine in the narrow strip of garden that was near the Mazibukos' front door, opposite the garage. She was on her knees with a spade, filling a large pot with soil. Benedict had never seen a *Mzungu* doing gardening work before: *Wazungu* usually just watched while gardeners like Samson did the work for them. Perhaps he should offer to help her.

'Hello, Mrs Levine.'

'Hi there, Bennie.' She looked up at him and smiled. Over her clothes she wore an apron that was messy with soil and mud.

He didn't like the short cut she made with his name: it made him sound smaller than he was. But he didn't say. 'Is there anything I can do?'

'*Ja*, just pass me the ice-cream, hey?'

Benedict looked around for an ice-cream, but couldn't see one anywhere. Mrs Levine was now busy tipping soil from a bag into a long pot that was shaped like two shoeboxes end to end.

'Um... What does it look like? The ice-cream.'

She didn't look up from what she was doing. '*Ag*, the pink and green, little specks of white.'

Benedict knew that meant strawberry and peppermint, with a bit of vanilla. He looked again. He could see a box of cigarettes, a box of matches, a cell-phone, some plants growing in black plastic... But there wasn't any ice-cream anywhere. Wherever it was, it must surely be melting.

'I can't see it, Mrs Levine!'

She had stopped emptying soil into the long pot, and was levelling it off with her hands. She looked up now. 'There! Just next to you!' She pointed with a finger covered in dirt to somewhere near Benedict's feet.

But there really wasn't any ice-cream there.

With a loud tutting sound, Mrs Levine walked on her knees to where Benedict stood, and lifted a small bush with its roots encased tightly in a black plastic bag. '*This* is an ice-cream bush, hey?'

His face feeling suddenly hot at his mistake, Benedict helped her to tear the black plastic away from around the roots of the bush. She was planting it in the soil of the big pot, and Benedict was admiring the different colours of its small, pretty leaves, when the cell-phone on the grass next to the box of cigarettes started ringing.

Mrs Levine looked at her hands, and then at Benedict's, which he had wiped clean on his shorts even though Mama kept telling him not to.

'Should I bring it?' he asked.

'*Ag*, just look who it is for me.'

Benedict squatted down and looked at the phone's small screen. 'It says Solly.'

'*Hah!*' she said angrily. 'Solly can bloody *whistle!*'

The phone continued to ring. Ignoring it, Mrs Levine picked up the spade and used it as a pointer in the same way that Benedict had used his ruler with his bilharzia poster. 'Those little ones there, Bennie. And the other two smaller ones behind.'

Benedict picked up those plants and brought them to her. All the time, the phone continued to ring. Benedict felt uncomfortable. Mama would never not answer her phone! What if it was business? What if somebody needed help?

He helped Mrs Levine to fill the long pot with the little plants, and at last the phone was quiet. When they were done, he helped her to put the pots of plants where she thought they'd be best.

Then Mrs Levine reached into the large pocket on the front of the skirt part of her apron, and brought out a small sign painted on an oblong of wood. The sign had an ice-cream-stick stand, which she pushed into the soil of the long pot. *Bees and butterflies welcome*, it said.

'*Eh!*' said Benedict, who had never seen anything like it. 'Don't they know they're welcome?'

'Sometimes,' said Mrs Levine, dusting the soil off her hands and reaching for her cigarettes, 'sometimes it's nice to be told.' She lit a cigarette, sucking hard on it. 'Sometimes,' she said, exhaling, 'people need to make it clear that you're wanted.'

Her mouth settled into a tight, straight line.

Benedict and Titi went with Mama on Sunday afternoon, Titi so that she could spend time with Henry, Benedict so that Henry could show him Sheba's Breasts.

Henry drove, on account of Mama not being supposed to have passengers until she got her licence, and they made their way slowly down the Malagwane Hill towards the tall distant mountains, passing the beautiful green folds of the high hills on the left before they turned onto the old road through the Ezulwini Valley.

'My friend!' said Henry, eyeing Benedict in his rear-view mirror. 'Your head is going to twist off your neck! I told you there's no need to keep looking. The place we're going has the perfect view.'

'You can sit still,' said Titi from the seat beside him, patting his knee. 'Henry will show us.'

'Why don't you sing for us, my friend? Your mother needs cheering.'

In the seat next to Henry, Mama said nothing.

'Sorry Uncle went away, Auntie.'

'The week will go fast, Angel. Pius will be back with you in no time at all.'

Mama sighed.

Benedict tried to think of something to say, but couldn't. If he and his brothers and sisters hadn't come to live with Mama and Baba, Baba would soon be retiring from his university job in Dar es Salaam instead of having to work hard as a consultant in different countries on account of consultants being paid much more money. Mama and Baba would be relaxing at home together over the weekend instead of Baba driving to Johannesburg after church and Mama staying behind with the children for the whole entire week.

But Mama was sad about more than just Baba being away, Benedict knew that. Just as he had expected, Mrs Zikalala had not ordered an expensive cake. A plain vanilla sponge baked in Mama's tin that had the shape of a heart, it had been boring for Mama to decorate, and it had ended up just plain ugly to look at. White. Pure white. And on top of the smooth white icing on the top, Mama had had to pipe Queenie's name in more white and surround it with a sprinkling of tiny white flowers. *Eh!* At least if there had been two layers, Mama could have put icing in a lovely colour between them. But no, Mrs Zikalala had wanted one layer only.

When Mrs Zikalala had collected the cake on Saturday afternoon she had been very excited, opening her mouth and flashing her tongue from side to side, ululating loudly enough to make the cows lift their heads from their drinking at the dam. Mama had tried hard to feel happy about that, and she had told anybody who would listen that the most important thing in any business was for the customer to be happy. But that evening she had gone down to the other house to get a headache tablet from Auntie Rachel.

Henry adjusted his rear-view mirror to get a better look at Titi. 'A song, Titi! Please!'

Titi looked down, smiling into her lap. Quietly, she began to hum one of the hymns they had sung at Mater Dolorosa that morning.

Two bars into the hymn, Henry readjusted his mirror, said a loud *eish!* and began to slow down and pull off the road. Two motorbikes then five, six, seven, eight big black cars with dark windows sped past them, their lights flashing and sirens blaring.

'*Eh!* Where is he going in such a hurry on a Sunday afternoon?' asked Mama.

Henry laughed. 'Anywhere he wants to go!'

They were quiet for a while as Henry pulled back onto the road and picked up a bit of speed. But the noise and rush of the king's cavalcade seemed to have shaken Mama from her low mood, so that when they passed a small group of worshippers ambling home after a Church of Jericho service, she clapped her hands together and said how beautiful they always looked in their bright red robes with their wide collars of royal blue.

'Titi would look too nice in that red!' Henry adjusted his mirror again to look at her.

'Me, I prefer the full blue,' said Titi.

'Ah! You say that only because you know I'm a Zionist! You should come to church with me one day, I'll get someone to borrow me a lovely blue robe for you.'

Titi looked down into her lap, but Benedict could see that there was a very big smile on her face.

Henry turned off the road and entered the large, open-air car park of The Gables shopping centre, where there were very few cars. The supermarket there was still open but almost empty. There was a lazy, Sunday-afternoon feel to the couple of restaurants, and there was very little activity in the car park. He pulled his Corolla into a parking bay far from the other cars, and they all got out.

'Right, my friend,' he said to Benedict. 'See that mountain to your left?'

Benedict looked. 'It's Nyonyane. Execution Rock.'

'And what did I say was opposite?'

Benedict swung his head the other way and breathed in sharply as he saw the mountain there. 'Is that...?' He had no breath to finish his question.

'Yebo. Those are Sheba's Breasts.'

Benedict stared at the mountaintop. 'But I see only one!'

Henry opened the boot of the Corolla and took out a number of orange traffic cones. 'They're side-on, nè? The other one lies behind.'

This wasn't the perfect view that Henry had promised, but Benedict hid his disappointment. 'Do you see, Mama?'

'I see.' Slipping her hand down the neckline of her blouse, she pulled out some folded emalangeni notes and peeled off a couple, handing them to Titi. 'You two have some sodas while you wait.'

Henry stopped positioning his cones and reached for his wallet from his back pocket. 'There's a nice place behind the butchery across the road, nè? Get some meat for a braai tonight while you're there.' He smiled at Titi as he handed her some money.

'What kind of meat?' Titi slipped the notes inside the top of her dress.

He shrugged. 'Some chops, some *wors*. Whatever you think. Enough for two, nè?' He winked at her, and she dropped her head and smiled.

'Be careful crossing the road!' said Mama, who was buckling herself in to the driver's seat.

'We will, Mama.'

Benedict turned and gave her a small wave as he and Titi headed towards the gateway out of the car park. Part of him wanted to give her a hug as he always used to when saying goodbye to her, but hugging her was starting to feel a bit awkward these days. Of course, he still did it when he was ill or upset. But he certainly wasn't going to hug her now in front of Henry, who saw that he was big.

Titi took his hand as they waited to cross the road, and he

let her. He didn't want to get an accident when he was so close to finding where the treasure might be. Auntie Rachel thought the treasure was pretend, but that didn't mean it couldn't be real. He wasn't exactly sure how he would go about finding it, but he knew from a storybook that there was a way of finding water that just needed you to hold two sticks, and the sticks knew where the water was buried. Maybe sticks knew treasure, too. Baba would be so proud of him if he came home from the conference and found the dining table covered with gold and diamonds! It wouldn't matter that Mama's business wasn't doing well, and Baba would be able to retire without worrying about the children. They could all go home to Tanzania, and Mama and Baba could relax. Imagine!

Inside the butchery at the end of a small row of shops next to the Why Not Disco Night Club – where people said ladies who weren't polite took all their clothes off as they danced – Titi took her time choosing the meat for the braai she would enjoy with Henry that night. While he waited, Benedict looked around. The large chunks of fresh meat hanging up on hooks behind the butcher, and the smaller cuts of dried beef, kudu and ostrich suspended above the counter reminded him of the shrike's butchery he had found one day in a tree near the dam. The bird had killed a lizard and hung it up on a thorn for later.

Braai was another word from South Africa, and it was the same as saying barbecue. Behind the butchery you could braai your meat over a fire inside half of an old oil drum lying on its side on top of the metal frame of an old school desk. Then you could sit and eat it at one of the plastic tables in the shady courtyard.

Benedict and Titi knew without discussing it that they should drink their Cokes at a table some distance from anybody else. That way they wouldn't be too close to somebody who might be drinking too much beer or too close to somebody who might hear their Swahili and shout at them for being *shangaans* or *makwerekwere*. Only two of the tables were occupied anyway, so it was easy enough to find one that stood apart under a shady tree.

Benedict picked up a couple of the small sticks that had fallen from the tree and played with them as he chatted and giggled with Titi, hoping that they might point to the treasure, if it was real and if it was here. But they didn't work, and he soon lost interest, tossing them to the ground and concentrating instead on a lone hadeda ibis that stalked nearby, pecking at the ground with its long, curved beak. When some ducks flew very low overhead, quacking loudly, the hadeda took flight clumsily, its large grey body seeming awkward as it squawked its loud racket into the afternoon air during take-off.

He looked up at the ducks. Black with orange legs and grey bills, they were the same kind as the duck that he had rescued. He imagined that his duck was amongst them, strong and happy, together with family. If she had come back to the dam, he hadn't recognised her – or she hadn't recognised him.

They were chatting about how exciting it was that at Baba's conference there were going to be people from all over Africa, including Tanzania, when they noticed a man moving from table to table with a large black plastic bag. When he got to them he put the bag on their table, pulling it open to reveal a large quantity of chopped pieces of meat. With an anxious

143

expression on his face, he asked them a question in siSwati, switching to English when he saw that they didn't understand.

'Does this look like a cow to you?'

'Sorry?'

'This!' He opened the bag a bit more to reveal more of the meat. 'If you saw all this being served, would you think it was a cow? A whole cow?'

'*Eh*, I don't know,' said Benedict. He looked at it carefully. 'It's hard to see when it's all chopped. Maybe half a cow? What do you think, Titi?'

Titi stood up and assessed it carefully. 'Half,' she said.

'*Eish!*' The man looked distressed.

'It's not even half!' called the butcher, who was smoking a cigarette outside the back door of his shop. 'I told him he needed to get at least half.'

Letting out a string of angry siSwati, the man searched through his pockets for more money as the men drinking beers at the other two tables began to laugh at him. Finding nothing, he closed up his bag of meat by tying a knot in it and went away looking very upset.

Shaking his head, the butcher ambled over to Benedict and Titi and asked them where they were from.

'We're *shangaans* from Tanzania,' said Titi nervously, and the butcher threw back his head and laughed, his fat belly jiggling up and down.

'Why did he need a whole cow?' asked Benedict.

'Cleansing ceremony,' said the butcher, dragging on his cigarette as he pulled out a chair and sat with them, keeping an eye on his shop. '*Eish*, these nowadays we cannot afford. It's one burial after another.'

'Sorry,' they chorused quietly.

Dropping the last of his cigarette, the butcher ground it into the soil with a shoe. He began counting on his fingers. 'First it's the casket, then it's the vigil. You've heard all the singing on Sunday mornings, nè?'

Benedict nodded. All-night vigils for the late usually happened on Saturdays, and on the way to church on Sunday mornings they often heard the mourners singing.

The butcher continued counting on his fingers. 'Then it's the funeral. Then after a month it's the cleansing ceremony. That's when we remove our bits of mourning cloth, cleanse ourselves of our mourning and ask the ancestors to protect the rest of our family. Now, how can we afford to slaughter a cow for that ceremony after all those other expenses, after all those other family gatherings where everybody needs to be fed?' He shook his head. 'Maybe once a year we can afford, but *eish*, these nowadays, it's too much.' Eyeing his shop carefully, he stood up. 'They come here asking for what looks like a cow. I sell them as much as they can buy, but I know – and *they* know – they're going to be judged. What will the ancestors think of them?' He shook his head sadly. 'Excuse me, nè?'

'Times are hard,' said Titi after he had gone back into his shop to serve a customer.

'Mm.' Benedict drew the last of his Coke up from the can through his straw. Baba had told him that in the whole entire world there were only seven factories that made Coca Cola syrup, and one of them was here in Swaziland. It was in Matsapha, the industrial area close to Manzini, but you couldn't go to visit it because it was confidential just like Mama's business. Nobody was allowed to know its secret.

'Benedict!' Titi's voice was angry, and he realised that he had been making a noise with his straw, sucking at the empty can for any last remaining bubbles. He knew that wasn't polite.

'*Samahani!* Sorry!' Then he gave a little burp and said *samahani* again, and when Titi burped too they collapsed into giggles.

Mama was excited on the way back up the hill. She had squashed only one cone and knocked over only another two, and Henry had declared her ready for the test. Henry laughed a lot and Titi's eyes were bright with expectation. Benedict was quiet, though, and he wasn't sure why. Something was hiding somewhere in his head. He would find a quiet place later on and see if he could coax it out.

But it was some time before he was able to do that. As Henry swung into the garage to pull up behind the red Microbus, Moses and Daniel stood up from the lowest step, their cheeks striped with tears, and ran to the car. They threw their arms around Mama as she stepped out.

'Sorry!' called Auntie Rachel, coming towards them from the other house carrying the youngest of the Mazibukos, the one who had been a baby that somebody had found in a dustbin. 'They had a falling out with Fortune. Can't for the life of me tell you what it was about, but they insisted on waiting here for you to come home.'

Mama embraced the two snivelling boys. '*Eh*, I'm sorry, Rachel.'

'*Ag*, no problem, hey?' She turned to go back to the other

house. 'The girls are still with us, I'll send them home later when you've dealt with those two.'

'Thank you, Auntie Rachel!'

They went up to the house, Benedict holding Daniel's hand and Mama struggling with Moses who held on to her with both of his. They left Titi behind in the garage to plan her evening with Henry. Benedict heated some milk in a saucepan for the boys and spooned some honey into two mugs. The jar of honey had to stand inside some water in a dish so that the ants couldn't get to it. Benedict felt sure that the ants would one day find a way to build some kind of bridge across the water to get to the honey; they spent long enough walking around the edge of the dish thinking about it.

Benedict and Mama would have tea later, but what mattered now was calming the younger ones. Warm milk and honey usually did the trick.

When he carried the two mugs into the lounge, the boys were sitting on either side of Mama on the couch. She had given each of them a tissue and they had wiped their eyes and blown their noses.

'Dominoes,' Mama said to him. 'Somebody cheated at dominoes.'

'Fortune!' declared Moses hotly.

'Uh-uh!' Mama's voice was firm. 'It doesn't matter who! It was just a game.'

'Yes,' said Benedict, putting their mugs down on the coffee table. 'A game should be about laughing and having fun. A game isn't something important, like real life. You mustn't make the mistake of taking it seriously. Tears don't belong in a game.'

Mama smiled at him warmly. 'You are sounding just like my Pius,' she said.

Benedict's chest swelled with pride. 'But Baba would be able to give an example of countries making the mistake of going to war over a game, or families never speaking to each other again because of something that started as a game.'

Titi came in at the front door and passed quickly through the lounge without looking at them. They heard a door slam.

'Titi?' called Mama. But no answer came.

'I'll go,' said Benedict.

He knocked on the door of the girls' bedroom. Titi didn't answer, but he heard her blowing her nose inside. He opened the door a little way and called her name softly.

'*Karibu*. Come in,' she said, her voice wet with tears.

'*Eh*, Titi!' Benedict sat down next to her on her bed.

'The meat is for Henry and his wife,' she said, sniffing loudly. 'He's having the braai at home with her.'

Benedict took her hand that wasn't holding the tissue. 'Sorry, Titi.'

Her tears came more strongly, and she said nothing, sniffing loudly into her tissue. Henry having a wife had been making her unsure and not very happy right from the very beginning.

Benedict stood up. 'I'm sending Mama, see?'

He changed places with Mama, leaving Titi in Mama's care while he did his best to cheer his brothers. He wondered if he should offer the boys and Titi some drops of Auntie Rachel's rescue medicine, but on the whole he thought it was better not to. Mama didn't really like to have any medicine in the house, even though this was just made from flowers and it wasn't pills that a child could mistake for sweets.

When his brothers had finished their milk and honey, he took them out into the garden with their football and played at being interested in kicking it around with them. It was a boring thing to do, but it gave him time to think.

In Swaziland a man was allowed any number of wives, and he often had girlfriends too. So far King Mswati had seven wives and a fiancée, but people said he was still young. He was born the same year that Swaziland was born, 1968, and if you minused that from this year, 2001, it told you that the king and Swaziland were both thirty-three now.

Henry already had one wife, and he acted like he wanted Titi to become his wife number two. But he never said. He had certainly acted like the meat was for him and Titi, but had he actually said? Benedict wasn't sure. Was it polite for Henry to ask Titi to choose meat for him and his wife? Was it right? Benedict wished that Baba was here. Baba would know.

Benedict knew what Mama would be telling Titi now, as he kicked the ball as badly as Sifiso would and it went into the flower bed, almost toppling over the edge of the garden into the wilderness of banana and pawpaw trees. She would be saying that *of course* Titi was upset, it was only natural to find the culture of many wives difficult when you had grown up in a culture of one wife only. She would be agreeing with Titi that Henry hadn't been clear about tonight's braai for two. And she would be assuring Titi, as Benedict had heard her do before, that *of course* she would be able to find somebody else, and *of course* Henry wasn't going to be her only chance at having a husband and children, so she really didn't need to accept something that didn't feel right.

Eventually Moses and Daniel grew tired of Benedict's half-hearted effort, tired enough to agree that it was time to go and say sorry to Fortune, who was much better at kicking.

His sisters were coming up the steps as his brothers were going down, and, anxious for them not to interrupt Mama's talk with Titi, Benedict sat them down in front of the TV and said he would bring them some tea. He put enough milk in the saucepan for all of them to have tea, and while he waited for it to boil, he looked in the fridge to see if there was anything special they could have for their supper. There was no chance of a braai. That kind of meat was much too expensive for such a big family – and besides, a braai would probably upset Titi when his intention was to cheer her up. With Baba away, everybody could do with cheering.

Cake.

Cake was the answer. As soon as the tea was made, he would sift some flour to get all the weevils out. Mama could bake some cupcakes, and they could all help with making icing in their favourite colours.

It was a busy evening with lots of fun and giggling, and plenty of mess. Henry, the argument with Fortune, and regrets over Mrs Zikalala's ugly white cake were all forgotten.

It wasn't until Benedict was lying in bed in the quiet darkness, waiting for sleep to take him, that he remembered that there was something hiding somewhere in his head. He thought back over the events of the day to see if anything would make it come out.

It began to step forward slowly, blurry at first, misshapen. It didn't look right. He concentrated hard, until at last it looked like something he could recognise, something that made sense.

Yes.

It was definitely an idea.

Climbing out of bed, he went to find Mama.

NINE

O N HER HANDS AND KNEES IN THE DOWNSTAIRS
bathroom, Mavis scrubbed at the shower floor with one
of the children's old toothbrushes and a mixture of Sunlight
and Jik. The Sunlight was for the small tiles, which were like
pieces of the plates and cups that she washed with Sunlight in
the sink, and the Jik was for the bits of black that had started
to grow on the white lines between the tiles. Madam had said
it was only bleach that would get rid of that. It had never been
there before, it had only come since Doctor had started sometimes using the shower instead of the bath.

Doctor wasn't happy these days. With her own ears Mavis
had heard him arguing with Madam behind the closed door of
their bedroom. This has to stop, he had told Madam, if it
doesn't stop then she'll have to go.

He had been talking about *Gogo* Levine, Mavis had known
that without even needing to guess. *Gogo* Levine knew dairy
farming, she used to do it with Madam's father. But Doctor
and the dairy manager knew dairy farming, too, they didn't
need anybody telling them do it this way not that way. Doctor
would stop down at the dairy on his way home up the hill, and
if the dairy manager told him anything about *Gogo* Levine he

would come very quickly into the house and go straight to the bathroom, where he would slam the door loudly and shower in cold water. Only after that would he say hello to everybody in the house.

One evening he had said to Madam, how long is she going to stay? She can't stay here forever. And Madam had said they had to remember that *Gogo* Levine and Madam's father had bought this farm for them, they couldn't just tell her to go. Mavis hadn't heard that with her own ears, it was Lungi who heard it. But helping the three smallest girls to bath upstairs, Mavis had heard the downstairs bathroom door slamming very hard, and she had heard the shower water running for a very long time.

What could Madam say? *Gogo* Levine was her mother and her mother wasn't happy, she needed to be with her daughter. But Doctor was Madam's husband, and Doctor wasn't happy with either of them. Mavis found herself worrying that maybe Madam and Doctor would leave their marriage, just as *Gogo* Levine had done. What would happen to the children then? They had already lost too much!

Vusi would maybe be okay, Petros was the same age as Vusi and Petros was definitely okay. Innocence would maybe not be okay. She wasn't as clever as Vusi, and she did silly things without thinking what might happen. She would rather sing and dance and laugh with the girls from the other house than think about making something of her life, meanwhile Madam and Doctor were paying for her to be schooled. Mavis wasn't even sure that Innocence would make a good cleaner, she was such an untidy girl. As for Fortune, it was impossible for Mavis to tell if he would be okay or not. That boy had never had a serious thought inside his head, not even for as long as it took to dust a windowsill. Olga was very easily upset, she would definitely not be okay if anything happened to her new family – but the three small girls were maybe small enough to be okay if they needed to go to another new family now. Maybe.

Eish!

A few evenings ago, while the family was eating at the table in the kitchen and Mavis and Lungi were waiting to wash the dishes and have their own supper, Mavis had slipped quietly into Madam and Doctor's bedroom and sprinkled two drops from one of Madam's special small brown bottles on their pillow-cases.

It was the one called Ylang Ylang, and Mavis knew about it from doing the ironing in the kitchen while Madam was telling a friend about it in the lounge when the whole of the rest of the house was quiet. It was exactly what Madam's friend needed because there was tension and distance with her boyfriend, and the Ylang Ylang was going to help them to relax and be romantic together.

Since Mavis had sprinkled the oil on Madam and Doctor's pillow-cases, Doctor hadn't used the shower, not even once. But, *eish*, the black marks on the shower floor just wouldn't stay away. As she scrubbed at them, her thoughts went to Titi.

It wasn't enough that Titi had seen the world and was part of her madam's family, now she had a boyfriend too. A Swazi, meanwhile she was a *kwerekwere*. He was rich, he had a business and a car, but that wasn't enough for Titi. No. She wanted him not to have any other wife or girlfriend. Who did she think she was? Mavis would be happy to get any husband at all, she wouldn't mind sharing, even if it meant sharing with any number of others. But it was never going to happen. It didn't matter, really. Not as long as *Gogo* Levine didn't make Madam and Doctor leave their marriage. Mavis loved her job here, she loved that there were children to take care of.

She was rinsing the bleach solution off her hands under the basin tap when somebody began to wail, and by the time she got to the big downstairs room still drying her hands on a towel, Madam and *Gogo* Levine were right behind her and three more children were wailing. Their mouths wide open, their voices louder than the cartoons they had been watching on the TV, Olga and the three little ones squirmed on the sofa, glaring angrily at the ground where the enamel bowl of popcorn that Lungi had made for them lay on its side, the white puffs of corn scattered everywhere.

Madam and Mavis did their best to bring comfort and calm, while *Gogo* Levine scooped up the bowl and went to ask Lungi to make them some more. Mavis bent and put the smallest one on her back, securing her there with the towel by draping it over the child's back then tying it around her own front. Leaving Madam on the sofa, she took the hand of the second smallest and, jiggling the one on her back comfortingly, she led the other towards the far end of the room, talking to her all the time. Children who were crying needed separating, other-wise they would keep setting each other off.

From the window at the far end of the room, Mavis could see the cows making their way past the side of the garden, on their way down to the dairy for milking.

Eish.

Titi had brought slices of cake for Lungi and Mavis. Lungi had said it was delicious, she wanted to learn baking from

Titi's madam. Titi's madam didn't just add eggs to a mixture from a box like Madam had taught Lungi. Mavis had saved her slice, putting it away on a shelf in the wardrobe until she could give it to Petros. Today was absolutely the last day it would still be nice, and once again she wouldn't be able to give it to him. She would have to eat it herself now.

The last of the cows were passing, and Petros walked with them, his dog dancing along at his side. As she listened to his coughing, Mavis's heart ached and she bent to hug the child whose hand she'd been holding. The pills Madam had bought for Petros from the doctor were no good, but she didn't want to say anything to Madam. Madam already had enough to worry about with Doctor and *Gogo* Levine, and Mavis didn't want to make Madam angry or upset. Madam had already shouted at Lungi for letting the pot of beetroot boil over, and then she had said sorry to Lungi and started to cry.

If anything happened to the family, Mavis wouldn't have this job, and then she wouldn't have a small child on her back and another in her arms.

TEN

AFTER SPORTS ON WEDNESDAY AFTERNOON, BENEDICT and Giveness went with Sifiso and his parents in the Buffalo Soldiers van for Sifiso's birthday. Auntie Rachel said that having his birthday at the end of July meant that Sifiso was a lion, like the king, so Benedict had drawn a picture of a lion for him. There was no need of a cake from Mama because Sifiso's birthday was at the restaurant where his big sister had a job as a waitress, and they were all going to have waffles with syrup and ice cream, which was Sifiso's absolute best. Sports every Wednesday afternoon was Sifiso's and Benedict's absolute worst, and they were jealous that Giveness was excused it on account of his skin not doing well in the sun. The waffles were going to taste especially good after the sports.

'*Eh!*' said Benedict, as the Buffalo Soldiers van passed Mr Patel's shop. 'Look!'

Somebody had sprayed red paint all over the walls and window.

'*Eish,*' said Mr Simelane, shaking his head behind the wheel.

Sitting next to him at the front, Mrs Simelane tutted.

'Why do they do that?' Benedict asked.

'Drugth,' said Sifiso.

'Drugs?' Benedict wasn't sure what drugs looked like, but he didn't think he had ever seen any for sale on the shop counter. He supposed they could be hidden inside something there. If Mama's cupcakes were still for sale there, they could even be hidden inside those. Once, back in Dar, Titi had eaten drugs by mistake, when a friend had given her a biscuit baked by the people she cleaned for. Titi and her friend didn't know, but drugs were hiding baked inside that biscuit, and after Titi ate it she felt very confused. Then she got frightened and started to cry, and Mama had to give her tea and wrap her in a blanket and sit with her until she was better.

Benedict couldn't imagine Mrs Patel selling anything like that.

'*Yebo*,' said Mr Simelane. 'Some years back now.' He clicked his fingers together rapidly a few times. 'When was it?'

Mrs Simelane helped him. 'Two years ago? Maybe three.' She turned to face Benedict. 'Their son... I forget his name...'

'Thun Deep,' said Sifiso.

'That's right! Sandeep. *Eish*, your memory is good, nè?' She beamed at Sifiso before looking back at Benedict. 'Sandeep got himself some bad friends, more especially boys who took drugs. They got caught at school.'

'Expelled!' Mr Simelane accelerated to get through the traffic light up ahead before it had been red for too long.

'*Yebo*. Then Mr Patel took Sandeep to the Hhohho police headquarters and made him tell them all the people he knew who sold drugs.'

'It was in the *Times*,' said Mr Simelane. 'Thereafter, Sandeep wasn't safe. They had to send him away to India!'

Eh!

So, it was the Patels' own son that had been sent away for doing nonsense, it was Mrs Patel's own heart that was broken. Her heart was all in pieces, just like the hoopoe's body when Jabulani pulled it from the funeral van's grille. Benedict imagined Jabulani making a special casket for Mrs Patel's heart, with a carving of Sandeep on its lid. He wondered if he should offer Mrs Patel a few drops of rescue medicine next time her saw her. But no. It wasn't right that he knew she needed rescuing, not without her telling him herself. Besides, he only ever saw her inside Mr Patel's shop; how could he possibly offer her medicine over curry and Russians and chips?

If he ever had to be sent away himself, he knew it would break Mama's heart, just as sending Sandeep away had broken Mrs Patel's. And how would his family survive without their eldest boy? *Eh!*

'Now ever since, they keep reminding Patel that he's not welcome. Moreover,' added Mr Simelane, changing gear to slow down behind a heavy truck, 'Sandeep can never return back.'

Mrs Simelane shook her head sadly. 'Nobody thought such a thing could happen to people like the Patels.'

'But at day's end, drugs as a scourge can occur to any family, nè?'

As Mr Simelane said it, Benedict felt an extra weight pressing on his shoulders. He had never before thought of the possibility of drugs coming to his own family. Okay, they had already come to Titi, just once, by mistake. But he had never before worried that they might come to his brothers or his sisters. Now, as the eldest boy, he had yet another danger to watch out for.

The restaurant was a little further than Uncle Enock's work, past where the pineapples were put into cans and in the same compound as Swazi Candles. Sifiso's sister had put a vase of plastic roses and a *Reserved* sign on an inside table for them, away from the sunny outside tables where *Wazungu* from a tourist bus talked loudly in a language Benedict didn't know.

While the grown-ups drank tea, Benedict chose to join the other boys in having sodas: he preferred his tea to be milky, spicy and sweet the Tanzanian way, rather than watery and plain the Swazi way. The waffles were soft and delicious, more especially because Sifiso's sister was kind enough to make sure that the boys got extra ice cream and plenty of sweet, sticky syrup.

When they had finished, the boys went into Swazi Candles, where only Sifiso had been before. The front part was a big shop, with shelf after shelf of candles in the most wonderful colours. Big, round, square, egg-shaped – and *eh*, there were candles shaped like elephants, hippos, tortoises, giraffes, buffalo! So many animals! Some were patterned in blues and greens, others in reds and browns, others in all the colours you could imagine. And so many birds! Some of them looked so real!

'They don't *look* like candles,' said Giveness.

'No, they are,' said Sifiso, pointing to the string sticking up out of the back of a warthog patterned in swirls of red, yellow, blue and green. 'Here'th the wick, nè?'

'*Eish*,' said Giveness.

Benedict could see that Giveness was battling to see the point of a candle that was anything other than straight and white. 'A candle doesn't have to look like a candle,' he said, 'just like a cake doesn't have to look like a cake. It can look like a bus or an aeroplane or a cow. Or anything else you want.'

'Come and thee them making them!'

Sifiso led them into the room at the back where a handful of people sat at work, and one of them called the boys over.

'I'm starting a new one,' the man said, handing Sifiso a perfectly round ball of white wax.

'It'th hot!' Sifiso passed it quickly to the other two, who passed it quickly back to the man.

'It's going to be an elephant,' the man said, and they watched him drape over opposite sides of the ball two thin disks of patterned colour so that the ball was entirely covered.

'That's going to be an elephant?' Giveness sounded like he didn't believe it.

'Imagine!' said Benedict, loving every second of the six or seven minutes it took the man to shape the ball into a head, ears, trunk, body, tail and legs before pushing in other pieces for eyes, stabbing a hole into its back for the wick and dropping it into a plastic tub of water to cool. Unmistakably an elephant, it floated there amongst the other elephants that the man had already made. And already he was busy with another ball of wax.

Outside the shop, Benedict and Sifiso waited for a few minutes on the small shady veranda at the entrance while Giveness went back inside to say that somebody had taken his umbrella, which he had left out there before going inside. Nobody should have taken it anyway, but on a day without any rain it was just silly. While the staff went in search of it, Giveness joined them on the veranda.

Hoop, hoop, hoop, came the call of a bird.

161

Benedict scanned the tall trees in front of the restaurant until a movement high up caught his eye.

'Look,' he said, pointing excitedly. 'It's a hoopoe.'

'Where?'

'There! Look.'

After a few minutes, the beautiful bird left the tree, flew over the roof of the restaurant and was gone. Benedict could hear Giveness and Sifiso making sounds of appreciation behind him, but when he turned round he saw that their appreciation wasn't about the hoopoe at all. Somebody had managed to find the missing umbrella.

Mama would love all the colours at the candle factory, and Benedict told her about it at supper to cheer her up. Baba had been away for three whole days now. Mama said that Baba had already been there for his work, and that he had said the candles were an excellent export to countries in the West, though most of the rest of Africa had only one requirement of a candle, which was neither decorativeness nor expense.

'Too many books can blind a person to beauty,' Mama said sadly, shaking her head. Then she smiled. 'We'll go there together, Benedict. You and me.'

Benedict beamed. Mama's driving test was tomorrow, and when she had her license they could go anywhere at all together.

'Why not us?' asked Grace, indicating herself and Faith. 'Can't we come too?'

'And us,' said Moses, almost choking on his mouthful of *ugali*.

'I'm sure you can't play ball in there,' Titi said to the boys.

'You'd be bored,' Benedict said to the girls. 'Like you were at the gorillas, Grace.'

'I was *not* bored!'

'Only because there was a girl for you to talk to about anything but gorillas!'

Grace shrugged as if Benedict had a point, and as she went back to making balls of *ugali* to dip into the spinach and peanut sauce with her fingers, Benedict thought back to the trip they had been on to the Virunga Mountains in Rwanda. A neighbour of theirs who was going with his daughter had had space for two more, and Mama and Baba had wanted Grace and Faith to be the ones to go.

'Gorillas are very big,' Benedict had told Faith in the bedroom all the children had shared with Titi back then. 'Much bigger than Baba.'

She had looked at him with very big eyes. 'Do they eat people?'

It would have been easy to lie, but that wasn't right. 'No. But they can chase you and then you can get lost in the forest. Specially if you're small.'

When her eyes had begun to fill with tears, Benedict had put an arm round her, feeling bad that he had scared her quite so much. 'I'm only joking, Faith. They're not so scary, but they *are* big.'

'I don't want to go,' she had whispered. 'Benedict, please don't let them make me go.'

Benedict had gone in Faith's place, and the gorillas had interested him so much that he had very quickly stopped feeling bad about scaring Faith so that he could go in her place. Grace had been only a little bit scared, but their neighbour's daughter had been there for her to hold on to and giggle with, and to talk with about things other than the gorillas, which really hadn't interested her much.

Benedict knew that if he hadn't found the gorillas so exciting, he would have felt lonely and sad on that trip. It was one thing for Grace to prefer the company of her sister, but when any girl at all was more interesting to her than he was, it really didn't feel nice. The neighbour's daughter was visiting Rwanda for less than two weeks, but she and Grace seemed closer than Benedict and Grace had been for a very long time. It didn't hurt him in the way that banging his toe or his elbow hurt, nor in the way that Mrs Patel's heart hurt now, being all in pieces about Sandeep never coming back, but in a way that made him feel like a small part of him had – like Sandeep – gone so far away that it might never come back. Whatever that part was that had gone, it had left behind a small space inside him that was filled with emptiness.

Benedict asked Titi if she'd like to go and see the candles with him and Mama, but she smiled shyly and said thank you but no, Benedict and Auntie should go together. She would ask Henry to take her there.

On the Friday of the week of Baba being away, Auntie Rachel was in a bad mood when she collected them from school, on account of having spent the whole entire morning taking Mrs Levine across the border into South Africa so that they could do a U-turn and come back into Swaziland again. A holiday visa lasted only so long, and whenever Mrs Levine's was going to expire, she had to leave and re-enter, and Auntie Rachel had to take her.

On the way home, Vusi Mazibuko told everybody about something that had happened during break at the high school. A group of boys in his class had found a scorpion amongst a pile of old bricks at the edge of the schoolyard. One of them had run to get some exercise books, which they had used to scoot the creature away from the bricks onto a patch of bare ground. Surrounding it with books to keep it there, they had then encircled its prison of books with a ring of dried leaves and small twigs, which they had set alight before lifting away the books.

'*Ag* no, man!' said Auntie Rachel. 'Shame! I hope you weren't involved?'

'Of course not—'

'And why did they have matches?'

'They smoke. Some of—'

'But not you, hey? Because if—'

'*Ngeke!* Never!'

'Why?' asked Benedict, who was sitting up front next to Auntie Rachel. 'Why did they do that?'

'To make it kill itself,' said Vusi, from the row behind him.

'*Eh!*' How could people be so cruel?

'*Ja,*' said Auntie Rachel, 'they used to do that on my parents' farm. Just for entertainment.' She shook her head. 'My mom would go ballistic when she caught them at it.'

'Why?' Benedict asked again. 'I mean... I don't understand.'

'*Ag*, the scorpion runs around inside the circle of fire, it sees there's no way out, so it gives up. Kills itself. Curls up its tail and stabs itself in the back with its own sting.'

'*Eh!*' Benedict thought about how frightened the creature would have to be to do that.

'That's stupid,' said Innocence, who was next to Vusi. 'Why doesn't it just wait for the fire to go out?'

Vusi began to laugh.

'What?' asked Auntie Rachel, looking at him in her rear-view mirror.

'I'm just thinking of those boys not letting the fire go out, trying to keep it going forever,' said Vusi, still laughing. 'More and more sticks, then chopping down trees. Soon there's no more forest left—'

'Just desert!' said Benedict.

'Meanwhile those boys have become old men, they've had no schooling, all they can think about is keeping that fire burning!' Vusi shook his head, grinning widely.

'Stupid,' said Innocence again.

'*Ja*, hey?'

A woman with a baby on her back and a huge basket on her head tried to flag down the yellow Hi-Ace and everybody chorused, 'We're not a bloody taxi!'

'The scorpion,' said Benedict. 'Did it… Is it late?'

'No!' said Vusi, slapping one of his legs and leaning forward as far as the seatbelt would let him. 'A girl saved it!'

'*Eh? A girl?*' Benedict twisted right round to look at Vusi.

'Nomsa from my class,' said Innocence, flicking something out from under one of her fingernails. 'She's mad.'

Vusi told them that Nomsa had pushed between two of the boys who were standing around the ring of fire chanting for the scorpion to kill itself. She had stomped on some of the flames with her school shoes, scooped the creature up in her hands and put it down safely amongst the bricks where the boys had found it.

It had all happened very quickly, and while most of the boys had been too shocked and surprised to say anything, a couple of them had shouted at her. But Nomsa had said nothing back. Then one of the teachers, Mr Thwala, had come and shouted at Nomsa as if everything was her fault, and he had told her to stay after school.

Then Olga Mazibuko and Grace began to tell Auntie Rachel about Mr Patel upsetting a lady outside the high school by searching through the sweets that she was selling, and Benedict looked out of the window and allowed his mind to wander as the vehicle filled with the children's chatter.

'They say it's not true,' Auntie Rachel said to him quietly as she slowed the Hi-Ace and eased it over the cattle-grid at the farm's gate. 'It's just a myth.'

'Hm?' Pulled from his thoughts, Benedict had no idea what she was talking about.

'Scorpions don't really commit suicide. You mustn't be upset, hey?'

Benedict gave her a smile to show her that he was far from upset. He knew the spider-girl's name now, and he turned it over and over in his mind like a smooth pebble in his hand.

Nomsa.

Later that afternoon, Benedict made his way down past the Mazibukos' house towards the dairy. Mrs Levine was busy in the garden, pulling some plants out of the flowerbeds.

'Hi there, Bennie,' she called, her eyes shining brightly.

'Hello, Mrs Levine. What are you doing?'

'Just getting rid of these.' She pulled so hard on a plant that when it finally let go of the ground it happened so suddenly that she landed on her buttocks on the grass. '*Eina*, man!'

The shock of it made Benedict want to laugh, but when he saw tears in Mrs Levine's eyes, he went and sat next to her, asking if she was okay.

She nodded, dabbing at her eyes with a tissue from the pocket of her gardening apron, suddenly seeming to have no energy left.

Benedict looked at the plants she had pulled out. 'Are they weeds?'

She smiled. 'In a way. They were all flowers at my wedding. I don't want to see them.'

'Um...' Benedict tried to think of a polite way to ask, but he couldn't. He asked anyway. 'Mrs Levine, you do know that this isn't *your* garden?'

Her smile grew wider. '*Ja*. I'm allowed in the garden, as long as I don't go near the dairy.'

Benedict wasn't sure what to say next. He looked at the plants again. 'I'm sorry about you and Mr Levine.'

She let out one of the longest sighs he had ever heard in his life. '*Ja*. I thought it would last forever, hey. Every bride does, I suppose.' She gestured towards the plants that lay wilting on the grass. 'When we danced in that hall, with those flowers everywhere... man, that was the happiest day of my life!'

Benedict smiled with her. 'How did you meet Mr Levine?' Maybe Mr Levine had seen her rescuing a scorpion or a spider.

Mrs Levine lent back so that she was lying on the grass, and propping both hands behind her head, she spoke as if she was having some kind of a dream. 'I was working at the hospital. Solly's sister had had a premature baby there.' Benedict didn't know what *premature* meant, but he didn't want to interrupt. 'The baby didn't know how to suck.'

Now he *had* to interrupt. What kind of baby doesn't know how to suck? It was what babies *did*. But Mrs Levine explained that no, a baby can be born too early, before the instinct to suck is there. Benedict knew about instincts; all animals had them.

Anyway, Mrs Levine was qualified to teach babies to suck, and she taught Mr Levine's sister's baby. Mr Levine came to the hospital every day to see his sister, and then when his sister went home but her baby stayed, he came every day to see the baby. When the baby went home, Mr Levine still came to the hospital every day, on account of falling in love with Mrs Levine.

'He treated me like royalty back then, Bennie. *Royalty!* I was crazy about him, gave up everything when we married.' Mrs Levine sat up. 'Career, the lot. Went and lived on his farm, gave him two beautiful, wonderful kids. Rachel came here to marry Enock, Adam moved to Australia so he didn't have to fight in the army for apartheid.' Her face suddenly changed, and so did her voice, like she had woken from the lovely dream she was in. 'And still I stayed on the farm with Solly, spending my life doing his bloody accounts.' She got to her feet, bending to gather up the plants she'd pulled up. 'Then he only goes and runs off with some little tart who—'

'*Mom!*' Auntie Rachel was suddenly behind them. '*Please!*'

Mrs Levine busied herself with picking up the rest of the wilting plants, ignoring her daughter's hard stare.

169

Auntie Rachel helped Benedict to his feet and gave him a small squeeze. 'Can you find something else to do while I talk to my mom?'

He continued on his way down the hill, past the dairy where he could hear the cows being milked, and where he could hear a dog barking and Petros coughing. He wanted to go and talk to Petros, to see how he was and to ask him again about the mines and the gold, but talking to Mrs Levine had already delayed him, and he didn't want to miss Baba coming home.

As he carried on down the driveway, he thought about Mr Levine running away with a tart. Was that like the queen of hearts baking some tarts and then somebody running away with them? Who was it who ran away with them? The king of hearts? He couldn't remember. There was a dish that ran away with something. What was it? A spoon? Something like that. Anyway, Auntie Rachel sometimes made little tarts called Bakewell, which were pastry spread with jam and then filled with cake, with a thin layer of white icing on top. They were okay, but really, cake didn't need pastry and there should be thick butter icing on top in a nice colour.

He came to a halt at the gate, where he spent a long time looking at the cattle-grid.

No.

He couldn't bring himself to cross it and run all the way up to the edge of the highway to meet Baba's white Corolla, no matter how badly he wanted to do just that. He knew that it was silly to imagine that he was small enough to fall through the gaps between the strips of metal.

But still.

When he had been much smaller, Grace had sat with him and helped him to read a story about three goats called Billy. They had to get across a bridge without being eaten by a big, ugly monster that lived underneath and looked very scary in the pictures. Benedict knew that the monster wasn't real, it was just pretend, and there was no monster waiting to eat him under the cattle-grid or under the narrow bridge leading to the pump in the middle of the dam. Anyway, even if there *was* a monster – which there wasn't – he knew from the story of the goats how to escape being eaten. The trick was to tell the monster that he was very small – which he wasn't – and that there was somebody bigger coming along who would be a bigger meal.

Of course, that would only work if Baba really was coming along behind him. Baba was big enough to scare away any monsters, even the ones that were real and not just pretend. There had been three goats, and the first two had both said that somebody bigger was coming. But there were only two Tungarazas, on account of Benedict's first baba being late.

Then Benedict breathed in sharply. What if the three goats weren't from three generations? What if they were three brothers? Okay, it would be silly for all three brothers to have the same name, but maybe that was normal in goats. Daniel, his smallest brother, would cross the bridge first. Daniel was a year older than Moses, but he was smaller on account of having the same sort of shape as Faith, little and solid. Then Moses would cross, and both of them would rely on their biggest brother coming up behind them to save them.

Eh!

He would have to be big enough to save them!

Taking a deep breath, he stretched out his right foot and rested it lightly on the metal bar of the grid that was closest to him. At once that leg felt like he had been sitting on it badly for too long and it had gone to sleep. That same feeling flooded up his whole body, and he struggled to breathe as he felt himself beginning to fall down, down, down between that bar and the next.

Dizzy with fright, he sat down hard on the ground and scooted away from the grid on his buttocks, his shallow breaths coming quickly. He could feel his heart pounding in his chest the same way it had when he had run all the way from the dam with his duck in his arms, calling to Uncle Enock.

Blinking back tears, he took a few deep breaths to calm himself. How he wished he had the little brown bottle of rescue medicine in his pocket! It had been after he had taken his duck to Uncle Enock that Auntie Rachel had given him some drops of it for the first time. He really could do with a few drops now! But all he had was his breathing, and he had to make do with that.

There had been no monster coming for him. No, he was sure of that. Just the feeling of sliding down into a dark place where he would be lost forever. Unnoticed. Forgotten.

He forced himself to look over at the grid. The spaces between were really so small! But he did not stand up until Baba's white Corolla was right next to him and Baba was asking him what he was doing there. He climbed in beside Baba and said he'd been waiting to tell him the good news about Mama, that she'd passed her test.

Her test had been the day before in the afternoon, so it had

172

been Titi alone who had greeted them at home after school, and Titi alone who had listened to their stories about their school day as they had their fruit and tea.

When Moses and Daniel had finished their homework, they had played in the garden, not wanting to go down to the other house in case they missed Mama coming home with Henry, and the same worry had kept Benedict and his sisters at the dining table with their books much longer than they needed to be there.

The hooting from the Quick Impact Corolla all the way up the long driveway had told the whole entire compound what the Tungaraza household had been waiting to hear: Mama had passed!

'As easy as cutting a slice of cake!' Mama had declared with a big smile as all of them had hugged her. 'Okay, maybe not a sponge cake. A heavy cake thick with dried fruit.'

'And nuts, too!' Henry had declared happily, laughing as he grabbed Titi and twirled her around in a dance. 'Let us not forget that three-point turn with its five points, nè?' Mama laughed. 'Or that cone that will never again be able to stand straight!'

Mama had flopped down on one of the couches with a loud *eh* and kicked off her smart shoes. Benedict had sat down next to her.

'We're all proud of you, Mama!'

Mama had put an arm around him. 'I'm proud of me, too, my boy. I'm proud of me, too.' Then she had pulled him closer and planted a kiss on his forehead.

It was Benedict's idea that Mama could learn driving, and it was Benedict who had brought her Henry. Tucked under

Mama's arm then, he had felt proud of himself, too. But he never said.

Now, in Baba's Corolla, he said, 'She got her licence, Baba!' His voice sounded like he didn't have much breath inside him. Part of that was still about the cattle-grid, but more and more of it was about how excited he was to see Baba.

'That is very good.' Baba seemed a little sad.

'Mama and Titi are cooking a special supper to welcome you home.'

'That is very good.'

As they waited for the cows to finish crossing the driveway in front of them, Benedict wondered why Baba wasn't more pleased. Perhaps he was tired. The drive from Johannesburg to Mbabane was long, and perhaps Baba hadn't slept so well in the hotel, away from Mama.

Petros walked with the cows from the milking shed to their sleeping shed, giving Benedict a small wave. When Benedict returned it without thinking before he remembered he wasn't supposed to know Petros, Baba didn't even notice. His mind seemed very far away.

'Was the conference good, Baba?'

Baba nodded. 'Very good.'

'Did people come from Tanzania?'

'Yes. They brought me—' Baba clicked his tongue against the roof of his mouth as the last cow stopped right in front of the Corolla and Petros and Krishna came back to move it on. Then the way was clear and they headed up towards the house.

'They brought you what, Baba?'

'Hm?' Baba seemed to have forgotten that he was in the

middle of a sentence. 'Oh. Yes. News from home.' He sighed. 'They brought me news from home.'

As they tucked in to their supper of spicy chicken pieces with mashed potatoes, boiled gem squash and spinach, Baba smacked his lips together and said how delicious it was, and how happy he was to be back with his family, more especially his beautiful and brilliant wife. Mama smiled and patted her hair, and said how happy she was to have her husband home and how proud of him she was for having spoken at a pan-African conference.

But Mama was moving her food around on her plate rather than eating it, and Benedict knew that something was wrong.

She had been fine when Baba had arrived, proudly showing him her driving licence, telling him all about the test and reminding him how clever he had been to have the idea that she should learn to drive. But then Baba had led her into their bedroom and closed the door, and whenever the other children's noise had died down and Titi's clattering and splashing in the kitchen had stopped for a moment, Benedict had heard that they were talking in hushed voices.

At the end of the meal, when Mama brought in her dark chocolate cake with the yellow shape of Africa on it glittering with Dusting Powder (Gold), Baba said how lovely it was. As he sliced into it, he joked about what a crime it was to be cutting Africa up into random pieces as the colonials had done in the past, and Mama laughed, but her laugh was too big for Baba's joke and her eyes shone a little too brightly.

Mama and Baba both took tiny pieces, and while Baba

managed to finish his piece in between telling them all how powerful Africa could be if African countries would unite and trade with one another rather than with the West, Mama ate little more than a mouthful before quietly dividing her piece up between Moses and Daniel.

The children moved to the couches to watch TV, Benedict went to his cushion next to the bookshelf, and with Titi washing up in the kitchen, Mama and Baba were alone at the table.

They were silent.

Half-heartedly, Benedict looked for Krishna in one of the encyclopaedias. What was it that Mama and Baba weren't talking about that was stopping them from talking about anything else? They had talked about it behind their bedroom door, so it was obviously something they didn't want the children to hear.

Was it something *about* the children?

About *one* of the children?

Was it about *him*?

Eh!

What had he done wrong?

He began to cast his mind back over the week that Baba had been away. But no. Mama had been fine until Baba had come home and talked to her in their bedroom. Was Baba disappointed in him for waiting at the gate instead of going all the way up to the highway? He thought about that for a few seconds before dismissing it: Baba would probably have been angry with him if he had put himself in danger by going near the fast highway traffic. What could it be?

Was Baba angry that Benedict and Petros had greeted each other?

When Mama's cell-phone rang, Benedict felt as relieved as Mama and Baba looked.

It was Zodwa.

Eh! How could he have forgotten? Getting up from his cushion, he stood looking at Mama hopefully, clasping his hands to his chest. Without him even noticing, two of the fingers on his right hand crossed.

Listening to Zodwa, Mama began to smile. It was a proper smile, a real one, not pretend. *Yes!*

Pushing the button to end the call, she nodded at him and he rushed to hug her, then they told Baba about it together. He hadn't wanted to tell Baba about it before, when it could have turned out to be just another disappointment.

'Benedict has had a wonderful idea,' Mama began. 'A way to save my business.'

'*Eh!* I need some good news like this!' Baba looked genuinely pleased, and Benedict beamed.

'Baba, you know that lots of people here become late?' Baba nodded. 'And you know that afterwards, after a month or two depending on their church, their family does a ceremony to wash away their sadness and to ask the ancestors to protect them?' Baba nodded again.

'Pius, they have to slaughter a cow! When they've already spent so much on burial. It's not just once in a while but too, too often. People are struggling!'

'Baba, I asked my friends at school. If somebody really doesn't have money for a cow, they can kill a goat instead, or even a chicken. The important thing is the ancestors want some blood, else they won't protect the family. But the family has all come together, and a small thing like a chicken doesn't give them much to eat. Now, what if they have a cake as well as the chicken?'

'*Eh?*' Baba scratched his head. 'A cake? But now you are talking of changing people's culture. That is not an easy thing to do.'

'But a cake costs a lot less than a cow, Pius.'

'And culture is not simply a matter of cost, Angel. A practice can be expensive, outdated, even dangerous, but if people justify it as culture it will still remain.'

'It will remain only as long as there is nothing better to replace it! Please listen to Benedict, Pius. He put it to Zodwa and Jabulani so beautifully.'

'Baba, it's not about changing a culture, it's not about replacing what people do now. It's about starting a new fashion. It's a way of celebrating somebody's life after all the sadness about him being late. A cow is just a cow, Baba. Okay, they can slaughter it for the ancestors, but that's about the ancestors looking after them. What about the late person who's gone? The cow doesn't say anything about that person, about who he was in his life. Say he worked as a pineapple picker. His family can remember him with a cake like a pineapple. Or say he was a teacher. He can get a cake like a giant piece of chalk—'

'Or a chalkboard duster,' said Mama.

'Yes. And then everybody can be looking at the cake and remembering him and talking about his life, and they won't see that the meat they're getting isn't a whole cow or is just a goat or a chicken.'

'Or they won't mind,' said Mama, 'even if they do see. The cake will be so lovely they won't complain.'

'I see. And Zodwa agrees with this?'

'Yes.'

'Did they vote, Mama?'

Zodwa had said that she wanted the decision to be made by everybody at Ubuntu, on account of people needing to get democracy wherever they could in a place where votes didn't count for very much.

'Yes. And tonight she took the idea to the late Ubuntu's brother, the man who actually owns the business.'

'He agreed?'

Mama nodded, and Benedict knew that Zodwa had helped her brother-in-law to see that he had had the idea himself, just as Mama and Zodwa had planned. 'He just wants a percentage of the new branch of the business.'

Over the tea that Titi made for them, Mama told Baba that they would start with a pilot project, the kind of small trial that Baba always said was the way to begin any new venture, and that Mama would do the baking at first, training other ladies to bake and decorate in the second phase as the project grew, so that by the time Mama left Swaziland the business would have two feet of its own.

Benedict counted on his fingers. 'It helps people to celebrate the life of their late nicely, it gives Ubuntu Funerals an edge, and it gives Mama more business. It's for winning and winning and winning, Baba.'

'*Eh*, I have not been speaking into empty air!' declared Baba. 'My words have not been wasted. I am a proud man tonight. Very proud indeed.'

His chest swelling, Benedict knew that it was time to make Baba even more proud. He cleared his throat before he spoke.

'Mama, I want a percentage, too.'

'*Eh!*'

He expected Baba to slap him on the back, shake his hand, laugh with joy, clap his hands together. Anything. Anything except shake his head, which was what he began to do. Baba told him he should have built up to it, he should have talked about how the idea had been his and about how much money could come to the business – and to Mama – because of his idea. Then he should have said exactly what percentage he wanted – two, five, ten – and justified why it was right for him to ask for it. That was how a man negotiated.

Baba didn't need to say it, but that was how Benedict had shown he wasn't yet a man.

Mama was in trouble, too. She hadn't negotiated any financial arrangements with Zodwa, and Baba was going to have to step in and put something on paper. He would need to—

'Pius,' Mama tapped on Baba's watch. 'News.'

When the tea he had shared with Mama and Baba woke him in the night and he tiptoed across the passage to the toilet, Benedict heard Mama and Baba talking in the lounge in the same hushed voices they had used in their bedroom.

'Angel, this disappointment is cutting through me like a machete through a ripe melon.'

'Uh-uh-uh.'

Benedict used the toilet quietly, not flushing in case the noise of it woke up the whole entire house. The voices were still there as he slipped silently back across the passage towards the boys' bedroom.

180

'How will we manage, Pius?'

'We'll find a way. What choice do we have?'

Crawling sleepily into his bed, Benedict knew for sure that something very big had happened.

ELEVEN

WHEN DANIEL AND MOSES SHOUTED FROM THE garden that the Ubuntu Funerals van had arrived, Benedict was at the dining table chatting with his sisters as they tidied away their homework books.

'My mama always had homework of her own,' Faith remembered. 'She was always preparing tomorrow's lessons.'

'*Eh!*' said Grace, nudging Benedict with her elbow. 'Imagine if *our* mama had been deputy head of a school!'

Benedict rolled his eyes for Grace's sake, though in truth he wouldn't have minded. He imagined all the books that might have been in Faith and Daniel's house.

'Remember how exciting it was when we got to spend time with our baba?' Grace's hands stopped what they were doing as her eyes seemed to focus on something far away. 'It was so nice when he wasn't at the factory morning to night. Eh, it was a real treat when he was home with us.'

'*My* baba was *never* home.' Faith's voice was sad. 'I don't really remember him.'

'Our mama's a bit blurry for me, too,' said Benedict, 'even though she was home all the time.' He glanced at the framed photograph on the wall. Because it was always there to look at, the two people in it – his baba and his baba's sister – were very clear in his mind, which meant that his baba's sister – Faith and Daniel's mama – was less blurry than the picture inside him of his own mama. But he didn't want to say.

'She was always sewing,' remembered Grace, 'and trying to knit. Eh, do you remember my blue jersey? Short short short.' She indicated somewhere high above her waist. 'She got bored and stopped here.'

Benedict didn't remember. 'Do you think Daniel and Moses remember much?'

'Not Moses.' Grace shook her head. 'He wasn't yet three, and it's more than four years since.'

'Daniel wasn't seven yet,' said Faith, 'and for us it's only two years since. He remembers things, but he doesn't want to talk about anything from before.'

'*Eh*,' said Benedict. 'What is in those boys' heads but football?'

'Like our baba,' said Grace. 'When it wasn't work, it was football.'

'Mm. And he used to run to keep fit.'

Faith began to giggle, and Grace joined in.

'What?' Benedict couldn't see what was funny.

'Imagine Baba running!' The girls couldn't stop giggling.

Benedict smiled as he tried to imagine Baba trying to bend down past his round belly to tie the laces of a pair of running shoes. Baba would bend to pick up a book, yes. But running shoes? Uh-uh.

He was still smiling when his brothers called from the garden.

He had long since returned *King Solomon's Mines* to the

public library unread, but he had made a drawing of the map that was in the book. He folded his copy of the map now, putting it in his pocket before carefully re-folding Baba's large map of Swaziland.

Mama wanted the girls to clear the table quickly and go to their bedroom, where Titi was having her afternoon nap, but Zodwa and Jabulani said there was no rush, there was something they needed to do outside first. Benedict went out with them while Mama made tea.

Their faces were very serious.

'Maybe...' Jabulani looked at the two boys wrestling on the grass.

Benedict sent his brothers to play down at the other house.

Then, placing the plastic bag he was carrying on top of the stack of plastic chairs on the veranda, Jabulani removed from it a large bottle full of golden liquid, which he handed to Zodwa.

Zodwa examined the bottle carefully. 'You see this?' she said, showing it to Benedict. 'This is for you.'

'For me?' Looking at the label, Benedict didn't understand. He was never going to drink whisky! It was only for grown-ups!

Zodwa's finger underlined the words *Famous Grouse* before tapping at the label's picture. 'This is a grouse, nè?'

Benedict nodded. He hadn't seen a grouse, but he had seen a guineafowl, which looked a similar sort of shape.

'We went to a *sangoma* to ask the ancestors about this new part of the business,' said Jabulani, locking his hands together and shaking them up and down. 'She threw the bones for us.' Jabulani's hands flew apart, and Benedict imagined the

184

sangoma's collection of bones and shells scattering all over a grass mat, just like in the picture in one of the books about Swaziland in the bookshelf. The place where each thing landed could tell a *sangoma* what the ancestors were saying about how everything was and how it was going to be.

'She gave us some *muti*,' said Zodwa. 'You know *muti*, nè?'

'Medicine,' said Benedict.

Zodwa nodded. 'She said that for the business to succeed, ours is to slaughter a chicken—'

Jabulani interrupted, putting a hand on Benedict's shoulder and speaking quickly. 'Don't worry, nè? We're not going to slaughter a chicken at your house!'

'No, no. That is why we have this.' Zodwa tapped at the bottle again. 'It's modern. We used a chicken at Ubuntu Funerals, but for here we'll use this. We knew it would upset you to have the blood of a chicken sprinkled around the outside of your house—'

'Though I don't mind making another small casket!' Smiling, Jabulani squeezed Benedict's shoulder.

'A grouse is family with a chicken, nè?'

Benedict nodded. How kind they were to think of him! He knew that when he ate a piece of chicken it meant that the chicken had been slaughtered, but he really didn't want to watch it happening right in front of him. Their concern for him made him feel a bit like Abraham must have felt when God told him no, he didn't have to sacrifice his son Isaac after all, a goat would do just as well.

Tears stung at the back of his eyes as they all became solemn.

Giving the neck of the bottle the kind of sharp twist that

would end a chicken's life, Zodwa unscrewed the lid and released the spirit, all three of them walking all the way round the outside of the house as she sprinkled the liquid slowly onto the ground.

Benedict wasn't quite sure what his mind should be doing, if he should be praying or what. He decided to think about beautiful cakes and high piles of Cake Order Forms, and whenever Zodwa poured a little more quickly and the bottle of Famous Grouse made the same *gloop-gloop-gloop* sound as the call of a Burchell's coucal, he tried not to focus on listening for an answering call from behind the hedge of yesterday, today and tomorrow bushes. The bottle emptied as they finished a full circle of the house.

Inside, the girls had gone to their room and Mama waited alone at the dining table with tea and cake. Benedict took his to have at the coffee table, where he sat on one of the couches with the bird book, keeping an ear on his percentage.

Now that the ancestors had blessed their new business, they could have their first proper meeting. As they had already agreed by phone, Zodwa and Jabulani had chosen the first three cakes that they were going to provide for free on account of having to spend money to make money as Baba always said, and just to see what people thought.

The first cake was for the family of a man who was late from a car accident. Mama said she didn't want to know about the car accident, thank you very much, she was in the celebration business, so could they please just tell her about what they were celebrating, which was the man's life.

'Sorry, nè?'

The man had worked at the casino at the Royal Swazi Sun

hotel in the Ezulwini Valley, and his family had been very proud of him for having such a good job. Mama said they should suggest to his family a cake shaped like a casino table covered with casino chips with one of those wheels that spun round. Or they could have a treasure chest that was partly open, with casino chips tumbling out. Jabulani liked Mama's treasure-chest idea, but it would be up to the family to choose.

Then there was a man who had worked cutting sugarcane in the sugar plantations in eastern Swaziland, and that made Benedict think of Mrs Patel's ancestor cutting the British colonials' sugarcane with his dentures. Swazi children loved to chew on sugarcane, he had seen them running alongside the sugarcane trucks trying to get a piece. But Miss Khumalo told them that chewing on it too much was bad for their teeth. Maybe their teeth would fall out and they would need dentures like old Auntie Geraldine in Bukoba.

Zodwa said a cake that looked like a big, thick piece of cane would be nice, and Jabulani suggested one that looked like a whole bundle of pieces of cane tied together. Mama said it would even be possible to make a cake that looked like one of the lovely yellow cane-gathering machines that the Tungarazas had seen in that part of the kingdom on their way to their new home on the Malagwane Hill.

The last cake was for the family of a young girl.

'Benedict's age,' said Zodwa sadly and, sensing all their eyes suddenly upon him, Benedict concentrated hard on trying to find a grouse in his book. There was a sandgrouse, but it didn't look much like the famous grouse, and it didn't live in Swaziland. He wondered what the grouse had done to make itself famous.

Jabulani cleared his throat. 'This one we chose because it's difficult.'

'Tell me what we're celebrating,' said Mama. 'What did this child love to do? How did she make her family happy?'

For a long time, nobody said anything. The only sound was Jabulani clearing his throat.

Then Mama said that it was good that they had chosen this case because it gave them the opportunity to see what difficulties lay ahead. She told them that they needed to go back and speak to the child's family, to find out what the child loved to do, what it was about the child that the family loved, what it was about her that made them happy. The family wasn't yet ready to order a cake if they didn't yet know what they could celebrate, if they didn't yet feel ready to celebrate.

'In the cake business,' Mama added, 'you are not yet ready to make a cake if you yourself don't yet understand why there is a celebration, why your cake is necessary.'

'You are right, Angel,' said Jabulani. 'Ours is to go back to the mother and then report back.'

'Right,' said Zodwa. 'Now let us be clear. We are done with talking about cakes and celebrations, nè? Because as a woman I have to talk about this child and why she is late.'

'Maybe...' said Jabulani, and again Benedict could feel everybody's eyes upon him.

Sitting on the kitchen step while he tied the laces of his old pair of shoes, listening to pieces of what Zodwa was saying as her voice came faintly through the kitchen and a little more clearly through the open window near the top end of the dining table, Benedict didn't see why Mama had asked him to go outside. It wasn't as if he was too small to understand. He knew exactly what had happened to that girl on account of having witnessed it happening to his duck.

She had been swimming by herself near the edge of the dam, happily dipping her bill into the water to scoop up something to eat, when suddenly, without any warning, male ducks had come and attacked her. Five, six, seven, eight, one after the other, landing on top of her, forcing themselves on her, even though she had struggled and quacked and tried to get away, even though he had shouted and run up and down on the muddy bank, looking for stones to throw at them to make them stop.

When it was over, she was left floating barely above the surface, patches of her feathers gone, one wing outspread, too exhausted to stop herself from drowning. He had run out to her as quickly as he could, the mud sucking him down, the water pulling at his shorts as he bent and scooped her up into his arms, anxious not to cause her any more pain, desperate to save her, frantic to get her down the hill to Uncle Enock.

He thought about her now as he made his way up to the dam. He hoped that she was okay. Uncle Enock had told him that only ducks could do that, they were the only birds that had a pipi. As he emerged from the trees onto the plateau, he remembered the programme he had watched on TV about hyenas, and he thought perhaps that was why female hyenas chose to have a pretend pipi. Was that how they kept themselves from getting hurt by the males? Was that why the males let the females be in charge?

He wished female people could have a pretend pipi, too.

Then they could be in charge, and it wouldn't be his shoulders that had to carry all the responsibilities that came with being the eldest boy. Grace would have to be the grown-up one, the one who had to watch out for dangers, the one who always had to make sure that the whole entire family was okay.

Petros was kneeling at the edge of the dam, scooping up handfuls of water to drink. His golden-brown dog wagged her tail as Benedict squatted to pet her.

'*Sawubona*, Krishna. *Sawubona*, Petros.'

'*Yebo*.' Petros stood up, smiling shyly and wiping his hands on his trousers. '*Unjani?*'

'*Ngikhona*. How about you?'

Petros squatted down next to Krishna. 'Better,' he said, rubbing his chest with his hand. His shirt was open, and Benedict could see his ribs under his skin. 'I have new doctor. Better than Auntie's.' Reaching into the pocket of his shirt, he brought out a piece of newspaper, unfolded it and handed it to Benedict. 'Somebody, he help me to read.'

It was an advertisement, the kind that Benedict had seen plenty of in the *Times of Swaziland*, near the announcements that told friends and family that a certain person had demised, and when they were going to have the vigil and burial. This one said: *Are you sick/in pain? Lost a loved one? No problem to big or to small. Clear evil spell with magic stick. Get lover back in 1 hour, lost job back in 3 days. All sickness cured, TB, Aids. Win at casino garanteed.* The advertisement ended with the number to call.

'You went to this doctor?'

'*Yebo*.' Refolding the piece of newspaper, Petros put it back in his pocket and took out something else. 'Now I can get a baby with my girlfriend.' He showed Benedict a small, black-

and-white photograph of a young woman. 'He live near Nhlangano.'

Baba had been to Nhlangano. It was the big town in the south, in the Sishelweni region.

'She looks nice.'

'Yes. Now I am the size to marry, but *eish*, Auntie's doctor, he say no, I mustn't marry.' He shook his head. 'That doctor, he tell me no, I mustn't get a baby.'

'*Eh!*'

'This one,' he tapped his shirt pocket, 'he say I can marry my girlfriend, we can get a baby.'

'That's nice.' Benedict gave the photograph back. 'Will she come from Nhlangano?'

'Uh-uh.' He slipped the photograph back in his pocket.

'So you'll go there?' from his squatting position, Benedict eased himself onto the ground, stretching his legs out in front of him.

'Soon. When I'm already tip top.'

Not wanting Petros to think he had no plans himself, nothing in his own pocket, Benedict brought out his drawing of the map to the caves full of gold and showed it to him.

'Do you want to help me to find this gold? We can share it.'

Petros looked at the piece of paper, turning it sideways then upside down, just like Benedict's sisters did whenever they tried to work out a map.

'Here,' he said, getting to his knees. 'I'll show you what it says.' Reaching for a bendy stick, he placed it on the grass. 'This is the Kalukawe River, only I don't know what its name is now. And these,' he put two stones next to each other, some distance from the stick, 'these are Sheba's Breasts, just down the hill.' He pointed in the direction of the peaks. 'And all the way here,' on his knees, he crawled towards the dam and slapped a piece of ground, 'here is where the treasure is.'

'Here?'

'Well, no...'

'Here?' Petros's eyes had grown very big.

'No. You see—'

'This paper,' Petros looked at the map, 'it say treasure is here? On this hill?' His breathing was fast now, and he began to cough. Krishna drew close to him, squashing her body up against his legs.

As the loud, bubbly sounds of coughing continued, Benedict waited patiently, thinking that the new doctor's *muti* hadn't yet had time to make the dementia in Petros's chest better. At last the coughing eased, and Petros turned his head and spat onto the ground. It wasn't nice to spit, but Benedict didn't say.

'No, it's somewhere else, some other place. That paper says where.'

Petros was calmer now as he stood up, handing the map back to Benedict. 'My ancestor, he have this.'

'This map?' Benedict stood up too.

'No.'

'A different map?'

Petros nodded before making Benedict jump by whistling and whooping loudly. Cows began to appear around the end of the clump of trees from the field beyond them, and Krishna walked to meet them, her tail wagging slowly. Petros began to move away.

'Did he find it?'

Walking away, Petros gave no answer.

Benedict called after him. 'Your ancestor. Did he find the gold?'

But Petros was coughing again, and by the time he stopped he was some distance away with the cows, and he seemed to have forgotten that Benedict was there.

On the Saturday afternoon when Innocence Mazibuko had her birthday party, all the Tungaraza children were invited. Benedict wasn't keen to go but Baba said he must, and he went because he could see that Mama and Baba wanted some time alone to talk. They seemed a little happier than when Baba had first got back from the conference, but Benedict could see that something was still wrong.

He had looked in Auntie Rachel's book, the one where she had shown him that Sifiso's birthday meant he was a lion, but Innocence's birthday at the end of August just meant she was a maiden, a young girl. That was boring for a birthday picture, so he had drawn some flowers for her instead. Feeling shy to give it to her himself, he had given it to Grace to pass on.

As he had expected, there were lots of girls at the party for his sisters to talk loudly and dance with in the big, added-on room, and there were also plenty of younger children. Mrs Levine was in the garden trying to organise games to keep the young ones busy, while Auntie Rachel and Uncle Enock chatted and laughed with a few parents in the lounge.

Helping himself from a bowl of cashew nuts flavoured with *pilipili*, Benedict looked at the cake that Auntie Rachel had made. It was a big oblong covered in chocolate and sprinkled with tiny pieces of dried coconut. Benedict counted the four-teen candles on it. Lungi told Titi and Titi told Benedict that Auntie Rachel always used a cake mix that came in a box. Mama said that was cheating, but Baba said it was just about saving time and money. But Auntie Rachel didn't need to make a special cake for Innocence, not for a birthday that wasn't special.

Grace was going to be thirteen next birthday, and her cake was going to be special on account of her becoming a teenager. Benedict's last birthday cake had been special on account of him getting to double numbers. Mama had made him a big butterfly, she had copied it from one of his books. Not his favourite, the African monarch, which didn't have enough colours for a cake, but one called blue pansy, which was black with big patches of bright blue, small patterns of white and round circles of bright red that looked like pretend eyes.

Pouring himself a throw-away cup of bright orange Fanta from a big plastic bottle, he moved round to the piece of the garden at the far side of the house where it would be quieter. As he rounded the corner his mouth flew open and he almost spilled his drink. A girl was sitting there with her back to the wall of the house, her knees pulled up to her chest.

It was Nomsa.

'*Sawubona,*' he said.

She looked up at him. '*Yebo.*' Her voice was surprisingly soft compared to the hardness of her eyes.

They told each other their names, then neither of them said anything for quite some time. Benedict wasn't sure what to do.

'Should I...?' he began. 'Do you want me to go?'

'It's okay, you can sit.' She looked at him carefully as he

found a place across from her on the grass. 'Did her mother make her invite you, too?'

Benedict wasn't sure. 'I suppose. We live in their other house further up.'

She nodded, and they were both quiet again.

'I saw you saving a spider,' said Benedict. 'And I heard you saved a scorpion.'

She shrugged her shoulders. 'People can be cruel.'

'Yes. But the scorpion could have stung you. You were brave.'

She shrugged her shoulders again. 'It was nothing.'

They were quiet for a while before Benedict said, 'We can look for lizards if you like.'

'Here?'

He nodded, pointing to the wild, rocky area beyond Auntie Rachel's vegetables. The rocks marked the edge of the garden and kept the cows from straying into it on their way past to the dairy down the hill. Lizards loved rocks.

'Are they poisonous?'

'Not really. But a big monitor lizard can give you a bad bite.'

Standing up, they walked together towards the rocks, stopping to greet Lungi and Samson who were sitting on chairs next to the outside room that Lungi and Mavis slept in. It wasn't a work day for Samson, but he was visiting on account of Lungi being his sister. Titi thought that Lungi was actually Samson's girlfriend, even though Lungi wasn't allowed. She had to wait for two whole years to pass after her husband became late, and only then was she allowed to stop wearing her black clothes and cleanse herself of her mourning. Only then was she allowed a boyfriend.

195

While Nomsa lifted small rocks without any fear, Benedict was much more careful. Uncle Enock had warned him that anything could be under a stone, anything that could jump at you and bite you or sting you, and it was best to leave stones unturned unless you knew what you were doing. They uncovered a nest of ants and quite a few centipedes, but any lizards were chased away by the noise they were making.

Then Benedict froze. Very close by, in the long grass in front of the large rock on which they were standing, lay the thick coil of a snake.

'Nomsa!' he hissed, pointing.

She drew in her breath. 'Is it poisonous?'

'Maybe.' He peered over the edge of the rock. 'It looks like it might be a puff adder.'

'*Eish!*'

'We should go. Come.'

But Nomsa wouldn't move. Instead, she squatted down on the rock to get a better look.

'No, Nomsa!' She was making him nervous now. 'Come *on!*' He pulled at her shoulder but she shook him off.

Then she did something you should never do near a snake. Bending down closer, she stretched her hand towards it.

Quick as lightning, without any warning, a flash of sudden movement shocked them both, and then there was a loud thud as the blade of Samson's spade hit the earth after passing right through the snake.

Benedict looked up at him in shock. He hadn't even heard him coming! The man spoke a string of angry siSwati at them, gesturing firmly at them to get away from the rocks.

Back near the house, Benedict felt a bit shaky, his hand

196

trembling as he picked up the throw-away cup of Fanta he had left there. But Nomsa's hard eyes were bright with excitement. She wanted to know all about snakes. How many kinds were there? Which ones were dangerous?

As Benedict told her all he knew, he was aware that she was a very strange kind of girl, the kind of girl he might like to have as a brother. Or, if necessary, a sister. He took her into the Mazibukos' lounge to show her Uncle Enock's snake book.

Auntie Rachel was serving tea to a few mothers, some of them holding babies.

'Auntie Rachel, can I show Nomsa a book?'

Auntie Rachel smiled as she looked at the two of them. '*Ag, ja*, help yourself.'

Excitedly pulling out the book he was looking for, Benedict made the bookshelf shake, and the slice of petrified wood on top of it bumped against another crystal, almost knocking both pieces of stone to the ground.

'Careful, hey!'

'Sorry, Auntie Rachel.'

They spent a long time on the floor in front of that book-shelf, and it seemed to Benedict that Nomsa thought he was the kind of boy she might like to have as a brother. But her mood changed suddenly when a man came into the room rattling his car keys. Benedict's mood changed suddenly, too, when he recognised him as the angry teacher from the high school, the one who had shouted at him and his brothers about using the big boys' toilets.

Auntie Rachel greeted him. 'Hello, Mr Thwala. Finished in Manzini so soon?'

'Yes, yes,' he boomed. 'Nomsa, go and find the others, nè?'

'I *hate* him!' she whispered into Benedict's ear as she stood up, leaving Benedict too shocked to say anything back. That was another thing that he and Nomsa had in common. Okay, he didn't *hate* Mr Thwala, he just didn't like him. But still.

Uncle Enock came in then and shook the man's hand. 'Thanks for giving them a ride, nè?'

'My pleasure,' he bellowed, rattling his keys some more. 'I was going past here anyway. Always happy to help out.'

As soon as Nomsa and two other girls had left with Mr Thwala for their ride home, Benedict decided to go back up to the Tungarazas' house.

Mrs Levine was sitting on the lowest step near the garage, smoking a cigarette.

'Hi there, Bennie. Had enough?'

'Mm. My friend's gone home.'

'Sit,' she said, shifting over a bit and patting the step next to her.

He did as she said, asking if Mrs Levine had had a nice time playing with the little ones.

'*Ja*.' She inhaled deeply, then her words came out in the smoke. 'For about five minutes. Kids don't know how to behave these days, hey?'

'I know how to behave!'

'*Ja*, Bennie, but that's you.' She bent and kissed the side of his forehead, smelling of smoke and the famous grouse. 'You're a good kid.'

Benedict thanked her for calling him good, though he didn't like being called a kid. Or Bennie.

They said nothing more until she'd finished her cigarette, put it out against the side of the concrete step and slipped what remained of it inside her cigarette box. Then she began to talk like a truck that was going down the Malagwane Hill without any brakes.

'God, but I'm bored! Enock won't let me help in the dairy, Rachel's more or less banned me from the garden except that little strip there by the front door, the kids don't need me, they were all doing just fine before I came, even Lungi gets upset when I try to help in the kitchen. Oh sure, Solly says he wants me back, but it's only because the accounts are a mess, does he think I'm bloody stupid? No, he can whistle. I can't go to Australia, Adam's made it clear on the phone I won't be welcome there...'

While Mrs Levine went on and on, Benedict tried to think of something helpful to say to her. She sounded a bit like Mama had sounded when her business was so slow, before Benedict had found Henry, and before Mama had helped Baba to suggest driving lessons for her.

Baba would suggest that Mrs Levine should learn something new. She already knew driving, she had hired a blue Golf now so that she didn't have to bother Auntie Rachel any longer. But there was no more room in the garage, so she parked it right outside the front door, and Benedict knew that Auntie Rachel and Uncle Enock got annoyed every time they had to walk around it to get into the house.

What other something new could Mrs Levine learn? Benedict struggled to think of one.

Then an idea came to him. Maybe, instead of learning something new, she could go back to doing something old.

Even if it was *very* old, she might be able to take it down from a shelf, blow the dust off it and give it a good polish.

'...and then he bloody—'

'Mrs Levine, you know teaching babies to suck?'

'What?' She looked at him as if she'd forgotten that he was there.

'Teaching babies to suck. What you used to do. You've got a certificate, right?'

Mrs Levine lit another cigarette. 'I've got a whole bloody degree in speech therapy! Teaching babies to suck was just about all the use I put it to before I threw it all away and married Solly. Now he says to me—'

'Speech therapy?' She didn't seem to mind when he interrupted.

'*Ja.* Getting rid of stuttering, helping people get all their sounds right. That type of thing. Anything to do with what goes on in the mouth and throat. Breathing, too.'

What she was saying was very exciting to Benedict, and he crossed two fingers of the hand that wasn't next to Mrs Levine.

'It's nice to have a skill,' he said.

'*Ag, ja,* but I haven't done it for years.'

'I bet you could still do it.'

'Hah!'

'There are people here who can't say all their sounds right.'

'No, I'm sure there are. But it was so long ago now. I probably only imagined I had the skill, just as I imagined I was married to a man who loved me, and I imagined I had kids who wanted—'

'There's a boy in my class who can't say *sss*.' Benedict was anxious not to let the opportunity pass. 'Everybody laughs at him.'

'*Ag*, kids are cruel, hey?'

'Mm. Maybe you could try helping him and see if you still know how.'

She was quiet for a while. Then, placing a hand on one of his shoulders, she pushed herself to her feet. '*Ag*, my throat's dry from all this talking, I need to find a drink.' She began walking towards the Mazibukos' front door.

'He's my friend, Mrs Levine! The boy who can't say *sss*, he's my friend!' He said it loudly to her retreating back.

Back at the house, he hoped that Mama and Baba had had enough time to talk by now and he wouldn't be disturbing them. But the house was silent. The door to Mama and Baba's bedroom was closed and he couldn't hear any voices behind it, so they must be taking a nap. He wouldn't disturb them. Titi would normally be sleeping at that time, too, but she was out with Henry.

Benedict went to the bookshelf. Standing in front of it, he thought he might look up Mrs Levine's ice-cream bush, but as he reached down for the plant book his eye was caught by the edge of a piece of paper under one of Mama's magazines next to the basket for keys. *Eh!* Was that already some sums about their cake business? Baba had told Mama she had to keep proper records if she was sharing her profits with somebody who was getting a percentage.

He pulled out the piece of paper. It was a letter, neatly typed. Had somebody written to place an order? He began to read it.

The address at the top was a school in Mwanza, on the shores of Lake Victoria, the place where he had lived with his first mama and baba before they were late. Was this an old letter? He checked the date. No, it was only about two months old.

It was addressed to Baba at the university in Dar es Salaam. How had it got here, to Swaziland? Of course! Somebody from that university had been to the conference in Johannesburg. He had brought the letter to Baba. This was the news from home that Baba had mentioned.

It wasn't anything about the cake business, so he shouldn't read it. He was putting it back under Mama's magazine when he saw that there was another page attached behind the first. He glanced at it quickly. It was a photocopy of some kind of form, with an official stamp. But it had nothing to do with him.

Wait! There was his first baba's name: Joseph Abednego Tungaraza.

But it wasn't right to read somebody else's things.

He put it back.

TWELVE

MAVIS WAS PROUD OF WHAT SHE HAD ACHIEVED. Most cleaners would sit around waiting till a party was finished and only then begin to clean. But not Mavis. No. All the way through, silent and unseen, she had moved from the kitchen to the big downstairs room where Innocence and the girls danced and pretended not to be looking at Vusi, to the garden where the younger ones ran about noisily and dizzily, to the lounge where Madam drank tea with the mothers, to near the garage where Doctor and the fathers stood around drinking beer, and back again to the kitchen. All along the way she gathered up glasses, cups and plates, discarding the paper ones in a large black bin liner, and washing the others at once, so that when she went out and collected more, the empty sink would be ready for them.

There were just the last few party-guests left now – one couple still with Madam, Doctor and *Gogo* Levine in the lounge, one or two girls still with Innocence – and after they had gone, Mavis would do one last round to clear everything. When Lungi came in later to find out from Madam who could still eat what for supper, she would not see a kitchen that looked like there had been a party.

As she waited for the kettle to boil, Mavis finished giving the big table a last wipe-down with a damp cloth. Then she rubbed at the part right in the middle with a dry cloth before putting the basket back there. It was a very beautiful basket with bold zigzags of red, black and cream, and Mavis didn't want to let it spoil by getting its bottom damp. She liked to think that her cousin had made it, meanwhile she knew it could have been made by any of the ladies who worked for the same project as her cousin. But maybe it really was her cousin who had collected the *lutindzi* grasses from the fields, exchanged them for the dyed ones brought by the project, woven the basket in her home and then waited for the project to come and fetch it for selling to tourists – or Madam – in the shop near Doctor's animal clinic.

Nobody could see how beautiful the basket really was unless they came to look while all the stones that Madam kept inside it were in the sink. The stones were many and a duster couldn't clean them nice-nice, they needed washing. *Eish*, the stones had too many colours, many more colours than all the wool that Mavis could buy in Mbabane. Each one was about the size of the top part of Mavis's thumb, and not one of them had any piece that was sharp or square. Madam had told Olga about them one rainy morning when Mavis was hanging the washing in the sheltered part outside the back door. Olga had stayed home from school with a bad cold, and she didn't want to leave the kitchen until Lungi's biscuits were out of the oven, so Madam had sat her on the table and talked to her about the stones.

They were tumbled, Madam had said, there was a special tumbling machine that made them keep falling and rubbing against each other until their sharp edges became smooth and round, it was what happened to stones at the sea. Mavis had never been to the sea, it was far away in Mozambique. When life pushes you around and knocks you, Madam had told Olga, it makes you smooth and special like these stones so that you can shine and everybody can see how beautiful you are.

Checking that she had done all she could in the kitchen for now, Mavis made herself a cup of tea and went outside with it. The chairs that Lungi and Samson had been sitting on were empty, but the door to Mavis and Lungi's room was open. Lungi was probably walking down to the gate with Samson. Mavis settled on one of the chairs to drink her tea.

The *kwerekwere* boy, the eldest, she had seen him in the lounge during the party, looking at books with another child. Life had certainly tumbled him, both of his parents were late. But look how he was shining! Titi said he had started a new business with his *gogo*. Imagine that! He was going to grow up to be a fine young man, one who could take care of all his family's needs.

Her own boy would have been like that, Mavis was certain. Not in exactly that way. No. That way needed knowing the world and having parents with more schooling than just primary. Her own boy would have been like Petros, who already had a good job and was kind and generous, giving things to others like a rich man who needed nothing. Her own boy would be saving his money for his mother in a tin under his bed, he wouldn't be asking anybody for anything. He would be making it okay that Mavis didn't have a husband to be an adult for her and to sign things for her, he would be in charge of her himself.

But, *eish*.

There would be no husband for Mavis.

And there was no boy.

Holding her cup of tea tightly, Mavis closed her eyes.

Push, the midwife had told her. Push! But she was just four-teen and she was way too small and the baby wouldn't come. It was a long time before anybody went to look for a car, and another long time before a car came. When they picked her up to put her in it, the pain was so great that her mind had said no, stop, and it hadn't let her wake up again until she was in the hospital with her belly already stitched shut. Her baby boy was late, and her womb was gone.

That was how life had tumbled Mavis.

Madam never said, but Mavis knew that if she asked, Madam would say that she shone as a cleaner. Nobody could ever run their finger along the top of a door and find dirt there. Nobody could ever look at one of Doctor's shirts and say that it hadn't been washed and ironed nice-nice. No. Life had tumbled her, and she was shining.

Her boy would be the same age as Petros now, almost seventeen. She couldn't stop herself wishing that her own boy was alive, and that he was Petros. How lovely it would be to have her boy working on the same hillside where she could see him every day though he was grown and working and not living with her.

The cows were already down the hill now, and yesterday they had been with somebody else, the one who always waved and called cheekily to Mavis. She wasn't going to bother with that one, he wouldn't bother with her when he found out about her womb. Or maybe he would bother with her, meanwhile he was looking for a woman who could give him a baby, a woman worth marrying. Mavis didn't want to be somebody a man just passed his time with while he looked for somebody else.

She hadn't spoken to Petros for three days now, and she wondered how he was. She had found a new doctor for him, a doctor who was advertising in one of madam's newspapers. She had cut the piece out of the newspaper with the kitchen scissor and given it to Petros, but he hadn't gone at first because of money. *Eish*. So she had given him some money from her Cobra floor-polish tin, and now he had gone. Now his cough could start to get better. Madam's doctor wasn't any good, he was like the doctors in the hospital who hadn't been able to save her baby or her womb.

Hearing a car starting up and some voices shouting good-bye, she stood up and swallowed the last of her tea. It was time to go in and clear up the last of the party mess.

THIRTEEN

BENEDICT FELT LIKE HIS WORLD HAD TIPPED OVER – and it wasn't just because he was staring at the TV while lying on his side on the couch.

Looking back at everything that had happened, he tried to make sense of it by doing what Miss Khumalo always told them to do when they were writing a composition: give it a beginning, a middle and an end.

Beginning

Auntie Rachel was stuck in another roadblock, and Benedict waited outside the high school with the Tungarazas, the Mazibukos, and several other children.

Moses needed the toilet.

Benedict told him to wait.

Then Daniel needed the toilet, too, so the three of them ran to the far side of the school grounds, terrified of bumping into Mr Thwala. Instead of waiting outside the toilets where Mr Thwala might see him, Benedict went in with his brothers. Moses was too nervous to go, so they were in there for some time.

When they came out, they were glancing around quickly to see if it was safe to run back to the gate, when a classroom door opened. They froze.

To everybody's relief, it was Nomsa who came out. Pulling her schoolbag onto her back and heading off without noticing them, she sniffed loudly.

Benedict called to her, but she didn't hear. Running after her, he called her name again, but she began to run away from him towards the school gate.

And then a large hand grabbed at the back of Benedict's collar, pulling it up and back in a movement that stopped him dead and tore the top button off his shirt.

The angry voice of Mr Thwala boomed above him. 'Why are you small boys here again? Did I not tell you to stay away?'

When the teacher released his grip, Benedict struggled to get back his balance before turning to face him, respectfully avoiding looking him in the eye.

'Sorry, sir. My brothers needed the toilet.' He hated that his own voice sounded so small, so childish, after Mr Thwala's. His brothers stood very close to each other, their eyes big. Moses looked like he needed the toilet again.

Mr Thwala's large hand forced Benedict's chin upwards. 'You!' he declared. 'Nomsa's friend from the party!'

Without looking at him, Benedict nodded as best he could with the man's hand under his chin.

'Are you spying on me?' Falling away from his chin, the hand balled into a fist and jammed against the teacher's hip. 'Did she tell you to spy on me?'

'No, sir.' Why would he spy on Mr Thwala? He didn't want to be anywhere near the man!

Daniel spoke up bravely, as Moses began to cry. 'We needed the toilet, sir. Auntie Rachel didn't come for us yet.'

'You didn't look in the classroom?' he boomed angrily.

All three boys shook their heads, keeping their eyes on the ground as Mr Thwala paced up and down. Benedict was aware of his heart hammering inside his chest.

At last the man spoke. 'Come with me.' Benedict stooped quickly to pick up his shirt button, and the boys walked nervously towards the school gate behind the teacher.

'Straighten your shirt,' Mr Thwala said to Benedict. 'Untidy boy!'

Outside the gate, Mr Thwala addressed all the children who were waiting in the shade of the thorn tree. 'This small boy,' he said, pointing at Benedict, 'came into the school looking for his *girlfriend*.' Benedict's face became hot as he felt everybody's eyes upon him. 'Who does he think he is to have a girlfriend big enough to attend high school?' Then he began to laugh in a way that wasn't about finding something funny but about wanting to hurt somebody.

One by one, the other children began to join in the laughter. Then Mr Thwala walked away, leaving Benedict feeling smaller than ever.

'Benedict has a girlfriend,' Grace announced at supper that night.

'*Eh!*' said Mama and Baba.

'She's not my girlfriend!' he said, for what seemed like the hundredth time that day.

'It's okay to have a girlfriend,' said Titi, giving him her widest smile, the one that told him he had done something very good. 'A girlfriend is a nice thing to be.'

'She's not my girlfriend,' he said again.

'Nomsa,' said Grace. 'She's in class with Innocence.'

'*Eh!*'

'She's not my girlfriend.' He really didn't feel like eating his tinned pilchards and rice. His stomach hurt, and his head didn't feel right. He looked at Mama, his eyes begging her to make it stop.

'*Eh*, did I tell you?' Mama said to everybody, clapping her hands together. 'They loved my cakes! More especially the treasure chest for the family of the casino man.'

After supper he sat staring through the book that lay open in his lap, feeling miserable. Mama and Baba were talking in whispers.

'Are you not concerned, Pius?'

'Why should I be concerned? I cannot tell you how happy this makes me!'

'But he's just a boy. She's older—'

'She's a *girl*, Angel. It's been a worry to me that he doesn't like sports like a normal boy, that he prefers to hang around you talking about colours and cakes. Then today I came home from work and I found him sewing a button on his school shirt. *Sewing!*'

'Pius—'

'No, Angel, I'm proud of him for getting a girlfriend!'

Tears splashed down onto his book.

The next day, Nomsa made it worse by rushing up to him outside the school gate, handing him a folded piece of paper, and telling him to read it later. Everybody saw, and everybody said that she was giving him a love letter. Of course it wasn't a love letter, but he put it in his schoolbag and said nothing. And just to show everybody that he didn't care, he left the letter there for two days.

Then Nomsa came to find him. 'Well?' she asked breathlessly, even though other children were watching.

'Well what?'

'Did you...? My letter...'

'Oh,' he said loudly, to everybody who was listening rather than to Nomsa herself, 'I haven't read it yet.'

Tears welled in the hard eyes that stared at him until he looked down, ashamed of himself, the dull pain that had been in his head the past couple of days feeling so much worse.

Before bedtime, he hid the torch under his bed, bringing it out only when he could hear from his brothers' breathing that sleep had taken them. As quietly as he could, he dug the letter out from the bottom of his schoolbag, so aware of how badly he had behaved. Thanks God Baba was away for the night in Pigg's Peak, in the northern part of Swaziland, and wasn't there to be as disappointed in Benedict as Benedict was in himself.

In the round beam of the torch, the letter surprised him. It wasn't what Miss Khumalo would call a letter at all. There was no address, no Dear Benedict, no proper ending. It was just a question and a name: *Can you get me some weevil tablets from the Mazibuko farm? Nomsa*

Eh!

What?

Switching off the torch, he climbed into bed to think about it.

Okay, she wasn't his girlfriend, and the way he had behaved today, she couldn't even think of him as her friend. But she had given him the letter before he had behaved badly, when they *were* friends. Friends who both liked rescuing small creatures and looking at books about snakes.

But this letter was more like one of Mama's shopping lists. It wasn't like one of Mama's phone calls to Baba asking him to stop for more bread on his way home from work; those calls always had a please and a thank you. This letter was not polite.

And it didn't even make sense. Farmers used weevil tablets to gas the weevils that were living in the grain they were storing. Uncle Enock's farm didn't grow or store grain. It was a dairy. If there were weevils in Nomsa's mother's flour or rice, she needed a sieve or a flat basket to separate them out.

He had thought the children in Nomsa's class were unkind to her because she was a little different. But maybe what Innocence said about her was right. Maybe she *was* mad.

Shaking his head against his pillow, he was aware that the ache was still inside it.

Then a new thought rushed into his head, bringing with it stories from the *Times of Swaziland*, stories that Mama and Baba talked about at the far end of the dining table, stories that pressed against the ache and made him sit up quickly.

Eh!

Could it...? Could she...?

No. Not seriously.

But still.

Mama was watching a film on TV, and when he showed her the letter and told her about Nomsa, her face turned from its lovely deep brown to grey. With Baba away and Titi out with

213

Henry, Mama had no choice but to phone Auntie Rachel, even though it was late, to ask if Lungi or Mavis could come and sit in the Tungarazas' house.

It was Mavis who came, straight from her bed with one side of her hair sticking up in the air and a blanket of brightly-coloured squares outlined in black wrapped around her. With her was Uncle Enock, taking the keys to the red Microbus from Mama's shaky hand and telling her that he wasn't going to let her drive in the night to a part of Mbabane without any lights, more especially with such a new licence.

They went in Uncle Enock's bakkie, Benedict sitting between him and Mama, directing him as best he could from the little that Nomsa had said about where she lived. They went very fast, Mama telling Uncle Enock she had lost count of the number of stories in the *Times of Swaziland* about people suiciding themselves by swallowing weevil tablets, and Uncle Enock telling her, in between shouting at vehicles, that, yes, it was what Olga's mother had done.

Once they were in the right part of Mbabane, where the houses weren't very nice and many were more like shacks, somebody told them exactly where to go, and they found Nomsa living alone with a mother who couldn't get out of her bed on account of being too sick to do anything for herself. She could barely open her eyes to look at the visitors in the night who were there with their torches, hugging her daughter. Benedict had never seen anybody so thin in his whole entire life.

Nomsa said it would be too painful for her mother to try sitting up, she needed to be lying down. It took no strength at all for Uncle Enock to pick her up and lay her down gently in the back of his bakkie, but it was another matter entirely getting Mama in there.

'Rather sit inside, Angel.'

But Mama insisted. 'It is not a child's job to comfort the sick, Enock. No, let the children sit inside with you.'

Nomsa brought a chair from the house, a neighbour managed to find a low stool, and together the neighbour and Uncle Enock got Mama from the stool onto the chair and then into the flatbed of the bakkie, where she settled herself next to Nomsa's mother, straightening her blanket and holding her hand. Benedict was glad that Mama wasn't wearing one of her smart, tight skirts that would have made getting her in there so much more difficult, but he felt bad for her, knowing that she must feel ashamed for having come out wrapped in a *kanga* and with her flat house sandals on her feet.

With Nomsa's mother admitted at the government hospital, they headed back down the Malagwane Hill, Mama in the front this time with Benedict half on her lap and Nomsa between the two grown-ups, the small bag of her things in the back of the bakkie. Uncle Enock had told her that she would stay with the Mazibukos until her mother was well again.

Benedict was sure that everybody in the bakkie knew that Nomsa's mother was never going to come home from the hospital, but nobody said. His own first baba had taken his first mama to stay in the hospital in Mwanza until she was well again, but she was never well again, and she had never come home. It was easy to become late in a hospital, even if the hospital was nice like this one, where the nurse had given Nomsa's mother a mattress on the floor instead of making her lie head to toe in the same bed as a woman she didn't know.

Uncle Enock said there weren't enough nurses on account of many of them going to England to do the same job for more money, but he was sure that the few who remained would do their very best for Nomsa's mother.

Benedict wasn't happy now that Nomsa was at the other house. Never mind all the business about her being his girl-friend, he didn't even want her as a friend. He had thought he had found a girl who was very like him, a girl who loved all of God's creatures, even the ones that were poisonous or danger-ous. But instead she was just a girl who was looking for something to make her late.

But as for Benedict's world tipping over, that was all just the beginning.

<u>Middle</u>

Mama was going to have a baby. Titi heard it from Mavis, who had heard Auntie Rachel and Uncle Enock talking about it.

Benedict didn't know if Mama thought it was a blessing or trouble, but he knew for sure it was trouble for him. Okay, it can't be nice to live by yourself with just one parent, like Nomsa. But he already had two big sisters and two little brothers. Wasn't that enough? Did Mama and Baba want their house to become like the Mazibukos', full of children and noise?

Uh-uh-uh.

And what about money? Baba was going to have to be a consultant for ever. He could never go back to his old job at the university in Dar, not with another mouth to feed. He would never be able to retire, and all the Tungaraza children

216

were going to keep moving to one country after another, wherever Baba got a job with lots of money, on account of Mama
and Baba wanting the family always to be together.

There was going to be a long string of first days at new
schools, an endless big effort to fit in and belong, and there
would be more and more struggles between wanting other
children to like him and not wanting to like them too much on
account of having to say goodbye to them soon.

Benedict's head hurt.

He looked at Mama, wondering when it was going to
happen. She didn't look any different. He wanted to ask her
about it, but that would get Titi and Mavis into trouble for
gossiping. And him, too.

He worried and fretted about it until his head was pounding and he felt hotter than he should then suddenly cold and
shivery, even though winter was over and the full heat of
summer was baking their house on the hill. At last he had to
know.

'Mama,' he said, pushing his supper around on his plate
and feeling sick at the thought of eating it, 'when is our
brother or sister coming?'

'What?' The piece of sweet potato that Mama had been
about to put into her mouth fell from her fork, landing with a
splat in the small heap of boiled blackjack leaves on her plate.

'What are you talking about?' asked Baba.

'Everybody says we're getting a new brother or sister.'

'Who is everybody?' Reaching into the neckline of her
T-shirt for a tissue from her underwear, Mama dabbed at the
bit of her supper that had splashed up onto her front.

'Everybody.' Benedict's face was hot.

But Baba wanted to know exactly who, and Titi came to Benedict's rescue, saying it was Mavis and Lungi. Then Mama and Baba looked at each other and Mama said it was time, and Baba nodded.

Baba took a deep breath and cleared his throat. Mama covered his hand on the table with her own.

At the conference in Johannesburg, Baba told them, somebody from the university in Dar had brought him a letter that had been sent to him there by the principal of a school in Mwanza. The letter told him that he had another grandchild, and it included a copy of the child's birth certificate.

'A girl,' said Mama, sinking Benedict's heart. 'Josephine.'

'Grace's age,' said Baba, sinking it further.

Josephine had been living with her mother, a secretary at the factory in Mwanza where Benedict's first baba had been manager. But now her mother was very ill and had gone to the hospital – Benedict knew from when his own first mama had gone to the hospital, exactly what that meant – and another family had taken Josephine in.

'For the time being,' said Baba.

'She'll come and live with us when her school year ends.' It was only Mama's mouth that smiled; her eyes looked tired.

Benedict felt very tired himself, very sick. He wanted to go and lie down, or maybe he needed the toilet, but when he stood up from his chair his legs couldn't hold him and everything went dark.

That was the last he remembered of the middle of his world tipping over.

End

It was malaria. Probably not a new malaria: they said you only got it down in the eastern part of Swaziland, though Benedict was sure he had seen the black-and-white spotted mosquitoes that gave it to you in their house on the hill. This was probably old malaria visiting him again, which could happen on account of it sometimes never fully leaving your blood.

Lying in his bed, with Mama and Titi taking turns to drape a fresh damp cloth over his hot forehead and trying one after the other to tempt him with food that he didn't want to eat, he thought feverishly about what had happened.

First Nomsa. A girl.

Then Josephine. A girl.

Now malaria. Which you could only get from a female mosquito.

Girls? Uh-uh-uh.

It was days and days until he was well enough to get out of bed.

Lying on his side on the couch, staring at the TV, he felt much better, though not yet well enough to be at school. He hadn't even been outside yet, and that was what he missed the most. Mama knew that, and she had opened half of the glass sliding door onto the veranda so that he had plenty of fresh air as he lay there.

He didn't have to be lying down, he was perfectly well enough to be sitting up, but the TV was boring him. It was on a news channel and he wasn't allowed to change it. Mama would have let him change it if it was just her, but it was

Mama and five other ladies, ladies Mama was training now that the Ubuntu cakes business had started to do well, and the news channel was what they all wanted to look at as they worked at the dining table. Benedict had no choice but to watch the same two aeroplanes getting an accident over and over again.

On his side, it looked a little different from the way it had looked when he was sitting up. Instead of flying into the sides of the tall buildings, the aeroplanes seemed to fall down from the sky into buildings that were already lying down. Then the buildings scooted up to the left in a big cloud of smoke and dust. But what Mama and the ladies said was the same every time.

'*America?*'

'*Eish!*'

'Ooh, nè?'

'New *York?*'

'Uh-uh-uh.'

Mama was teaching them decorating, and they were working on a cake to celebrate the life of a man who had worked for many years in the Bulembu asbestos mine at Havelock in the north. He had spent a long time trying to help the miners to get money from the mining company in Britain because the asbestos had made them sick. He had been a hero in the community, and lots of people had contributed so that his family could get a very beautiful cake to remember him.

The ladies were making a large copy of what the town of Havelock looked like in a photograph: a dark green mountainside beautifully decorated by the mineworkers' compound of small homes in pastel yellows, pinks, blues and greens. They were oohing and tutting about the aeroplanes getting the same accident again when Benedict heard a small thud on the glass of the sliding door.

Sitting up, he could see nothing unusual. Then the thud came again, and he got up and went out to the veranda to look for a small bird that might have got an accident by flying into the glass in the same way that the aeroplanes on the news had flown into the buildings. There was nothing on the ground next to the glass except a tiny pile of wet soil.

An owl hooted.

Owls weren't usually awake during the day. What was going on?

The hoot came again, from down near the garage, but Benedict could see nothing there. Then something moved, exactly where he had been looking. It was Petros, beckoning to him.

Calling to Mama that he was going to be in the garden, Benedict made his way down the steps to meet Petros. He hadn't seen him for such a long time! Petros took him all the way down to the shed where the cows slept at night, his dog trotting along next to them until Petros shut her out of the shed. Inside, he pointed up one of the wooden walls to somewhere near the ceiling, and when Benedict's eyes had adjusted to the gloom, he breathed in sharply.

Perched high up on a ledge was the most beautiful owl! Its big, dark eyes looked down at them from a white, heart-shaped face above a cream-coloured chest speckled with brown. The edge of the wing that they could see was black striped with orange-brown.

'*Eh!*' Benedict's voice was a whisper.

Petros smiled. 'Look,' he said softly, reaching for a stick that was leaning against the wall. Then he took something from his pocket and balanced it carefully in the small fork at the end of the stick. It was a late mouse.

'Give it,' he said, placing the other end of the stick in Benedict's hand.

'*Eh!*' Shaking a little from having been so ill, and also on account of the huge honour that Petros was giving him, he held the stick up high so that the top of it rested against the owl's perch. The bird looked at the mouse carefully, then bent down, took it in its beak and straightened up. The mouse hung there for a few seconds while the owl looked at them. Then it put the mouse down on the perch, holding it there with one of its feet.

'Come,' said Petros. 'It don't eat when we look.'

Outside, Benedict thanked him for showing him such a lovely bird.

'You were sick, *bhuti*?'

'Mm. Malaria.' Benedict wasn't sure if Petros had called him *bhuti* because he'd forgotten his name, if it was just because Swazis tended to call all men *bhuti*, or if he really meant to call Benedict his brother. Would Petros like them to be brothers? *Eh*, Benedict would love to have a brother who showed him owls!

'Malaria? *Eish*.'

'How about you?'

Petros smiled. 'Better. Soon I go get a baby with my girl-friend.'

'That's nice.' They were walking slowly up towards the garage, Krishna circling around them, her tail wagging.

'My baby will get gold from my ancestor.'

Eh! Benedict hadn't thought about the gold the whole time he was sick. He had been too busy thinking about how girls had tipped his world over.

'Did your ancestor find the mine? The gold?'

Petros shook his head. 'Long time ago, my great, great, great… *eish*, I don't know greats, nè? My ancestor. He work for Portuguese, in Mozambique.'

'You're a *shangaan*?' In Mozambique, Shangaans were just one of the groups of people who lived there, but in Swaziland a *shangaan* was the same as a *kwerekwere*, and a Mozambican was the worst kind of *kwerekwere* to be. It didn't just mean you were stealing jobs from Swazis, it meant you were bringing guns.

Shaking his head, Petros laughed without coughing. The dementia in his chest really did seem to be better, though when Benedict looked carefully he could see that Petros's face had sores and his body was even skinnier than before. Thinner even than Nomsa's mother, he reminded Benedict of the skinny, skinny person in the white robe in the picture on the United Nations wall. He really couldn't have been getting enough to eat.

'Portuguese come here,' he said, 'they want slaves.'

'*Eh!* Slaves?' Slaves were taken from Tanzania, too, Benedict knew that from Baba. They had to work in the clove plantations on Zanzibar, the island off the coast from Dar. That was back in the days when Zanzibar still belonged to Oman.

'*Yebo*. They bring gifts from India. To buy slaves.'

'From India?'

'Portuguese also live in India.' Benedict was going to have

to check that with Baba or Mrs Patel. It didn't sound right, and maybe it was something Petros didn't have right in his head. 'My ancestor, he take one gift.'

'He stole it?'

Petros nodded. 'He plant it here in Swaziland. Then he go home to Mozambique.'

Plant? Benedict remembered what Uncle Enock had said about Swazi Gold being the funny-smelling tobacco that Petros smoked. Was that what he was talking about? 'And you found it?'

Petros shook his head again. They were at the garage now, and it was best not to go nearer the house.

'They make railway here. They find it.'

'Who?' Benedict moved into the shade of the garage to lean against the red Microbus, and Petros did the same. 'Who made the railway?'

'English. They find it. Then my grandfather, he come, he take it.'

'He stole it?'

Petros looked surprised. 'No. It belong great, great, great...' with each great his hand gestured over his shoulder. '*Eish*. His ancestor, nè? He take it. Now he marry, he get a baby. He want to take them to Mozambique. They walk through bush to cross.' Petros coughed, shaking his head. 'A lion, it take my grandfather.'

'*Eh!* Sorry, Petros.'

Petros coughed again, his chest sounding bubbly. His mind seemed to wander away from their conversation, and Benedict wasn't quite sure how to bring him back. After a while, he came back by himself.

'That baby, nè? He's my mother.'

'And she gave it to you? The gift?'

Petros nodded.

'It's gold?'

He nodded again, coughing. 'Old,' he said, and Benedict wasn't really sure if he had been talking all the time about something old or something gold. Or Swazi Gold. It really wasn't easy, with Petros having so little English and Benedict so little siSwati.

Petros looked very tired now, and Benedict felt tired and a little shaky himself.

'What exactly is it, Petros?'

Petros's mind seemed far away again. His dog was sniffing a back tyre of the red Microbus, and he squatted to pet her. 'Krishna,' he said to her softly, smiling. 'My treasure.'

Then a voice called from the house.

'*Benedict!*'

'Mama?'

'Come and see how beautiful our cake is!'

FOURTEEN

IN THE SHADE BEHIND THE ROW OF CLASSROOMS, Sifiso and Giveness looked at Benedict with very big eyes.

'What thound did it make?'

'*Boom!*' said Benedict, trying his best to get the sound of it just right. 'But not loud like on TV. We weren't very close by.'

'It wasn't a plane like in America?'

'Uh-uh, a car.'

'I hope there'th nothing like that here!' Sifiso scanned the sky.

'It wasn't just in Dar es Salaam,' said Benedict. 'There was another one in Nairobi that same morning, also at the American embassy. That one was a truck, it was much bigger.'

'*Boom!*' said Giveness, his pink hands flying apart.

'Mama's been talking about it a lot with the ladies she's training. She lost an in-law in the Nairobi one.'

'Nairobi's also in Tanzania?'

'Uh-uh, it's in Kenya. But Mama's in-law was visiting there, she was in a bus going past when it went off.'

'*Eish.* Sorry, nè?'

'Mm. What's happened in America makes it feel like yesterday for Mama, meanwhile it was three years ago.'

226

Much more recently, two things had gone boom in Benedict's own life, but he didn't want to say. He just wasn't ready yet to tell anybody about his new big sister; he still needed to keep that inside him until he had stopped feeling like water that somebody had sent a stone skipping across. When the stone had finally sunk and ever further circles of ripples had stopped disturbing him, then he would say. And he didn't want to talk about Nomsa, either; if anybody were to overhear, they might start up the story again about her being his girlfriend. Anyway, he couldn't tell Giveness and Sifiso the story about rescuing Nomsa in the night, that wouldn't be right. It wasn't nice to gossip about somebody wanting to be late, and it wouldn't be right to talk about Nomsa's mother being sick. He wasn't entirely certain, but he guessed from the looks between Mama and Uncle Enock that it was the kind of sick you didn't talk about, the disease you didn't say.

Still scanning the sky, Sifiso changed the subject and asked Giveness if he knew yet when his mother was going to come.

'*Eish*, don't make me get nervous again, Sifiso!'

Giveness had been getting nervous for over a week now. His mother had left him with her sister when he was still a tiny baby, so he had never really met her. But now she was going to come and visit, and he and his aunt weren't sure why.

Sifiso patted his arm. 'Thorry, nè?'

'What if she wants to take me away?' It was what Giveness dreaded most.

'*Eh!*' said Benedict, as if they hadn't already had this conversation.

'No, Giveneth! It can't happen! I told you!'

'But it can! She's my mother, she can take me.'

227

'Your aunt is your mother,' Benedict reminded him patiently. There was nothing wrong with that: Mama was his mother, even though she was his grandmother. 'What did she say to your aunt?' He asked it in a way that said he hadn't asked it before.

'She said she wants to come and say sorry.'

'Maybe it'th true. Maybe she really ith thorry for leaving you behind.'

'Maybe. But she could say sorry on the phone, or in a letter. She doesn't have to come.' His pink hands twisted together.

'Say she comes,' Benedict asked again, 'and she says sorry. What will you say to her?'

His answer was still the same. '*Eish*, I don't know.'

That was the *boom* that was sounding in Giveness's life.

As the children neared Mr Patel's shop on their way to the high school, they saw that there was a policewoman just outside the entrance. Across the road, a handful of people stood looking at her.

Knowing that police meant trouble, which it was best not to go near, Benedict made all of them cross to the far side where they could walk behind the people who were looking. From there, they could see that somebody had painted *Bin Liner* across Mr Patel's window in big red letters.

'*Eh!*' said Benedict. 'Bin Liner?'

A man in a smart suit shook his head sadly. 'Some people are too, too ignorant, nè?'

'Nothing to do with Patel,' said one of the ladies there. '*Nothing!* Where is his beard? Where is his headdress?'

'Ignorant!' the man repeated. 'And in the middle of day-light!'

'Those thugs don't care!' declared another man. 'After all this time, who is going to arrest them? *Who?*'

Somebody said that the thugs' behaviour was un-Swazi, and somebody else agreed that they were a disgrace to the Swazi nation.

'They'll try anything, nè?' said the man in the suit. 'Any opportunity to hurt Patel.'

As the children continued on their way, Benedict wondered how much it really hurt Mr Patel to be called a bin liner. Okay, it wasn't nice for somebody to say that you belonged in a dustbin, but there were probably worse things that had been said to Mr Patel before.

At least the police were taking it seriously now. But maybe other people would also cross to the other side when they saw the policewoman outside Mr Patel's shop, maybe they would rather go and buy KFC or some other kind of take-away. Benedict knew from Mama how bad people felt when their business did badly. He hoped that Mrs Patel was okay.

Later that afternoon, he was getting ready to go up to the dam when he saw Mrs Levine making her way up the steps towards the Tungarazas' house. He went to say hello.

'Hi there, Bennie! Going somewhere?'

He didn't want Mrs Levine coming up to the dam with him, it was his special place for being quiet and thinking and being with other creatures.

'Um...'

'Glad I caught you. Listen, that friend of yours, the one with the lisp.'

'Yes?' Benedict's eyes lit up.

'What's his name?'

'Sifiso Simelane.'

'*Ag* no, man! Serious?'

'Mm.'

'Do you have his parents' number?'

'Mama has it.' Mama hadn't wanted him to go with the Simelanes for Sifiso's birthday without knowing how to reach them to say thank you. 'Are you going to help him, Mrs Levine?'

'I'll give it a go. But listen, I don't have a work visa, so Enock says I'm not allowed to charge any money for it.'

'I'm sure Mr and Mrs Simelane won't mind.' Benedict's smile was very wide.

'*Ja.*'

'Thank you, Mrs Levine!' Benedict went to her and she bent to accept his hug before pushing him away.

'Go do whatever you were going to do, and I'll get that number from your mom. If I don't ring right now I might never find the courage again.'

Benedict smiled all the way up to the dam, then he smiled some more when he settled in the shade of a water-berry tree and saw that on the grass very close to him was a large green praying mantis. Very gently, he encouraged it to climb up into his hand, which it did, settling unmoving into his palm.

He thought about the very nice *boom* that would go off in Sifiso's life if Mrs Levine could help him. Okay, he would still be fat, and he would still be bad at sports, but nobody would be able to laugh at the way he spoke, and that would make a big difference. A very big difference indeed.

As Benedict relaxed, his mind began to wander over other kinds of differences.

Mama said the whole world was going to be different now, but Baba said they should wait and see, on account of there being a different that's truly different and a different that's just more of the same but with a different name. Benedict wasn't sure what Baba meant, but he knew that things might be truly different at home very soon, much sooner than his new sister Josephine coming to join their family. Henry had asked Titi to marry him, and after thinking for a week about her answer, Titi was telling him yes or no this afternoon.

Grace and Faith had advised her to say yes. Henry had his own car and his own business, and he loved her.

'No girl can ask for more than that,' Faith had said.

'Except maybe Brad Pitt or Shaggy,' Grace had said, and the two girls had giggled.

'He's already married,' Titi had reminded them. 'Do you want to share your husband with another lady?'

'*Eh!*'

'Never!'

'Then why should I?'

Changing their minds, they had advised her to say no.

Daniel and Moses were too small to give advice, but Benedict knew they didn't want Titi going anywhere. Neither Mama nor Baba would tell her what they thought, no matter how many times she had asked them.

'Listen to your own heart,' Mama had told her.

'Listen to your own head,' Baba had told her.

Benedict hadn't known what to say to her. There were many reasons why he didn't want her to stay behind with Henry when the Tungarazas left Swaziland, but his main reason was entirely selfish: with a new big sister *and* a new place to get used to sometime soon, he wanted as much as possible to stay the same. Titi had been with him at his first parents' house, she had been constant in his life longer than any other grown-up. But the decision she needed to make was big, and it shouldn't be about anybody other than herself.

The praying mantis in his hand moved slightly, beginning to sway forward and back in a similar sort of way to a chameleon. Chameleons would extend a hand and move forward as if to take the next step, then sway back again, hesitating. That was what made them so slow: thinking too much about every step before taking it. They were such cautious creatures, fearfully swivelling their eyes in every possible direction all at once, and constantly changing their camouflage to keep themselves safe by not looking different.

Baba had said that Americans were looking in every direction at once now, just like a chameleon – one eye looking to the front and the left at the exact same time as the other eye was looking to the back and to the right – only they were probably going to move as fast as a snake rather than being slow like a chameleon. Baba didn't really manage to talk much sense about animals, but it was nice that he tried.

Mama had made a cake once that looked like the flag of America. Benedict thought about how a chameleon would look if it sat on that flag and tried to change its camouflage so that it looked the same. *Eh!* Its body would have long stripes of red and white, like a thick squeeze of toothpaste, while its head would be blue with lovely white stars.

There were big lizards with blue heads in Swaziland,

Benedict had seen them. Their body was yellow and orange and their head was blue. If something dangerous came, they just hid behind a tree, they couldn't change their colour like a chameleon to make themselves look like they weren't there.

Praying mantises had their own kind of camouflage, not the chameleon kind that could change. No, a praying mantis had to stay in one place to be safe. The green one in his hand was safe amongst leaves and grasses, but there were other kinds, ones that looked just like the bark of a tree, and others with lovely colours and shapes that made them look exactly the same as a flower's petals.

People said mantises looked like they were praying, holding their big front legs up in front of them the way people did when they were talking to God. But Benedict wasn't sure. To him they looked more like boxers waiting to land a punch. They ate other insects, so maybe they were doing both: attacking something then saying grace; fighting and praying.

Some people also said that a praying mantis was a god, the god of the San people who lived in other parts of southern Africa. The San people used to be called Bushmen, but Baba said that wasn't correct any more on account of politics. Now their name was San. It made sense to Benedict that people who hunted other animals for food would worship an insect god that killed other insects.

Thinking of killing other insects, his mind came back to Vusi's story about the boys lighting a fire around the scorpion, trying to make it kill itself, hoping to see it stab itself in the back. Imagine! It was normal for animals to kill other animals, but not to kill themselves. Okay, sometimes grasshoppers drowned themselves, but that was only on account of worms getting into their brains and making them do it. It wasn't right for animals to make life so bad and so frightening for other animals that they rather suicided themselves.

Benedict wanted to believe what Auntie Rachel had said about scorpions killing themselves, that it was just a made-up story, just pretend. But part of him believed it had to be real, and that made him feel uncomfortable because it made him think of Nomsa, which he tried not to do.

He hadn't spoken to Nomsa since that night. Auntie Rachel wasn't letting her go back to school before Mr Magagula had fired Mr Thwala or at least suspended him. Benedict didn't understand why, except that Nomsa hated him. Okay, he had frightened Benedict and his brothers, but it turned out that he wasn't such a bad man, really: he had been helping Nomsa with pocket money. But thinking about Nomsa made him feel like the inside of his head had stumbled into a thorn bush.

Quickly, he took his mind back to thinking about camouflage.

Maybe, once upon a time, the Patels had been good at camouflage. They hadn't stood out from any other Swazi. But what Mr Patel had made Sandeep do had made people notice them, the kind of people who didn't want to be noticed themselves. And now they were in trouble. It was too late for Mr Patel to hide behind a tree like a blue-headed lizard, so he may as well go out and attack the food ladies who might be selling drugs for the people who were attacking him. It really wasn't a peaceful way to live.

The mantis flew off Benedict's hand when Krishna started barking on the far side of the dam. He had been wanting to see Petros – who was very, very good at camouflage – to try to find out more about his confused story about his treasure.

Benedict wasn't sure if he'd got it right, but it seemed that one of Petros's ancestors had come to Swaziland from Mozambique with the Portuguese, who were looking for slaves. They were going to buy the slaves with gold from India, though why a Portuguese somebody would have an Indian somebody's gold, Benedict didn't know. Then Petros's ancestor stole some of the gold and buried it. Petros had once mentioned a map, so maybe his ancestor drew a map to help him to find the gold again. But something must have gone wrong, and an English somebody found the gold many years later when they were digging for the railway.

Eh! Mr Quartermain was an English somebody! Was it him? Benedict thought about what Auntie Rachel had said about Mr Quartermain's story. Was there a railway? He wasn't sure.

Anyway, Petros's grandfather came from Mozambique to steal the gold away from the English somebody, but when he was trying to get back home with his wife and his baby, a lion ate him. The baby grew up to be Petros's mother, and now the gold was with Petros.

Maybe that was the story, but Benedict wasn't sure. Maybe it was really a story about planting funny-smelling tobacco and an English somebody digging up the plantation to build a railway. Maybe what Petros had was seeds for growing Swazi Gold, like the seeds for growing giant beans in the story about Jack. Or maybe he was talking nonsense, just like everybody said. Maybe Petros really wasn't right in his head. Because if he really did have gold, and if the gold was real and not just pretend, why did he work here on the hill with cows, without any shoes or any nice clothes? And why wasn't he getting enough to eat?

Benedict wished he could ask Mama for some cake for Petros, but he couldn't, on account of the Tungaraza children not being supposed to talk to him. He thought that Petros might be somebody he could talk to about Josephine. Maybe he was somebody who would understand what Benedict meant without needing to understand all his words, and that might help Benedict to work out for himself exactly what it was that he did mean.

Getting a new sister meant so many things, but he hadn't yet worked out exactly what. Daniel and Moses didn't seem at all concerned about it, though Benedict knew they would have been excited to get another brother, especially one who knew how to kick a ball. Grace and Faith were excited, simply expecting Josephine to be just like Innocence. None of his siblings seemed to feel the way he did, like he was suddenly in the middle of a minefield with a loud boom echoing in his ears, unsure where to put his foot down next.

Krishna's bark came again from the far side of the dam. There were days when the cows went to one of the other fields, either beyond the milking shed or down near the chickens, and there were days when somebody else was with them. But with his dog here, Petros wasn't far away.

Maybe he was somewhere smoking one of his funny cigarettes. Uncle Enock had said it was *dagga*, which Benedict knew from school was bad on account of it being drugs. It wasn't nice that Petros had drugs, but maybe when you didn't have parents or a teacher to tell you no, you could easily do wrong things. You could do wrong things even if you *did* have parents and a teacher. Look at Sandeep Patel. Anyway, *dagga* wasn't un-Swazi: it grew here, it was called Swazi Gold. But the people standing across the road from Mr Patel's had said that the drug-sellers were un-Swazi. Maybe the *dagga* they sold was imported from somewhere outside Swaziland.

As he waited for Petros to appear, he glanced at the narrow bridge leading to the pump in the dam's centre. He was sure that Petros felt big enough and brave enough to walk along it. He wondered if he ever had. On the whole, he thought probably not. Petros would have no need to try, and no need to prove that he could. Besides, he wouldn't feel comfortable out in the open like that. No. Petros was at home on the edge of things, where he wasn't noticed. It was a safer place to be, really, and perhaps the Patels should have stayed there.

Benedict waited a long time for Petros, and he began to lose patience, wanting to go down to the house to check on the ladies Mama was training. He didn't want just to sleep through getting his percentage the way Zodwa's brother-in-law did, he wanted to know what was happening. When he finally stood up and called to Krishna, the dog didn't come and Petros didn't suddenly make it clear that he had been there, unseen, all the time. Benedict gave up waiting.

But by that time, Zodwa had already come to fetch the ladies, and Mama was working on a cake of her own, one she had decided to make even though nobody had ordered it. It wasn't a beautiful cake, but it was important to Mama. She had read in the *Times of Swaziland* that the British High Commission was giving a special gift to the Swazi police, a machine that could destroy all the illegal rifles and guns that were in the kingdom. In the whole of Africa there was only one other machine like that, in Kenya, Tanzania's neighbour.

Mama was making the cake as a thank-you gift for the

British High Commissioner. It was going to look exactly like an AK-47, and when it was complete she was going to cut it into three pieces, which she was going to move apart on the board to show that this gun would never again take the life of any mother's child. Benedict knew that it was really a cake about the gun that took the life of Mama's own child, Benedict's first baba. But he never said.

Waiting in the kitchen for the milk to boil for their tea, he read through the newspaper article lying on the counter, that was Titi's English homework from Auntie Rachel. She always chose something for Titi to read that they could talk about in English afterwards, after Auntie Rachel had helped her with any difficult words. This article was about the king buying twenty-five new luxury Chevrolets for himself; it said how much they cost and also mentioned about the king wanting to buy a private jet.

Benedict knew that Auntie Rachel would say that maybe it would be better to spend the money on Swazis who were sick or hungry, and he also knew that Titi would argue that it must be very nice to sit in a car that was completely new, or to fly in any kind of aeroplane at all.

He wondered what Titi was saying to Henry right now. When Henry had come for her at teatime, he had seemed nervous. He must have been anxious to hear Titi's answer, and it can't have helped that Mama and her cake students hadn't let him leave with Titi until he had contributed to the money they were collecting for the families of America's late.

Benedict crossed his fingers, hoping that Titi wouldn't say yes and trigger another loud *boom* in his life.

*

The thunder began while Benedict and Mama were drinking their tea, and the other Tungaraza children ran home from the other house between large drops from very black clouds. They had barely managed to close all the windows when the rain began battering the tin roof and lightning flooded the sky. Benedict knew from when Baba had helped him with his English grammar practice of making sentences with words ending in *–est*, meaning most, that Swaziland had one of the highest incidences of electrical storm activity in the whole entire world. It also had the world's oldest mine, though that mine had been for iron, not gold.

When the power went off, Moses and Daniel offered to help Mama and the girls with cooking supper on Mama's gas oven, but only because there was no TV to watch and the storm was so big that it frightened them. Benedict stood staring out through the glass of the sliding door, praying that Baba and Titi would both make it home safely, and that anybody who didn't have a home or whose home was made of mud or grass would be okay. With every stab of lightning, he prayed that nobody was late because of it, and as the wind tore at the trees, he prayed that it wasn't sending any more creatures to Heaven, whether it was Monkey Heaven, Bird Heaven or any other Heaven that Uncle Enock could imagine.

It was Uncle Enock who got home first. Benedict saw the lights disappearing into the garage and then, lit up by a flash of lightning, a dark, huddled form ran towards the other house and dodged around Mrs Levine's Golf to get to the front door. At last another pair of lights swung into the garage. Was it Baba or Henry? Benedict couldn't tell. Mama brought a lit candle in from the kitchen and used it to light some more for the dining table.

'Somebody's here, Mama. In the garage.'

'Who?' Mama joined him at the glass door.

Benedict shrugged. 'Should I go with the umbrella?'

'No, no, they'll come when the rain eases. The food will still take time.'

But when the food was at last ready the rain was still pounding, and, afraid that Baba or Titi might spend the whole night in the garage waiting for it to ease, Mama let Benedict go. The steps were slippery, water gushed over each of his bare feet in its haste to get down the hill, and wind pushed the umbrella this way and that so that he needed both hands to hold on to it and battled to keep the torch focused on the way ahead.

When at last he managed to get into the shelter of the garage and something dark and wet leapt at him, he almost screamed like one of his sisters! *Eh!* He dropped the torch. It went out.

'*Baba?*'

Nothing. The rain on the tin roof was so loud!

'*Henry?*'

Trying to push whatever it was away, he stumbled in the total darkness into the back of the vehicle, banging his elbow hard against it. One of its doors swung open, switching on the light inside it. He could see a figure climbing out as something wet slapped his face.

'*Baba?*'

'Benedict? Is that you?'

'Baba!' He could see now what was jumping up against him and licking him. 'Krishna!'

'What?'

'It's a dog, Baba. I brought the torch, but I dropped it.'

'Wait. Titi, bring the torch from the cubbyhole.'

With the help of that torch they found the other one, and with a bit of shaking and fiddling Baba got it to work again. Benedict shone it around the garage, but saw no sign of Petros.

Although the umbrella was large, there was no way three people were going to fit under it. Titi didn't want to be left alone with a dog, so she went first with Baba and then came back for Benedict. Krishna didn't try to follow them up to the house, which was a good thing: Mama would never have let her in, and at least she was out of the rain in the garage. Besides, Petros must be sheltering somewhere nearby.

The noise of the rain on the umbrella made it impossible for Benedict to ask what had happened with Henry and why Baba and Titi were together. He had to wait until they were all dry and seated round the candle-lit table for supper.

Then Titi told them that she had said no.

Benedict felt so relieved!

But he couldn't help feeling sad for Titi, and also for Henry, whose company he had always enjoyed.

'I thought I could do it if we all stayed together in one house, I thought I could be friends with his other wife. But no. He was going to put me in my own house. *Eh!* When he was with her, I was going to be alone. If he wasn't with me to show everybody that I was a Mrs Vilakati, I was going to be just a *shangaan*, a *kwerekwere*.'

Everybody at the table said how glad they were that she wasn't going to leave them, and she smiled bravely. But Benedict could see that there was something more that she wasn't saying.

'What did Henry say?' he asked her.

Titi sniffed. 'He...' Tears began to flow, and Mama handed her a tissue from inside her T-shirt.

'He told her he didn't have to accept that answer.' Baba had already heard the story. 'He threatened to smear her with red ochre.'

'*Eh!*' said Mama, and when she explained to the children what that meant, they all said the same. If a man smeared red ochre on a lady, it meant that she was his wife. He didn't have to ask, and there was nothing she could do or say. It was an old Swazi custom.

'Imagine!' said Benedict.

'Surely he was joking, Titi?' It was Mama who asked. 'Smearing with red ochre is also part of a traditional wedding, where both parties are willing and the man's family has paid cows to the woman's family. Was he not talking about that?'

'I don't think so, Auntie. I told him no, he couldn't make me his wife by smearing me, I'm not a Swazi. He told me no, a *kwerekwere* has even less rights than a Swazi lady. He was laughing, but *eh*, I was afraid.'

'She took a taxi to my office,' said Baba. 'Left him sitting there at Quick Impact.'

'I didn't want to go in the car with him.'

'He could have taken her anywhere, Angel!'

'I can't believe he would do anything bad, Pius! That is not the Henry I know!'

It wasn't the Henry Benedict knew either, but maybe any man could behave badly when it came to girls. Look how badly he had behaved himself when people had said that Nomsa was his girlfriend. And look – though he really didn't want to look

– look how his own first baba had behaved. When people had looked at his first baba, they had seen a man with one family, a man with a wife and three children. But that had been just a story, just pretend.

Benedict knew from Uncle Enock that almost no animals stayed together in one pair their whole entire lives, and the bird book said most birds stayed in one pair for just one season, just long enough to raise their babies. But when it came to other animals, pairs didn't seem to matter very much. People were supposed to be different, though. But maybe that was just a story. Although, really, how could it be just a story? Mama and Baba had been in a pair for ever. It was all very confusing, and maybe you had to be big to understand it fully.

After the meal, with the power still off and the rain still pouring, Benedict's brothers went to bed and his sisters tried to make Titi feel better by helping her with the washing-up. Benedict knelt in front of the bookshelf with the torch, choosing a book to take to bed with him to read by torchlight. Mama and Baba were talking.

'But which is better, Angel? Allowing a man to have many wives, or telling him he can have only one, and then he sneaks around and his parents learn they have another grandchild when she's already part grown?'

'No, Pius, you cannot say the two are the same.'

'I'm not saying they're the same, I'm just saying we have no right to think our culture is any better.'

'It's not exactly our culture!'

'And where exactly do we draw the line between culture and custom?'

'Don't try to confuse me like an educated somebody, Pius.

Just look at the consequences of many wives here. Zodwa's business is doing so well because so many are late from so-called natural causes.'

'And calling it natural causes is the real problem, Angel. It's a matter of being reluctant to say what is actually what, to acknowledge how big anything really is. Just look at this Malagwane Hill we live on. It's a high mountain, but it's called a hill. And women are treated as minors, not the grown adults that they are. When you reduce a mountain to a hill, when you reduce a woman to a child, then of course you're going to reduce the crisis of this disease to something minor. And then you end up with the highest rate of so-called natural causes in the world!'

Benedict pulled a book from the shelf.

'Yes. And what can people do about it if it's natural causes?'

'Nothing. Natural causes are something that simply cannot be helped, something that people are powerless to prevent.'

Benedict chose the *Jumbo Guide to Swaziland*. There was a nice photograph in the back of it of some children and a *Mzungu* looking at a picture that some San people had painted on a rock hundreds of years ago. That was before the other people who came to settle in Swaziland chased them away or made them late, and their praying mantis god hadn't been able to rescue them.

Maybe the San people had painted on the walls of caves. Maybe the *Jumbo Guide* would say where to find those caves.

And maybe they were the same caves that were on Mr Quartermain's map.

FIFTEEN

CROCHETING IN HER BED AS LUNGI SLEPT, MAVIS felt a small shiver of excitement. *Umhlanga* would soon be here, the Reed Dance that she so enjoyed. The colours! The songs! Her crochet hook seemed to be dancing with the bright pink wool of the child's jersey she was making. As she did every year, Mavis would spend the day of the dancing for the king with her sisters, proudly watching her nieces among the thousands upon thousands of other young girls who had come from all over the kingdom to dance. But this year she had a reason to feel even more excited.

This year Innocence had decided that she wanted to take part. Innocence, who never really seemed to think about anything at all, she had thought about this and she had gone to Madam and said she was thinking of joining in. Madam wasn't Swazi, she had never done *Umhlanga*, what could she tell her daughter to help her decide? Madam could have asked one of her friends to talk to Innocence. She could have asked one of Innocence's teachers. She could have asked the mother of one of Innocence's friends. But no.

Madam had asked Mavis.

Eish!

Mavis had sat with Madam and Innocence at the kitchen table, drinking tea together. Imagine that! The same kitchen table where the family sat for their meals, where Titi sometimes sat for her lessons with Madam, and where Madam sometimes sat for lunch with a friend who was visiting, that was where Mavis had sat with Madam to tell Innocence.

You'll be gone for eight days, she had told Innocence, and, as Innocence's eyes had begun to sparkle, Madam had reached for the basket of stones and chosen one to hold on to. You'll start at Ludzidzini, at the royal village of Indlovukati, the Queen Mother. That's where all the girls will go to, from each and every region. There are schools near, you'll sleep in the classrooms and there's a river near to wash in.

Eish, that night you'll meet many, many new friends! The next day you'll be in two groups, the small ones up to thirteen, then the big ones from fourteen, that will be your group. The small ones will walk to somewhere near, maybe around Malkerns, but the big ones will walk to somewhere far.

Madam had asked how far, and Mavis had said not to worry, if it's very far there will be trucks to take them there. But always the girls are going to arrive there at night, they have to show they have come from far. The big tents for them to sleep in will already be there.

Madam and Innocence had asked was it true there were no grown-ups, but no, not to worry, there were men there supervising the girls, they were chosen by the chiefs. Madam had chosen a second stone to hold on to, and Mavis had told them that another night some few lady elders would come to tell the girls about how to behave in their marriage, how to be dignified, how to make friends with other wives and work together the way they were doing with all the other girls now.

When you wake up, Mavis had said to Innocence, you'll see that the reed beds are near, and then you'll cut reeds. The number you cut must be even, otherwise it's unlucky for the royal family, nè? And you mustn't cut many, because they're more taller than you and you have to carry them all the way back to the royal village. *Eish*, they can be too heavy! You must bind your reeds together in a bundle for carrying. These nowadays you can bind with bits of plastic bag, but the real way to do it is to plait a rope from grasses.

The next day, Mavis had told Innocence, you'll go back carrying your reeds and you'll come at night to show you've come far, and you'll sleep in the classrooms again. Then you'll have a day for preparing for the dancing, fixing each other's hair, checking that your attires are nice, talking, talking, talking. Innocence had smiled. When you're ready to buy your attires, Mavis had told her, I have a friend who sews them nice-nice, nè?

Mavis had used her hands to show a line from over one shoulder down to the other hip when she had talked about the narrow sash adorned with woollen tassels that would pass between Innocence's naked breasts, and then she had used her hands again to show a short piece across her front when she had spoken about the beautiful *indlamu* skirt.

Madam had asked does the skirt have to be so short, and Mavis had laughed and said not to worry, the front part is covered, it's only the naked buttocks that can show, just a little bit underneath the skirt, that was the tradition.

The next day, she had told Innocence, you'll all take your

reeds to the Queen Mother's house and then you'll dance, all of you in your groups, all of you singing your songs and blowing your whistles. *Eish!* Be sure that you're in the middle of your line of dancers, if you're at the front or the back of the line, it's too hard to sing your song meanwhile the other group in front or behind is singing a different song. The next day the king will come to watch you dance, he'll talk to you.

Madam had asked can Innocence come home then, but no, she would sleep in the classrooms again, then the next day she was going to come home with meat because the king's men were going to slaughter some cows for the girls. But it wasn't just meat she would have, she would also have new friends, and pride that she'd done work for the Queen Mother's new reed fence.

And words in your head, Mavis had told Innocence, about not doing bad things with boys. Madam had said yes, not even silly things like hiding their drink in your schoolbag, and then they had all laughed. Madam had said it was good that Innocence had a grown-up to tell her what to expect, not just her friends at school, and then Madam and Innocence had thanked Mavis, and Innocence had hugged her and said yes, she was going to do *Umhlanga*.

Eish!

Mavis had been too sad when she'd had to stop doing *Umhlanga* herself. There were girls who still did it, girls who pretended they were still pure. There were girls, too, who said that your mother could even take you to Zululand for testing, and you could put a small bit of Colgate inside you, then when you lay down and opened for the ladies to check, they would see the white toothpaste and they would give you the certificate that said you were still pure, meanwhile you weren't. That was what those girls said, but Mavis and her sisters weren't sure. If the ladies saw that it was Colgate, then those girls and their mothers would be shamed in front of everybody who was there, just like any other girl and her mother if the girl was impure. Mavis never wanted to try that. What would it be for? Here in Swaziland you didn't need that certificate. And anyway, everybody already knew she wasn't pure, they had seen her belly growing. No, she could no longer take part.

She had always enjoyed each and every day of *Umhlanga*, but she had loved best the two days of dancing, the Reed Dance itself. The rhythms of the movements and the songs, over and over all day long, the rows and rows of girls snaking up to the front and then falling back again, singing again and again, dancing over and over, it had all made her feel like her body was there meanwhile her mind was in another place. It had made her feel like she was part of something very big, not just a small girl on her own.

Doctor was too happy that Innocence was going to do *Umhlanga*, she hadn't wanted to in all the years before. And Doctor and Madam hadn't argued about *Gogo* Levine for almost a week. Mavis had heard nothing, and neither had Lungi.

But Doctor and Madam had something new to talk about now, and so did Mavis and Lungi. Mavis and Lungi both thought it might somehow have something to do with why Innocence wanted to do *Umhlanga*. There was a new girl in the house, Nomsa, and since she had come, Innocence had been different. Not unhappy, just different. More serious, maybe. Thinking about things more. *Unsettled* was the word that

Madam had used. Innocence is unsettled, she had said to Titi's madam.

The day after Nomsa had first come, Mavis had been cleaning in the children's bathroom upstairs and she had heard Madam talking with Nomsa in the bedroom next door.

Nomsa, Madam had said, you know that there's no punishment here, no anger, no judgement. You don't have to tell me anything you don't want to, I'm only asking because I can help you better if I know. Nomsa's voice was very soft and quiet, but Mavis had heard her saying yes, she understood, and then Madam had asked her what was she planning to do.

Mavis had stopped scrubbing at the toilet bowl with Harpic so that she could hear Nomsa's answer. Nomsa was going to feed weevil tablets to her mother, her mother had asked her to. She had been in so much pain, and there was nothing else that Nomsa could do. She had been begging Nomsa for many, many weeks.

Madam had asked her if that was all, and then Nomsa had cried for a while before saying no, if the tablets worked for her mother then she was going to take some herself because of Mr Thwala at school. Then Nomsa had cried and cried, and she was still crying when Mavis had finished cleaning the bathroom. As she had passed quietly by the open door of the bedroom, she had looked inside and seen Madam holding Nomsa tight-tight.

Later, Lungi had heard angry voices outside near the garage, and she had looked out of the window at the side of the kitchen and seen Madam and Doctor arguing. Doctor wanted to get into his bakkie and go and fetch his gun, he wanted to shoot Mr Thwala for violating Nomsa, and Madam was begging him not to go. Then *Gogo* Levine had gone out and shouted at them both. What kind of bloody example for the children is this, she had asked them, how are you going to raise them from jail? Then they had all come inside and asked Lungi to make them tea.

Mavis and Lungi had both heard about such a thing happening, sometimes it was even in the newspaper. A teacher or even a headmaster would help himself to one of the girls, and then – to make him feel okay or to keep the girl quiet – he would give her a hundred emalangeni. It was always a hundred emalangeni. Madam and Titi had even talked about it for Titi's lesson when it had been in the newspaper and Madam was teaching Titi about if this then that. If a teacher does this, then he pays that. And if he does this, then he must go to jail. Mavis and Lungi had asked each other, was it written somewhere that a hundred emalangeni was how much these men should pay? *Eish!*

The next day, when Madam took Nomsa to the doctor and Mavis went to give a very special clean to the bedroom Nomsa was sharing with Innocence, she saw that Madam had put one of her special stones on the chest of drawers next to Nomsa's bed. It was one of the big stones from the shelf in the lounge, the pale pink one that was the stone of love. Madam had told a visitor about it while Mavis was standing on a chair just outside the lounge, cleaning the top of the wood around the lounge doorway. If you had that stone, then it helped you to feel that you were worth something, and if you felt that you were worth something, then you knew that you were worth love. That was what Madam had given to Nomsa. It was a nice stone, but it had many sharp edges. It wasn't enough for a girl that life had tumbled the way it had tumbled Nomsa. No. It didn't yet talk about shining.

Mavis went back down to the kitchen and searched very carefully through Madam's basket of stones on the table. Three or four of them were the same pale pink, and she chose the largest. Smooth and rounded, it was already shining in her hand, but she gave it an extra polish with a few drops of Windowlene to help to bring out all of the shine that it had. Then she took it upstairs and put it beside the other one next to Nomsa's bed.

It was a much paler pink than the bright pink she was crocheting now. Any mother that bought this jersey at the market in Mbabane would have a very happy child. When the jersey was finished, Mavis would use a bit of the wool to replace part of a square of her blanket that was wearing rather badly. The wool that was wearing was a reddish brown, and the pink would look fresher, cleaner, next to the bright green that was in the same square.

As Lungi turned over in her bed and began to snore quietly, Mavis's thoughts went to Titi, who had spent many nights turning in her bed inside the *kwerekwere* house, trying to think what to say to her boyfriend who wanted to marry her. Mavis would have said yes before the question had even finished coming out of his mouth. But after all that thinking, Titi had said no. *Eish!* Then he had said he was going to smear her with ochre. That was a man's right, but it wasn't what any woman wanted, not any woman Mavis or Lungi knew or had ever heard about. As much as Mavis wanted a husband, she didn't want a man to marry her without even asking. No. A man who married her without asking would do anything he wanted without asking, and that wasn't nice. Mavis wanted a man to love her, she wanted to love him back. She and Lungi had told Titi she shouldn't worry, smearing with ochre wasn't something a man said he would do, it was something he just did. If he said he would, then he was just joking with her, or just saying it because he was angry that he didn't get what he wanted. There were men who were like that.

But Titi had lied to Mavis and Lungi about the men in her own country. They didn't take just one wife there, her madam's own son had taken another without even telling the first. Titi said no, he never married the second. But all those years he had never told! *Eish*, the men in Titi's country were not honest, Titi should rather marry a Swazi.

Petros was going to marry, there was a girl in Nhlangano. He had come to talk to Mavis about his dog, and he had told her about the girl. Look, he had said, and he had shown her a photo, an old kind of photo that didn't have any colour.

Holding that photo, looking at that girl, Mavis's hands had trembled. She hadn't known that there was a girl. She hadn't known that he was waiting until he was better before he went to negotiate with the girl's family. She had sent him to the doctor and paid for him to get better, and now he had gone. Doctor had given him some holiday, and he'd gone to Nhlangano to pay *lobola*. He had no cows to give the girl's family, so the tin of money under his bed must be very full.

He had come to tell her that his dog was going to stay with the dairy manager while he was away, and while he was away would she please give the food for his dog to the dairy manager instead. Mavis had tried not to let her face show how hurt she was that he had thought the food she gave him was for his dog rather than for him. While they had talked about how taxi drivers didn't want a dog inside their taxi because a dog could mess, and about how it was fine for a chicken or a goat to be tied to the roof of a bus but it wouldn't be nice for his dog, and about how he would come back and earn some more money on the farm and then Doctor would drive him and his dog in the bakkie to Nhlangano when the wedding time came, all the time they had talked about those things Mavis had pretended that she was happy for him.

But she wasn't happy, and when he came back, she was going to tell him.

She was going to tell him it would break her heart when he left again.

She was going to tell him it was like he was her own boy.

SIXTEEN

WHEN THE TIME CAME, ALL THE MAZIBUKO children got the day off school to support Nomsa at her mother's funeral. That day, Mama drove the Tungaraza children to school in the red Microbus, which she didn't like to do on account of the early morning mist and fog on the way up the hill into Mbabane. Baba said it wasn't mist or fog, it was actually a cloud sitting low on the mountaintop, but Mama said she didn't have to know what something actually was to know that she didn't like it.

Helping themselves from the small pile of bricks that Uncle Enock stored at the back of the garage, Benedict and his brothers built the small step to help Mama climb up into the vehicle in her smart, tight skirt, and then they put the bricks back again. Mama never needed help getting out: by turning sideways on the seat so that both of her legs were out of the door, she could slide to the ground gracefully.

Grace had suggested that Mama should consider wearing a trouser like Auntie Rachel did, but Mama had said no, it wasn't polite for a lady her age to wear a trouser, especially a lady who wasn't the right kind of shape for it. And besides, here a lady in a trouser wasn't allowed into a government building, which meant that Mama wouldn't be able to visit Baba in his office at the ministry. Mama never had visited Baba in his office at the ministry, but still.

After school, it felt strange not having to walk to the high school to wait for Auntie Rachel. But they did have to wait, and Benedict was disappointed: Sifiso had been hoping to meet Mama so that he could say how nice her cake was, but Mr Simelane was in a hurry to get Sifiso home in the Buffalo Soldiers van because Mrs Levine would soon be arriving there to help him for the very first time.

Sifiso was nervous, but he was also a little giddy with excitement. Even if Mr Simelane hadn't been in a hurry, Sifiso would never have had the patience to wait for Mama to arrive.

'Nekth time,' he said, as his father hooted again.

'Next time,' Benedict agreed, though he knew that wasn't likely to be soon. Mama was busy with training the ladies, and she was also making a number of the Ubuntu remembrance cakes herself. And something interesting was beginning to happen: people liked the remembrance cakes so much that they were starting to order them for people who weren't yet late, to celebrate special moments in their lives like retirements, anniversaries and the beginnings of new projects.

Getting his percentage from the remembrance cakes that Mama made herself was making Benedict feel big. It wasn't a lot of money, but it meant that he had been able to order a cake from Mama for Giveness.

The cake, which would be ready for the arrival of Giveness's mother that weekend, wasn't a cake to welcome her. No. She didn't really deserve a welcome on account of her calling Giveness one of God's mistakes. But Giveness and his aunt deserved to have something sweet and comforting to make them feel better and to help them to forget about being afraid.

Benedict wasn't afraid waiting outside the primary school: if his brothers needed the toilet, they knew where to go, and nobody was going to shout at Benedict and make him feel small. But he knew from Auntie Rachel that there was no need to feel afraid at the high school now, either, on account of Mr Thwala being gone. Two other girls had come forward and said that Mr Thwala had been doing bad things to them, too, and Mr Magagula had had no choice but to tell him to go.

Benedict hadn't been nice to Nomsa himself, and thinking about that sometimes made him feel like he'd bitten into a rotting prickly-pear fruit that had stung his mouth and flooded it with the taste of *kinyezi*. *Eh*, he just hadn't understood! He had even thought it was nice that Mr Thwala helped Nomsa with pocket money! Now that he knew, he didn't need Mr Thwala to make him feel small; he felt small all by himself.

When the red Microbus finally arrived, Mama wasn't alone inside it. A man they didn't know slid the side door open. Stepping out and tipping his seat forward, he ushered the surprised children into the back. The inside smelled deliciously of curry and chips.

'Sorry, for delaying,' Mama called back to them. 'I'm just dropping these people past the golf course.'

'Eveni Village for me, nè?' said the man who had let them in.

'We're not a bl—' Grace began.

'We're not a taxi!' Benedict shouted, and the five strangers inside the Microbus laughed.

'I've already told them that,' said Mama.

'Many times!' laughed one of the ladies in the front next to Mama.

Mama told them the story, shouting it to them as she drove. Titi was down at the other house, looking after the smallest Mazibukos so that Lungi and Mavis could go with the other Mazibukos and Mrs Levine to support Nomsa at the funeral, and Mama had been too busy with cakes to make lunch for herself or to prepare any fruit for the children's tea.

That part of the story thrilled Benedict: it had been a long time since Mama had been too busy with cakes to do something.

Mama had decided to treat everybody to take-aways, which they almost never had on account of the expense. When she pulled up across the road from Mr Patel's shop, she knew that if she got out to go into the shop, she would find it very difficult to get back into the Microbus and there would be a very real danger that her smart skirt might split.

'I called a lady over,' said Mama, and one of the ladies at the front turned to the children and raised her hand. 'I asked her to go into the shop and get the food for me.'

'I negotiated for a lift,' said the lady who had raised her hand. 'Then inside Patel's, I found my brother.'

'It's me,' said the man who had opened the door. With his elbow, he nudged the man next to him. 'I told my friend.'

When the lady got into the Microbus with the family's treat, many others got in with her.

'Taxi is never free like this,' said one of the other men.

'I've already delivered the others,' said Mama. 'Now it's just these for other side the golf course.'

258

'Eveni Village for me, nè?' the man next to the door repeated.

When they finally got home, Giveness's cake was waiting there for Benedict. It looked like a big gift, and it was beautiful. The square of two vanilla layers was draped in thin, smooth stripes of bright red, green and blue just like the gift-wrap you could buy at the news agency in The Plaza. Wrapped around it was a wide ribbon of sunshine-yellow marzipan that finished in a large bow on the top, and with a corner tucked under the bow was a white sugar-paste label on which Mama had piped in large purple letters: FOR GIVENESS. It was perfect!

Baba helped him to deliver it on Saturday morning, on the way to the public library. The other children waited in the Microbus as Baba opened the squeaky little gate to the small, neat garden and went to knock on the door, leaving Benedict to concentrate on carrying the beautiful gift-cake on its board.

It was Giveness's aunt who opened the door. Benedict had guessed that Giveness wouldn't open it himself on account of being scared that it might be his mother.

Baba and Benedict greeted his aunt, and Benedict said they'd brought something for Giveness.

'Giveness!' she called into the house, her eyes dancing over the cake. 'Come! It's your friend!' Benedict knew she added that in case Giveness thought it was his mother, here to take him away. 'Come in, come in.'

'No, no,' said Baba, holding his hands up with the palms facing her. 'Thank you, but I have children in the car and we're on our way to the library.'

Giveness appeared in the doorway, and when he saw the cake his eyes grew large and his mouth fell open into a big O.

'It's for you,' said Benedict, handing it over.

Giveness took it, the O of his mouth so big that he was unable to speak.

All of them were busy laughing as they looked at Giveness looking at his cake, and there was no squeak from the little gate on account of Baba having left it open, so it wasn't until the lady with the suitcase was right up close that they saw her.

Then so many things happened all at once that Benedict would struggle later on to separate them out in the right order for Mama and Titi, who no longer came with them to get dropped at the supermarket on Saturdays, now that Mama had her driving licence.

He was pretty sure that Giveness's aunt saw the lady first, stepping around Benedict and Baba to greet her, and that next the lady's eyes fell on Giveness and stayed there as she ignored Benedict's outstretched hand as well as Baba's. Giveness stared at her, the round O of his mouth no longer about joy and surprise but now about shock and fright.

Then Baba took the cake from Giveness quickly as the lady leapt at her son like a lioness leaping at a buffalo, embracing him, covering his pink face with kisses and speaking in a deep-voiced moan without any spaces between her words, in a way that made her sound like a chainsaw cutting down a tree.

Nobody else moved or said anything. Then the lady let go of Giveness and, straightening herself up, she noticed the cake that Baba was holding.

'Oh!' she cried, looking at it carefully. 'Oh! Oh! Oh!' Raising both her arms up in the air and looking up into the sky, she cried oh! some more, before falling on her knees at Baba's feet and shouting a string of joyful-sounding siSwati at the top of her voice.

Benedict noticed Giveness's aunt glancing around at the neighbouring houses at the same time that he saw Baba stepping back and shifting the cake-board sideways so that he could say something to the lady at his feet.

'*Angisati siSwati, sisi.*' Looking down at her, he shrugged his shoulders as best he could with the cake-board in his hands.

Benedict decided to take the cake from Baba and give it to Giveness's aunt as the lady switched to English.

'A messenger from afar!' she shouted. 'Praise the Lord! When I first met Jesus, when I accepted Him into my heart as my Lord and my saviour, I told Him what I had done!' Casting an arm dramatically in the direction of Giveness, she swung her head round to look at him. Benedict saw that the pink of his friend's face was darker than it usually was, much darker than the pink hands that now covered his mouth so that Benedict couldn't see if it still had the shape of an O.

'He told me to come!' she yelled to her son. 'Praise the Lord, He told me to come to you!' Turning back to Baba, she lowered her volume the slightest bit. 'And then he sent you to me! Oh! Praise Jesus, hallelujah! You have brought me the sign from Him!' Sinking down on her knees until her buttocks touched her heels, she flung her body forward and grabbed hold of Baba's ankles, making Baba's mouth an O and sending Benedict's hands up to cover his own.

'Forgiveness!' she cried, her lips now close enough to Baba's shoes to kiss them. 'I asked and the gift was given! Praise Jesus, hallelujah, I asked and it was given!' Then she said amen over and over and over until it was one long word without any spaces in between and she was sounding like a chainsaw cutting down a tree again.

Baba tried to step away, but she tightened her grip on his ankles, almost making him fall. Giveness took the cake from his aunt so that she could squat down next to her sister and try to get her to let go, but she held on more tightly, pulling sharply on Baba's feet, so that the left foot that Baba had been trying to lift and pull back suddenly shot forward, making Baba lose his balance and tumble backwards onto the ground with a very loud *eh!*

Almost at the same time that Baba's buttocks hit the ground, the side door of the red Microbus slid open, and the Tungaraza children who had been watching and laughing scrambled out and ran to Baba, each of their giggling mouths suddenly becoming an O.

But Baba was fine, and Giveness's mother was suddenly quiet, rubbing with both hands at the side of her chin where the toe of Baba's shoe had hit her as he fell. Embarrassed now, she joined her sister and Giveness in insisting that the Tungarazas lock up the Microbus and come inside for a soda and a slice of cake.

While Grace and Faith were pouring Coke into glasses and Moses and Daniel were brushing the last of the dust from the back of Baba's trouser, Benedict took Giveness by the arm and led him to beside his mother's chair, where she could look directly at them. Her face was turned to the side on account of her sister standing in front of her chair, dabbing some ointment onto the side of her chin where Baba's shoe had cut her.

'Excuse me,' said Benedict, feeling his friend's arm trembling.

'Yes, dear?' Her voice was calm now.

'Me and Giveness, we want to know something.'

'Hm?' She flinched as Giveness's aunt dabbed.

'Did you come here to take him away?' As he asked, Benedict saw Giveness's aunt stiffen.

'What?'

'Is that why you came? To take him away from us?'

'Oh, Lord, no!' She looked up at her sister, who had stopped dabbing. 'Is that what you thought?'

'*Yebo!* Why else would you come all this way?'

'But I told you. I told you I was coming to say my apologies!'

'There are telephones for that.' The lid went on to the tube of ointment.

'And if I had phoned? How would the Lord have told me I was forgiven? How would I have known?' As she began to tell her sister all about meeting Jesus, Benedict and Giveness moved away.

Giveness let out a breath that he seemed to have been holding for a very long time, and putting both of his hands on his stomach, he said, 'Now I can eat some cake!' Smiling, he took Benedict's brown arm in his own pink one, and led him to the table where Grace was serving slices from his very special gift.

Benedict was relieved that Giveness wasn't going to leave, but something else was making him feel uneasy. He was worried that Petros might be very sick, that his new *muti* wasn't working. He hadn't seen him for many days, although he had spotted Krishna a number of times. It was unusual for the two to be apart.

Then Mavis told Titi and Titi told Benedict that Petros had gone.

'*Gone?* Without his dog?'

'His dog is with the dairy manger. Petros is going to come back, he only went for paying his *lobola*.'

Eh! If Mavis knew he'd gone for *lobola*, Petros must have told her. Why hadn't he told Benedict? They were friends. They were going to look for Mr Quartermain's gold together, and if it was real they were going to share it. Okay, if Auntie Rachel and Uncle Enock were wrong about Petros, and if Auntie Rachel was wrong about Mr Quartermain, maybe Petros's gold and Mr Quartermain's gold were already the same thing. But they could still have an adventure together to find more, then Petros would have more for his baby to inherit.

'Nhlangano,' Benedict said. 'That's where his girlfriend is. He showed me her photo.'

'*Eish.*'

'What?'

'Maybe Henry has a new girlfriend now. Maybe he's already paying *lobola* for another wife.'

Men didn't always behave well when it came to girls, and it really wasn't nice that Petros hadn't said goodbye to Benedict. But there were other boy and girl things going on to take his mind off Petros for a while.

It was the middle of October, and there was a public holiday for *Umhlanga*, the Reed Dance that happened every year. Thousands of girls from all over the kingdom had already gathered bundles of reeds for mending the fence in front of the home of the king's mother, Indlovukati the Great She Elephant, and today they would sing and dance for the king. Innocence was joining in, so Auntie Rachel took Mama and the girls to watch it.

Benedict and the boys had an outing of their own: Uncle Enock and Baba took them to Mlilwane, the sanctuary for wildlife in the Ezulwini Valley. They went in Uncle Enock's bakkie, on account of the roads there being too difficult for Baba's red Microbus, and Benedict and his brothers sat with Fortune and Vusi in the open flatbed at the back, even though there were leopards.

Vusi went to Mlilwane with his father every year, so he knew what to expect and what to look out for. He promised that they were going to be safe.

'There are no elephants in this reserve,' he told them, 'and no lions.'

'What about tigers?' Daniel's eyes were starting to get bigger as they entered the reserve, and Benedict's eyes closed as they went over the cattle-grid at the gate, which didn't seem quite as safe from the back of an open bakkie as it would have from the inside of a Hi-Ace or a Microbus.

'There are no tigers in Swaziland, nè?' Vusi's voice was patient; he had plenty of experience at home with younger children. 'All the tigers live in Asia.'

Soon after the gate there were zebras, two on the dirt road right in front of them and four more in the wild grass at the side.

'*Eh!*' said Daniel and Moses, and Benedict held his breath, not wanting to scare them away.

'Burchell's zebra,' Uncle Enock called from inside the stationary bakkie.

265

Benedict was confused. 'Are they family with a Burchell's coucal?' His question to Vusi was a whisper.

'*Ag* no, man.' Vusi sounded like Auntie Rachel. 'A mammal can't be family with a bird! They get their name from the man who first saw them.'

'*Eh!*'

All the morning, all the way through stopping to look at hippos, crocodiles, ostriches, warthogs and blesbuck, Benedict tried his best to see something new, something that he was the first to see, so that it would be known as Benedict's something or Tungaraza's something.

'What about that?' he asked Vusi for what seemed like the hundredth time.

'That's an impala,' Vusi said patiently. 'A male. See its horns? Females don't have horns. How high do you think you can jump?' he asked Moses and Daniel.

'This high!' Moses indicated with his hand.

'This high!' Daniel put his hand much higher.

'My daddy is two metres, nè? That impala can jump three metres in the air.'

'*Eh!*'

'And eleven metres forward.'

'*Eh!*'

Vusi put his hand over Fortune's mouth. 'And what do we call October month in siSwati?'

Benedict gave his brothers time to think of the answer, and when they couldn't he said *Impala* himself.

Vusi high-fived him like an American, and Benedict glowed with pride.

'Because impalas have their babies in October month,'

said Fortune, his mouth free at last.

'I know June as well,' said Benedict, anxious to impress the older boy some more. 'It's *Inhlaba*, meaning aloes. On account of aloes getting their flowers in June. And September's *Inyoni*, on account of birds finding mates that month.'

'Speaking of birds,' said Vusi, 'it looks like we're going all the way up to Nyonyane.'

'Execution rock?'

'*Yebo*. Hold on tight, nè? This road is steep.'

Up at the top, they all got out and Uncle Enock pointed out Sheba's Breasts. From there Benedict could see very clearly the two separate peaks that looked just like a lady's breasts. It was a much better view than the one Henry had said was perfect. He became aware that Uncle Enock was staring at him.

'What?'

Uncle Enock smiled. 'I'm waiting for you to ask about the gold.'

'Is it—'

'No! Long ago some tin was mined here on Execution Rock, but there's no gold mine anywhere around.'

'But the book said—'

'It's just a story, nè? Pius, come and tell your boy the difference between a story and the truth.'

Baba left the young ones looking at a pile of something's *kinyezi* with Vusi and came to join them.

'Baba, if it's in a book, isn't it true?'

'Not necessarily.'

'Even if it says it's true?'

Baba shook his head. 'That's a warning sign right there. People can say something is true just to lead you into a pile of nonsense like that pile the boys are looking at.' He indicated the younger ones who were now watching Vusi sort through the *kinyezi* with a stick. 'And if you trust the person who says it's true, that person can mislead you.'

'Books can lie?' asked Benedict, checking to see if he was understanding Baba correctly.

'Anything can lie,' said Baba.

Uncle Enock tried to help. 'You know a stick insect, nè?' Benedict nodded. 'It looks just like a stick.'

'It lies to you,' said Uncle Enock. 'It tells you it's a stick, meanwhile it's an insect.'

Benedict thought for a moment. God had made the stick insect like that to protect it from anything that might want to eat it. But if camouflage was a way of lying, was God saying it was okay to lie? Surely not. He was about to ask, when he saw that Baba had the look on his face that said he wanted it to be time for news.

Then Baba looked as though he had just had a very good idea. 'Food!' he declared. 'Time to eat?'

'Tip top,' said Uncle Enock. 'Vusi, show the boys the crocodile, nè? Dr Tungaraza and I will get the picnic out.'

Vusi pointed to just behind Sheba's Breasts, where the mountain made the shape of the huge face of a crocodile looking right at them. Benedict saw it at once, but the younger ones struggled and needed help. Then Vusi pointed out the Mdzimba Mountains to the right of the Breasts, which were sacred on account of kings being buried there.

There was so much to eat! Titi had packed sandwiches and cupcakes for everybody, and Lungi had given them boiled eggs, cheese cut into little squares, and plenty of fruit.

Baba and Uncle Enock sat on the wooden bench to eat, while Fortune, Moses and Daniel ate as they walked around exploring.

Benedict sat with Vusi on a rock near the edge of the mountaintop. Perhaps it was the very place where the long-ago criminals had been pushed off. Benedict wondered if any of them, knowing that they were going to be pushed, had chosen to jump instead. If somebody was going to make you late, maybe suiciding yourself like a scorpion was sometimes the only way to stop them.

Eh, he didn't like that his thoughts kept coming back to ideas like that these days. Sometimes he felt like something had knocked his mind from the place it had found to sit comfortably, and now it was struggling to find its balance in a more difficult place. It was a place where Baba could be in an aeroplane and it could crash into a building without it even being an accident, a place where his sisters might not always be safe, not even in a classroom. And it was a place where the idea of his first baba that he had carried inside him for ten whole years lay torn at his feet.

Whatever it was that was going on inside him, it felt like something he wasn't yet ready to understand. Maybe a grown-up or an older boy like Vusi would understand, but Benedict didn't want to say.

He began to peel the shell from a boiled egg.

'Vusi, you know Nomsa?'

'*Yebo*.'

'Is she going to be a Mazibuko now?'

'Looks like it. There's nowhere else for her to go, so of course she can stay with us, be part of our family.'

Benedict thought about being one of eight children as he swallowed his mouthful of boiled egg. 'I don't think Innocence likes her much.'

'Maybe not.' Vusi took a big bite of sandwich and chewed it slowly. 'But she'll get over it.'

'What's it like getting a new sister?'

'Just...' Vusi shrugged. 'Normal. I mean, I was once the new brother everybody got used to. Innocence was once the new sister. *Eish*, now we all have *Gogo* Levine to get used to, and she's getting used to us. We've all been in that very same place.'

Benedict remembered getting used to Faith and Daniel. It hadn't always been easy, especially when they preferred Grace and Moses. But they had all met one another before, there had been photos of one another in their separate houses, it wasn't like they were strangers.

Eh! It was going to be very hard for Josephine.

'At least Nomsa knows you from school,' he said to Vusi.

'*Yebo*.' He began on another sandwich. '*Ag*, she'll find a way to fit in.'

They ate their food quietly for a while as they watched a black-shouldered kite hover almost motionless in the air before it swooped down on something somewhere below where they could see. Then Benedict asked Vusi what he was going to be, and he said a doctor.

'A doctor for people?' Benedict wasn't entirely sure why doctors for people and doctors for other animals had to be so different.

'*Yebo*. And you?'

Benedict sighed, fingering a square of cheese. 'I want to do

270

something with animals, but I don't think I can be an animal doctor like Uncle Enock.'

'Why not?'

'I'm not clever. Mama says I am, and Baba says I'm clever in my own way, but when he looks at my school marks I can see that he's disappointed. I'm not scholarship-clever, that's the problem. Baba can't pay for university, we're too many. We're getting another sister, too.'

'I heard. But you know? You don't have to go to university to learn working with animals.'

'No?'

'No. You can train as a game ranger, a guide for visitors. A game park will teach you.'

'*Eh!*'

How wonderful it would be to drive people around a place like this and tell them about all the animals and the birds! There were plenty of places he could do that back home in Tanzania.

'Vusi?' Uncle Enock called from the bench, pointing to some large birds circling slowly in the air far behind where they were sitting.

'*Eish,*' said Vusi. 'Vultures. There's been a kill.'

Afterwards, the girls were much more interested in telling Baba and the boys about their day than in hearing about fat hippos, hiding crocodiles and circling vultures.

'Baba would never let *us* wear skirts that short!'

'And nothing on top! *Nothing!*'

'Uncle, those clothes are not polite.'

271

'Rachel told us the king needs to see as much of each girl as possible, otherwise he can't choose which one to marry.'

'Not that he *has* to choose,' said Baba.

'But Pius, the colours were so beautiful! Tiny turquoise skirts dotted with buttons and silver studs, with little fringes of yellow beads at the bottom. And then a bright ribbon over one shoulder and across to the waist, with big woollen tassels hanging off in yellow and pink and green and white and—'

'And the princesses had red feathers sticking up in their hair.'

Benedict knew that those were feathers from the national bird, the *ligwalagwala*, which you weren't allowed to wear unless you belonged to the royal family.

'Show them Mrs Zikalala,' Mama said to the girls. 'Benedict, you remember her?' Mama rolled her eyes and her voice went flat. 'The white cake.'

Benedict nodded, remembering the lady who wanted her daughter to marry the king.

Standing next to each other, Grace and Faith put on their faces that said they were acting somebody else.

'Look at my girl!' said Grace, her voice high-pitched as she indicated Faith, who stood with her head down, her arms folded. 'Isn't she magnificent?' Grace tutted loudly as she pulled Faith's arms down by her sides. Then, roughly, she raised Faith's chin. 'Queenie, let him see everything, nè? Where is your beautiful smile?'

Rolling her eyes, Faith gave a smile that made her look like a growling dog, and everybody laughed.

Grace continued. 'Turn around, Queenie!' With a great show of not wanting to, Faith turned her back to the room. 'Look at this!' Grace grabbed one of Faith's buttocks. 'Magnificent, nè? *Magnificent!*'

Mama was shaking her head, but at the same time she was laughing so much that tears came to her eyes, and she needed a tissue from inside her smart blouse.

'This is the year, Mrs Tungaraza!' Grace went on, pulling Faith's shoulders back so that her chest leaped forward. 'This is the year he will choose my Queenie!'

'Oh, that poor girl,' said Baba, but he couldn't help smiling.

'Auntie, did he choose already?'

'I don't know, Titi.' They had left long before the end on account of Mama's smart shoes hurting and Auntie Rachel wanting to get back to Nomsa and the little ones, who were alone with Mrs Levine on account of Lungi and Mavis both being off.

'There's a story,' said Baba, 'but I don't know how true it is. They say that when the king couldn't attend the ceremony because he was still at school in England, the elders sent him a video of it and he chose a girl from that.'

'*Eh!*'

'Did you see the king?' asked Benedict. 'Was he dressed as Ngwenyama the Lion?'

Maybe Mswati dressed up as a lion because a lion was the king of all the animals. Maybe King Solomon used to dress up as a lion; maybe that was how he was able to talk to birds and tell them what to do. Benedict didn't know if King Midas or King Martin Luther Junior ever dressed up.

'No,' said Mama, 'today he just had a *kanga* round his

273

waist and lots of beads. And the red feathers.' Mama's hand indicated feathers spiking up out of her hair. '*Eh!* Talking of a *kanga*, I must get out of this skirt!'

When sleep tried to take Benedict that night, he pushed it away, too excited by the idea of becoming a game ranger. After his schooling he would go straight to a game reserve, and they would teach him everything there was to know, everything in the whole entire world about any creature that wasn't a person. Snakes, bugs, elephants, birds, he would know them all. And he would earn money from showing them to people and telling them all about them. Okay, he would have to carry a gun like every other game ranger did, and Mama wouldn't be happy with that on account of it being a gun that had made his first baba late, but Mama and Baba would be so proud of him! It didn't matter that he wasn't scholarship-clever. People were going to pay him money for doing exactly what he loved to do, and that was how he was going to help his family. Imagine!

But if King Solomon's gold was real, and if he could find it, he could help them right now.

He hoped that Petros was going to come back soon. He didn't know how long it took people to agree on *lobola*, but it seemed that Petros had been gone a long time. Maybe it was taking long because Petros didn't have any cows to pay with. Maybe his girlfriend's family was insisting on cows, and then Petros would have to come back to Uncle Enock's farm and work for a very long time until he could afford. Or maybe the girl was saying no. Titi had said no to Henry. Benedict knew that Petros wouldn't just smear the girl with red ochre and marry her anyway. No. Petros was kind, he was polite.

Okay, he had gone to Nhlangano without saying goodbye to Benedict, even though he had called Benedict *bhuti*. But Petros was on his own, he didn't live with brothers and sisters. He didn't know that when somebody is your brother then you tell him that you're going away, and you tell him goodbye.

Benedict wondered if Petros would like to get used to being a new brother in the Tungaraza family. Baba could change Benedict's bed for a double bunk like the one Moses and Daniel slept in, and Petros could share their bedroom. Auntie Rachel could teach him more English to help him to fit in more easily.

Krishna would have to sleep outside, though. Mama and Baba didn't want animals inside. It was nice for Krishna that Petros had arranged for her to stay with the dairy manager while he was away: the farm was her home, she wouldn't have felt as comfortable at the holiday home for pets behind Uncle Enock's work.

If Petros joined their family, Benedict would do everything he could to make him feel at home.

Eh! If Petros joined their family, Petros would be the eldest boy. That would mean that things wouldn't weigh quite so heavily on Benedict's shoulders, and he would be able to relax a little.

Relaxing a little into that thought, he surrendered in his battle against sleep.

SEVENTEEN

WHEN NOMSA FINALLY WENT BACK TO SCHOOL, Benedict sat next to her in Auntie Rachel's Hi-Ace.

'I'm sorry about your mother,' he said to her quietly. She nodded but said nothing back to him.

On the way home from school, he tried again. 'I'm sorry I was mean to you, Nomsa.' She said nothing. 'About your letter.' She nodded.

Benedict wasn't sure what else he could say. While the other children chatted and giggled, he and Nomsa sat in silence.

It wasn't until Auntie Rachel drove over the cattle-grid at the farm's entrance and Benedict saw the shed where the cows slept at night that an idea came to him.

'I can show you an owl if you like.'

She looked at him. 'Where?'

'Here in the shed. Do you want to see it?'

'Is it late?'

'Uh-uh. It lives there.'

'Okay.'

'Later this afternoon?'

'Okay.'

Nomsa thought the owl was exciting, even though it was sleeping and it didn't wake up to look at them.

'You should bring Vusi to see it,' he said to her.

'Why don't you bring him yourself?'

'He's your brother now. He'll be happy to know he has a sister who likes birds.'

'You think so?'

'Mm.'

'Really?'

'Mm. So will you bring him to look?'

'Okay.'

'Good.'

Benedict told her about giving the owl a mouse to eat, and then he told her about the hoopoe, King Solomon's queen, that was buried in the special royal casket under the lucky-bean tree in his garden. She didn't know what a hoopoe looked like, so he took her to the Mazibukos' lounge and showed her in Uncle Enock's book.

Benedict saw her smile that day, for the very first time. Even before, when they had looked in the snake book together, her eyes had still been hard. But when she smiled as she thanked him for showing her the birds, her eyes softened and he found himself grinning back at her.

Eh! What if his new sister was like her? Imagine!

He didn't want Josephine to feel uncomfortable, to struggle to fit in as he could see Nomsa was. And he didn't want to behave badly when it came to a girl, not again. He wanted to be very sure that he didn't. As he left the Mazibukos' house to go up to his own, the small sign welcoming bees and butterflies to one of Mrs Levine's flowerpots gave him an idea.

277

He went straight home to work on it, and after supper that night, when Mama and Baba were by themselves at the dining table, he went to them with his piece of paper already neatly folded.

'Baba, do you have an envelope for me? And a stamp?'

'At work. Why?'

'I wrote a letter.'

'A letter?' asked Mama. 'That's nice. Can we see?'

Benedict hesitated. It wasn't nice for somebody to read a letter that wasn't theirs. But it really wasn't a secret, so he handed it over to Mama.

She unfolded it carefully. It wasn't special paper or anything, just something that was going to be thrown away at Baba's work, but he had written in his neatest writing on the side where there wasn't any printing, and he had done a small drawing of an owl like the one he had shown to Nomsa in the shed.

'Read it to me, Angel.'

'Dear Josephine,' Mama began. She and Baba looked at each other, and she needed to clear her throat before she read on. 'Hello. Welcome to our family.'

That was as far as Mama read before she needed a tissue from the underwear inside her T-shirt.

Baba took the letter from her and carried on reading. 'When you come to live with us I will help you. I am the eldest boy.' Baba looked up from the letter to smile at Benedict. Then he read on. 'Grace and Faith like music. Moses and Daniel like sports. Me I like books and animals. What do you like? You are welcome here. Your new brother Benedict.'

'*Eh!*' said Mama, into her tissue.

278

Baba's eyes were bright. 'Good boy,' he said, patting Benedict's shoulder. 'Good boy.'

For safety, Benedict slipped his letter to Josephine inside the back of the bird book until Baba could bring him an envelope. Then he settled down on his cushion to read about different kinds of owls. The one in the shed down the hill was a barn owl.

Mama and Baba talked to each other softly.

'I never thought of writing to her, Angel. I wrote to her school principal, I sent money to the family that's taken her in, but I never thought of writing to her.'

'*Eh*, Pius, I feel ashamed! It isn't her fault who her father was.'

'Or who her mother was. We've been thinking only of ourselves, our own disappointment.'

'I'm going to write a letter, too. It can go in that same envelope. And I'll put in a photo of one of my cakes.'

'And a photo of all of us. I'll choose a nice one.'

'Yes.'

'Yes.'

After the owl, Nomsa didn't have much time to spend with Benedict. She had missed a lot of school, and Mr Magagula was making sure that all of her teachers gave her plenty of extra work to help her to catch up. Some days she even stayed behind at school for extra lessons supervised by Miss Dube, and then Auntie Rachel went back to fetch her or she came home with Mrs Levine.

Mrs Levine had Sifiso and two other children to help in

their homes after school now, and she had bought a pale blue Corolla with money that belonged to Mr Levine, who could whistle.

Sitting up at the dam late one afternoon, Benedict tried to choose the best things that he could show to Nomsa when she at last had time to come up there with him. The frogs and tadpoles, for sure. The weavers' nests hanging over the water, definitely.

When Petros came back, Benedict wanted to introduce him to Nomsa. Okay, he wasn't supposed to be spending any time with Petros, but he didn't think that Nomsa would tell. She seemed like somebody who knew how to keep a secret. Nomsa could speak to Petros in siSwati, and then she could translate into English for Benedict. Petros had so little English, and Benedict still had so little siSwati, but with Nomsa they could talk to each other so much better. Petros would be able to tell Benedict more about his ancestors, his girlfriend and his gold. Maybe all three of them could work together to understand Mr Quartermain's map, and go on an adventure to follow it. Nomsa could ask the geography teacher at the high school about what the Kalukawe and Lukanga rivers were called now. She mustn't show the teacher the map, though. The teacher might want some of the gold, and if it was real and not just pretend like Auntie Rachel said, it was already going to be shared between Benedict, Nomsa and Petros.

Eh, imagine if Petros and Nomsa were his brother and his sister! Benedict thought that might feel very good, better than having two big sisters who didn't pay him much attention and didn't even like animals, and better than having two small brothers who were only interested in boys who knew how to kick a ball and never wanted to talk about anything serious.

He wanted to talk to Nomsa about *umcwasho*, the new law for girls that the king had made on the Reed Dance day. Uncle Enock said it wasn't a new law, it was an ancient law that was back for a modern reason. If a girl was between fifteen and eighteen, she had to wear a string of blue and yellow beads around her head with a long, thick woollen tassel in blue and yellow hanging down from it at the back, and that was to show everybody that she was a good girl who had never fallen in love with a boy or a man. If she fell in love with a boy or a man from now on, then her family had to pay a fine of one cow. If they knew who the boy or man was, his family had to pay the same fine, too.

Girls who were older than eighteen, up to twenty-four, they had to wear tassels of red and black, and they weren't allowed to fall in love or marry, otherwise they paid a fine of one cow, just like the younger girls. The tassels were called *umcwasho*, and girls were going to have to wear *umcwasho* every day for the next five years.

The king said the *umcwasho* law was about stopping the spread of disease, but Auntie Rachel said it was about controlling women just as the hoopoe had advised King Solomon to do. Mama and Baba both said it blamed girls for spreading disease, but Titi said it meant a man couldn't marry her by smearing her with red ochre, and she had decided to wear the red and black tassels even though she was a *kwerekwere*. Innocence Mazibuko had chosen to wear the blue and yellow tassels, even though she wasn't yet fifteen, but Nomsa said she was never going to wear them, even when she got to the right age. Benedict wasn't sure, but he thought that might be because of Mr Thwala.

Two of the dairy cows had been stolen on account of people needing to pay fines, so Uncle Enock had hired a Buffalo Soldier to guard the shed at night, and now the cows had to go out for grazing with two men instead of just one.

Benedict waved to the two men now as they went past with the cows on the far side of the dam on their way towards the milking shed down the hill. When the noise of the cows sent a large flock of red bishop birds up from the reeds, Benedict decided he would go and look for nests there as soon as all the cows had gone past. He would love to show Nomsa a red bishop. With its black face and bright red head, back and collar, the male looked very much like a priest from the Church of Jericho.

The female was dull and brown, and difficult to tell apart from so many other kinds of bird. It was like that with birds: the males were bright and colourful, and danced around to attract the females. Which was just the opposite, Benedict recognised, of how it was with people. For centuries male birds had been having a Reed Dance ceremony of their own.

Male birds would never put on bright colours like *umcwasho* to tell females to stay away. No. For them, wearing colours was a way of marking themselves out and making themselves more attractive; that was entirely what a peacock's big, beautiful tail was for. Benedict wondered if the colourful *umcwasho* tassels might not make girls look more attractive to boys, too.

He didn't go to the far side of the dam very often: the cows trod a well-worn path there on their way to and from the field on the part of the plateau that was on the other side of the

282

clump of trees, so there wasn't much grass to sit on. The plateau ended a little way behind where the cows walked, and the trees and bushes there were thick and wild as they extended up the steep mountainside. Benedict squatted there quietly, waiting for the red bishops to settle back into the reeds at the edge of the dam.

While he waited, he wondered how long Petros would stay on the farm before he went back to Nhlangano again for his wedding. If his own family was still here, Benedict would ask Mama to make the cake for Petros's wedding.

Something pushed against his back.

Eh!

Jumping up in fright, he leapt away from the bushes, landing in a wet round of fresh kinyezi from the cows.

Krishna jumped up at him.

'*Eh*, Krishna! Look what you made me do!' Pushing the dog away, he looked around for a patch of grass where he could scrape off the *kinyezi*. But everywhere was just mud, soil and even more *kinyezi*. Krishna moved away from him and ran a small way into the bushes before turning back to him and whining. When Benedict walked away to look for some grass, she came at him again, jumping up and wagging her tail.

She must be missing Petros even more than Benedict was. The dairy manager was inside the dairy office or the milking shed all day, he didn't come up here with the cows like Petros did. Krishna was probably lonely for Petros. Down in Nhlangano, was he lonely for her, too?

'What is it, Krishna? Do you want to play?' Benedict looked around for a stick to throw for her, but she wasn't interested. Instead, she went into the bushes again and turned to look at him, whining. Thinking she might be hurt in some way, he went towards her. She ran ahead a little then turned to look back at him.

'Okay, we can play catch.' Following her, he plunged into the bushes.

Fighting his way through the thick undergrowth, he chased her quite some distance up the steep hill until he tripped over something and arrived head-first on the ground in an area where there was much more space between the trees. As Krishna barked at him, he looked around, leaping to his feet in fright before his mind had fully recognised that very near to his face was a snake!

Eh!

But no, it was only half a snake!

Very carefully, he nudged at it with the edge of a *kinyezi-*covered shoe. It didn't move. With Krishna still barking at him, he looked back and saw that what he had fallen over was a spade. Had Samson been up here, killing snakes? Krishna didn't give him time to think about whether or not it was a safe place to be. Hurling herself up at him, she barked right in his face then ran forward, wanting him to follow. As he did, he realised that something smelled very bad.

A small square of muddy white paper on the ground caught his eye, and he bent to pick it up. It was a black-and-white photograph that he had seen before, and it set his mind racing. Staring at it hard, he could almost hear Baba's voice telling him to check that he wasn't adding two to two and getting six instead of four, but his heart began to beat at the rate of a humming-bird's wings, and, seeming to leave his mind behind, his legs took him back through the bushes and all the way down the hill and into the Mazibukos' lounge without even wiping his feet or knocking, where Auntie Rachel took one look at him and wrapped him in her arms until he'd told her everything. Uncle Enock came home at once and organised some men from the dairy. They had to go right away, it didn't matter that it would soon be dark, and Benedict had to show them where, he was the only one who knew. But his legs didn't want to work, and Uncle Enock carried him on his back all the way up the hill. He didn't have to go into the bushes with them, though, Krishna was waiting there to show them the way, and Mavis from the other house was suddenly beside him, out of breath and holding his hand way too tight.

And when the men emerged from the undergrowth with a heavy shape entirely wrapped in a blanket and Mavis began to sob, Benedict knew for sure.

And he wanted Mama.

EIGHTEEN

NOT THE NEXT MORNING BUT THE MORNING AFTER that, Mavis opened her eyes slowly and began to focus on the wall that she was facing, curled up in her bed. There was something unusual about the wall, but she couldn't quite understand what it was. She lay still for a moment staring at it, confused.

Then it dawned on her.

The wall was bathed in light.

Sitting up quickly, she glanced around the room. Lungi's bed was neatly made and the curtain above it hung open, letting in a stream of daylight.

Eish, what time was it?

As she reached for the alarm clock that sat on the small table between her bed and Lungi's, her hand almost knocked over a bowl that was there, covered by a plate. It was after nine! Swinging her feet onto the floor, she looked under the plate. The bowl contained some *lipalish*, some green beans, a bit of meat. All of it was cold. What was it doing here?

The door opened and there was Lungi, handing her a cup of tea and telling her Madam didn't want to see her in the house today, she was giving Mavis an off. Lungi took the bowl away, it was last night's supper that Mavis hadn't woken up to eat. Mavis must stay in bed, and Lungi was going to bring her something nice for her breakfast.

But Mavis had to get up, she needed the toilet. Afterwards, she splashed cold water on her face and did her best to flatten the side of her hair that was sticking up in the air, before she went back to bed to drink her tea.

She remembered everything now.

After the men had found Petros, she had spent the whole night wandering about outside, wrapped in her blanket, shivering and weeping, trying not to sob loudly enough to wake somebody. All that time! All that time she had thought he was in Nhlangano negotiating *lobola*, meanwhile he was lying on the hill, late. Maybe for some of that time he was lying there sick, calling for help. And she hadn't heard. She hadn't known. All that time!

When morning had come, she had washed and changed, her bed still not slept in, and she had gone to work in the house. She had managed all morning, she was fine until she was cleaning the step outside the front door, the one that was painted red and needed polishing. On her knees, rubbing the step with Cobra, she had suddenly felt moved to pray for Petros, and then, without even thinking about it, she had found her prayer shifting and becoming a prayer for her own boy, and when she realised that she had never prayed for her own boy before, not even once in almost seventeen years, she had lowered her forehead to the step and started to weep.

Madam had found her there on her way out to go and pick up the children from school. Her head was still on the step and she was crouched right down, her bottom jammed up against the back wheel of *Gogo* Levine's car. Madam had called for Lungi to come and help her to take Mavis to her room, but Mavis could barely stand and *Gogo* Levine, who had been getting ready to go to her afternoon job, she had had to come and help, too.

Mavis had slept the whole afternoon and the whole night, not waking, not even once.

Now Lungi brought her a boiled egg and a slice of bread with peanut butter, and she ate hungrily. It was Madam who came to collect the plate and the mug from her tea, and she asked if Mavis didn't want the doctor. But no. Mavis wasn't sick, she was just shocked and upset from seeing Petros unexpectedly late. In any case, she didn't want Madam's doctor. Madam gave her another small bottle called Rescue, and told her to rest.

Not feeling like going straight back to sleep, and not comfortable with lying doing nothing, Mavis picked up her wool. Lately she was taking a break from crocheting to concentrate on making *umcwasho* tassels, there was a big demand for them at the market. They were quick enough to make, just simple thick bunches of long strands of wool without any knotting or knitting or crocheting, and with pompoms near the end. Mavis wasn't good with beads, but that didn't matter. Somebody she knew made the simple strings of beads for around the girls' heads, and Mavis bought them from her before adding her tassels and having her friend sell them for her at the market.

Madam had bought one of the pale blue and yellow ones directly from Mavis for Innocence, though Innocence was still a bit young. Nomsa couldn't wear *umcwasho*, it was only for girls who were still pure, and everybody could see, without asking, what the girls who didn't wear it had done. Titi had bought one of the red and black ones for herself. *Umcwasho* wasn't something for a *kwerekwere*, but Mavis wasn't going to tell her not to buy.

These nowadays everybody was talking about girls remaining pure. Mavis wished it had been like that when she was as young as Innocence. Maybe with *umcwasho* on her head she wouldn't have fallen in love and conceived. But if she still had, the boy wouldn't have been able to run away as he had, as if it was nothing to do with him. The girls in her age group would have gone to his family in their tassels and made them give a cow.

As she wove pale blue and yellow wool through the two rounds of cardboard she had cut from an empty Jungle Oats box, she thought about all the things that had brought her to collapse on Madam's front step the day before. Number one, it broke her heart in pieces that Petros was late, it was like her own boy was late for a second time. Number two, she hadn't slept for a whole night. Number three, *eish*, it was number three that had unravelled her like a fallen ball of wool and made her to weep.

Why had she never prayed for her own boy? How could that have happened? When she had gone home from the hospital without her baby, he had never been spoken about in her house, her mother and her sisters had acted as if he had never existed. Weeks before the delivery, her mother had crocheted a blanket for her baby, but when Mavis had come home from the hospital without him, she found that her mother had quickly added more squares all around it to make it bigger and to turn it into a blanket for Mavis herself.

Putting down the pompom she was making, she stretched both her hands forward and rubbed them over the central part of the blanket. Her mother had been so skilful, it wasn't possible to tell exactly where the part for the baby ended and the part for Mavis began.

Then a thought came to her, a thought that put an ache inside her heart.

Eish!

Did her boy want his blanket? Was it him waking her in the night, asking for it?

Her family had always pretended that he never existed. They had done that to protect her. She was only a child, what would talking about her loss be for?

But nobody in her family had allowed themselves to mourn, they hadn't allowed themselves to grieve. And they had never cleansed themselves of their loss. His blanket should have been burned, the ashes should have been mixed with the cleansing water. It should all have happened after just one month, and then her boy could have been released to be with their ancestors.

Eish.

When she went home for her Christmas, that was what she would do. Mavis, her mother and her sisters, they would all do what they needed to do to let her boy go.

NINETEEN

EVERYBODY WAS CLEAR ON WHAT HAD HAPPENED TO Petros: the snake had bitten him and then he had sliced it in two, most probably so that it wouldn't bite his dog, too. Krishna would have been trying to protect him by attacking it. It was a puff adder, which Uncle Enock knew for sure because he had picked up its two halves to show to the police. Benedict knew from the book that it was a lazy kind of snake that didn't like to get out of your way as most other snakes did. Its bite didn't always make a person late, but Petros was sick already and his body couldn't cope with anything more.

Benedict remembered the stormy night that he had found Krishna in the garage. Had she been trying to tell him that Petros was lying sick further up the hill? Or was he already late then? *Eh!* How could Benedict possibly have known?

The night of the day he found Petros, Grace and Faith had fussed over Benedict at supper, which he had still felt too shaky to eat, and then again at breakfast, which Baba accused him of eating like a refugee who had survived on nothing but leaves for weeks. Daniel and Moses kept asking him for more details, and he knew that they were going to be telling everybody at school the story of what their big brother had done. It

291

didn't matter to his brothers and sisters that he hadn't actually saved Petros: he was still their hero.

But it did matter to Benedict, and he didn't feel very much like a hero at all. How could he, really, when he hadn't rescued his friend while he was lying sick and hurt just up the hill? How could he feel proud of himself when his friend was late? Hurtling down the mountainside, he had been so panicked and afraid that he certainly hadn't been able to imagine himself running in slow motion dressed as a fireman or a paramedic. It had all felt too real for that.

But still, he couldn't help enjoying the attention and the praise.

He really was exhausted, though. Mama kept him home from school for two days on account of him having had a fright, and Baba said he deserved some days of rest as a reward for having been so brave. But it wasn't either of those reasons that made him glad to be staying at home. No. It was entirely because of the question that had woken him in the middle of last night.

Yesterday he had spent the whole entire day in his bed, drifting in and out of sleep. Mama had said he was worn out by shock, but she didn't know that he and Petros had been friends. She didn't understand that he was sad, that being asleep felt easier than being awake.

Uncle Enock had tried to understand. He had come to check on Benedict, sitting on his bed and asking him all about his friendship with Petros. How much time did they spend together? Did they ever play wrestling games together like Daniel and Moses played with Fortune? Had Petros ever actually coughed on him? Back when Uncle Enock was a boy, friends had sometimes made themselves brothers by cutting themselves and holding their cuts together to mix their blood. Since Petros had called Benedict *bhuti* and Benedict had wanted him to be his brother, had Benedict and Petros ever done anything like that?

Eh, it felt good to be able to talk to somebody about Petros! Uncle Enock said he would go to Nhlangano to look for Petros's girlfriend, even though he thought she might be late from being sick, or she might even be just pretend. The girl herself was real, she was in a photograph. But maybe the relationship was just a story that Petros had made up when his head wasn't right from being sick or when he was confused from his *dagga* in the same way that Titi had been confused from that biscuit. Uncle Enock said Petros had never before taken holidays to go and see the girl, he had never lent a phone from anybody at the dairy to call her, not even once.

Benedict had no trouble going to sleep that night, even after he had spent the whole entire day in his bed. But after he had sat up in the middle of the night with the question suddenly in his head, there was no going back to sleep. In the morning, he was impatient. He was impatient for the children to go off to school, and then he was impatient for Mama to start working on her cakes. Her cake students weren't coming today. They were done with their training, really, but they still came three days a week to work with Mama around the dining table on account of their new workplace not yet being ready. As soon as Mama was busy with her icing syringe and Titi was busy with her cleaning and dusting, Benedict slipped quietly out of the back door.

The shoes he had abandoned there two nights ago were still

caked with cow *kinyezi*, but it was dry now and he tapped it off quietly before slipping his feet in and tying the laces. Then he picked up the small spade that he kept out there for clearing the monkey *kinyezi* from the garden, and crawled on his hands and knees past the window of the dining area so that Mama didn't see him. Even more certain now of the danger of snakes, Mama would have told him to come back inside.

He didn't want to worry Mama, but he did have to go back up to the dam. He had to find the answer to the question that had woken him in the night, making him sit up in his bed.

Why did Petros have a spade with him?

The area around the dam was very quiet. The men had taken the cows to a different field today, there was no longer any reason for Krishna to be barking or whining there, and even the birds seemed to be holding a silent vigil. The only noise came from the traffic on the Malagwane Hill, and the quiet of the plateau made Benedict nervous.

He had worried that he might not be able to find the exact place in the bushes again, but there was a clear path now, flattened by Uncle Enock and the men from the dairy going in and then coming out again with Petros. Benedict followed the path, stamping his feet and talking loudly to himself in a deep voice so that anything that might be lying in wait would think that he was very big and had somebody else with him. Here was where he had fallen, and here was where he had found the photograph. The bad smell was gone now.

He looked around, scanning the ground for any signs of recent digging. There were none. Maybe the snake had attacked Petros before he had even started. Squatting down, he looked again. From that angle, looking back towards where he had tripped over the spade, he noticed a slight mound under some thick undergrowth just next to a tree. He might as well start there.

Shouting hymns from church now, he pulled at the branches on top of the mound to unearth them. *Eh!* They weren't growing there, they were just lying on top. He cleared them away. Then, with his small spade, he began to dig. It wasn't long before the tip of his spade struck something hard, and with his heart beating with excitement about finally finding the treasure, he hurried to clear the soil away. Whatever it was had an odd shape, and it took a long time to dig it up completely. By the time he was brushing off the last of the soil with his hands, he had moved on from hymns and had recited his way through every times table that he knew, and sweat was dripping from his forehead.

Turning it over, he stood to look at it, whistling now like Mr Levine. There were no arms, and the ends of its legs were gone, but it was definitely the figure of a small child. Was this the Indian gift that Petros's great, great ancestor had stolen from the Portuguese? It was made of stone but, like Mrs Zikalala's white plastic sandals, it still bore a few tiny patches of gold. Okay, so it had had gold on it once upon a time, but it was really just stone now. And it certainly didn't look special enough to be the kind of stone that Auntie Rachel could believe in. But Petros had thought of this as treasure! How could that be?

Benedict whistled and stomped as he thought.

Maybe if you had only one thing in the whole entire world that came from your family, maybe you could think that one thing was worth the same as gold. And maybe you could even think your girlfriend's family would accept it in place of cows for *lobola*.

Benedict looked at it carefully, trying hard to see it as valuable. Something at its neck caught his attention and he bent to examine it. It looked like a bubble of dried glue. He traced the join with his fingers. Yes, the head had been glued on to the body.

Suddenly an idea began to come to him of what it was that he had found.

What had first looked like an underpant carved onto the figure could just as well be a nappy.

Could it be...?

Eh!

Imagine if the story in the Bible wasn't true!

Imagine if King Solomon *had* cut the baby in two!

It had happened in ancient times, so long ago that the baby could easily have turned to stone, just like the slice of tree on Auntie Rachel's bookshelf.

Eh! This baby could prove that King Solomon wasn't wise after all.

How could he be wise, really, if he had followed the hoopoe's advice not to respect ladies?

Mama didn't believe it was once upon a time a baby, not even for one second. But Titi thought it was.

'The Bible tells us the baby was never cut in two,' Mama reminded them.

'But books can lie, Mama. Baba said.'

'Maybe other books can lie, Benedict, but the Bible is

the word of God. And anyway, how is a baby going to turn to stone?'

'A lady turned to salt.'

'It can be a miracle, Auntie.'

'Uh-uh.'

They sat together and talked and looked, until at last Titi and Benedict had to agree with Mama that what they had thought just didn't make sense, and that, really, it was just an old stone statue that once upon a time had been covered in gold.

Titi ran a finger over the last small traces of the gold. 'Can it be worth money, Auntie?'

Mama shrugged her shoulders and asked Benedict what he wanted to do with it.

For months he had dreamed of finding treasure, and now he had found some and it was disappointing. Okay, it wasn't a pile of gold that could stop Baba from having to work in countries all over Africa, but everything was always worth something, to somebody. Maybe it was even worth a lot. Somebody might want to buy it.

It wasn't Benedict's to sell, though, it belonged to Petros.

But Petros was late.

Eh!

At last he came to a decision: Petros's treasure must go to his grave with him. And it had to be a secret because, number one, it was always a secret for Petros, and number two, nobody could steal it if nobody knew.

There was also a number three, but Benedict didn't say: if the Bible *had* lied about King Solomon not cutting the baby in two, it was probably best that nobody else found out.

'Good boy,' Mama said, giving him a squeeze and planting a kiss on his forehead. 'Good boy.'

In the office of Ubuntu Funerals, Jabulani looked uncertain.

'I suppose it's possible,' he said. Then he smiled. 'Anything is possible, nè? But to be buried with your dog is too un-Swazi.'

'He was a *shangaan*,' said Benedict. 'From Mozambique.'

Benedict could feel Mama looking at him. She knew everything now. Okay, not everything, just that he and Petros had talked, even though he wasn't supposed to talk to Petros on account of Petros not being right in his head. But Mama couldn't say anything about that now. It wasn't right to say anything bad about the late.

'Jabulani,' said Mama, holding the bundle in her arms in the same way that she would hold a baby, 'that boy had no family except his dog. They were always together, like a brother and his small sister. Now, how would you feel if your sister was buried in the disrespectful way that a dog is buried?'

Jabulani tutted, shaking his head.

'His dog's name was Krishna,' said Benedict, 'but he called her his treasure.' He placed a hand on the bundle in Mama's arms. Titi had helped Mama to sew the statue up in the old blanket that Baba kept in the back of the red Microbus for just in case.

'His treasure,' echoed Mama, holding the bundle to her more tightly.

'They'll want to be together in Heaven, too,' said Benedict. 'Uncle Enock thinks there's a Dog Heaven and a People

Heaven, but I know there's only one Heaven for all of God's creatures. Our hoopoe is waiting for us there, Jabulani. She'll thank us both for burying her so nicely.'

Jabulani was smiling now.

'In that very beautiful casket that you made,' Mama added. 'Such excellent craftsmanship.'

'Mama and me, we knew you'd understand.'

'*Eish!* Okay, nè?'

'Thank you, Jabulani!'

'Not to mention.'

Jabulani called one of his staff over to organise for Petros's dog to go into his casket with him, and Mama mopped at her forehead with a tissue. Benedict knew it wasn't just the weight of the stone that had made her sweat. Mama always kept the secrets of her cake customers, but she didn't like having secrets of her own to keep. This was a secret that only Mama, Titi and Benedict knew.

It was the right thing to do. The treasure was all Petros had, and he had no child to give it to, no other family at all; Uncle Enock had said. Petros's only family was Krishna, who was lucky on account of not having to go and wait to be chosen at the dog orphanage: she was going to live permanently with the dairy manager. He was happy to keep a dog that was comfortable around cows, and her barking might tell him if somebody was trying to steal a cow to pay the fine.

The King had to pay the fine himself on account of breaking his new law by taking a fiancée who was only seventeen and bringing her to live at his palace. Hundreds of girls went and threw their *umcwasho* tassels at the King's mother's house to make his family feel ashamed.

The new fiancée wasn't Queenie Zikalala. Mama said Mrs Zikalala must be very disappointed, but Baba said she should be glad about not having to find more than a month's salary to buy a cow to pay the fiancée's part of the fine. Grace said, in a high-pitched voice, that this *wasn't* the year for Queenie, Mrs Tungaraza.

It was almost time for *Incwala*, the kingship ceremony that happened every year, and Uncle Enock and Vusi were starting to talk about it. In the middle of November, men had been sent on foot all the way to the coast of Mozambique to collect some of the Indian Ocean in a calabash, and when they and the other men who had been sent to rivers were all back with the waters for the king's *muti*, it would begin.

It was sacred and secret and confidential, and not even Uncle Enock knew everything that happened, even though he'd been taking part with his own age group since school. A black ox would be slaughtered to make the king's powers fresh and strong, and afterwards, when the bones of the ox were burnt, the ancestors would send rain to put out the fire and then it would be okay for everybody to eat the new harvest. Vusi was going to walk for many kilometres with other young men to gather *lusekwane* branches at night, and the elders were going to use those branches to build the special enclosure where the black ox would be slaughtered.

Benedict looked up the *lusekwane* in Uncle Enock's tree book, where it was called a sickle bush, but it didn't say anything there about what Vusi and his friends knew for sure: its branches would wither in the hands of any boy who had been naughty with a lady.

Auntie Rachel showed him a photograph of a big group of young men carrying the branches, all of them wearing just a *kanga* skirt with an apron of animal skin.

'It looks like a moving forest,' she said. 'Like Birnam Wood coming to high Dunsinane hill.'

'Sorry?'

'*Ag*, it's something that happens in a play. *Macbeth*. Soldiers carry branches to disguise themselves as a forest so they can sneak up on the king and kill him.'

Benedict was startled. 'King Mswati?'

'*Ag* no, man. It's just a story.' Leaning forward with a tissue, she wiped away a splodge of milk from either side of his upper lip.

Benedict wasn't so sure about stories: they could be just pretend, or they could be real. Uncle Enock and Auntie Rachel had said that Petros's talk of having treasure was just a story, just pretend. But it was real, he really did have treasure.

'Auntie Rachel, you know Petros?'

'*Ja?*'

'Whose ancestor is he going to be?'

'Hey?'

'He didn't have any family. Who's he going to look over?'

'*Eish.*' She shrugged. 'I guess he can be our ancestor here. And the dairy workers'.'

'And Krishna's and the cows'?'

She smiled. '*Ja*, why not?'

'So will you do the cleansing ceremony for him?'

'We haven't talked about it, but I suppose we can. But we not slaughtering a cow, hey?'

'No, it's okay, it can be just one of your chickens, and you can have a remembrance cake, too. I'd like to buy it for him from my percentage.'

'*Ag* no, that's so sweet!' Auntie Rachel looked like she might need the milk-splodge tissue for her eyes.

When the Ubuntu Remembrance and Celebration Cakes shop was ready, Benedict went with Mama and Baba to look. It was in the industrial area of Mbabane, just up the road from Ubuntu Funerals, and Zodwa and Jabulani were there to greet them and to show them around.

The front room of the shop looked more like a lounge, with several comfortable-looking chairs arranged around a coffee table. Benedict recognised the range of brightly coloured cloths covering the chairs from the roadside market in the Ezulwini Valley.

'We'll consult here,' Zodwa told them. 'People are better able to think about celebrating their loved ones when they're relaxed, nè?'

'Exactly,' agreed Mama. 'This is a very happy room.'

'For happy memories,' said Jabulani, smiling widely. 'And look!' he pointed to a screen attached to the wall, just next to the framed photograph of the king that every business had to have. 'This is our best.'

'*Eh!*'

One by one, photographs of the remembrance cakes they had already made were coming and going slowly on the screen. Mama flattened a hand against her chest. 'That makes my photo album look so old-fashioned!'

'But your photo album can work even by candle-light,' said Jabulani. 'Being modern is nice, but we cannot be modern without power.'

'Power is important,' said Zodwa. 'Change cannot come without it, nè?'

'Sometimes power cannot come without change,' said Baba.

'That is true,' said Zodwa. 'And neither can come without support, nè?'

As the grown-ups nodded, Benedict had the sense that they were talking about something more than just electricity and screens with pictures, something complicated that he wouldn't understand and should probably not ask about.

Zodwa led the way from the front room into the large kitchen behind it, where there were six ovens, each with a gas tank standing next to it. Down the middle of the room was a long table where the ladies Mama had trained were busy decorating cakes, and along one side were shelves where the cakes would sit when they were finished. While Mama chatted with the ladies and admired their cakes, Jabulani took Baba and Benedict to the far end of the room, pointing out the sinks for washing up and what he said was a kettle, though to Benedict it looked like an enormous tin can with a tap near the bottom.

'It's always hot, nè? So there can always be tea, instant-instant, without anybody who comes here needing to wait. A cup of tea plays a very important part in comforting a person.'

'*Eh*,' said Baba, 'you are sounding just like my wife!'

Jabulani grinned. 'She's a very good teacher, nè?' Then he showed them the pantry, which you could walk right into to get butter and eggs from a fridge or things like flour, sugar and icing colours from the shelves. The last room, with a toilet just off it, was a place where the staff could sit to have their break.

Mama, Baba and Benedict sat in the front room, the one that was like a comfortable lounge, to have tea with Zodwa and Jabulani. One of the ladies had made cupcakes for them. They were good, but no cake was ever going to be as good as Mama's.

'We want to thank you,' said Zodwa, spooning sugar into her cup of tea, 'all of you.'

'Yes,' said Jabulani, 'we wouldn't have this new part of the business without all of you.'

Mama smiled and Benedict beamed, but Baba said no, he deserved no thanks himself, he had done nothing.

'Pius, you are wrong,' said Zodwa, and when she saw that Baba's brow suddenly got a line across it, she said sorry, but he was very wrong. 'Benedict brought the idea,' she told Baba, 'and Angel brought the expertise. But you were a good husband and a good father. You supported them both.'

'Yes,' said Jabulani. 'You didn't have to accept having ladies in and out of your house for training.'

'*Eh*, that was not about accepting!' said Baba, folding the circle of paper his cupcake had come in. 'That was about welcoming! Angel was bored before, she had almost no customers. I was very happy to welcome a sense of purpose back into my house.'

'This new part of the business has brought a new sense of purpose to us, too,' said Zodwa. 'Before, we simply concentrated on burying the late with dignity and respect. But now we're also focusing on helping others to celebrate the lives of their late. We're helping to record why each and every one of those lives mattered.'

'And,' said Jabulani, 'we're even helping people to record why lives matter while those lives are still being lived. *Eish*, there are more and more orders for cakes that celebrate why people are important to others now, cakes that talk about what people mean to each other now before they are late.'

'Ubuntu is smiling down on us,' said Zodwa, smiling herself. 'The business he started is doing so well now.'

'Thank you,' Jabulani said to Benedict. 'The edge you brought to us is too, too good, nè?'

Then Jabulani's cell-phone rang, and he had to rush down the road to Ubuntu Funerals to sort out a delivery of wood for making caskets that was causing problems, and the Tungarazas left shortly after that when a young couple arrived full of smiles, wanting to order a cake.

On the way home, Baba pulled up outside Mr Patel's shop, just as Benedict had asked him to. Leaving Mama and Baba in the Microbus, he went inside quickly. Mrs Patel was behind the counter, where she always was. Benedict waited for her to finish with a customer who was buying a Russian and some chips before he spoke to her.

'I have something for you,' he said, reaching into the pocket of his shorts. Mrs Patel looked at him suspiciously, perhaps expecting a worm or a snail. 'I made it myself,' he said, handing her his small gift.

She examined it carefully, exploring the feel of it with a long, thin finger. He had spent a whole entire afternoon making it, an afternoon that had been full of rain and noisy, bored brothers and sisters. It wasn't as beautiful as it could have been, but it was the best he could do with what he had, which was an empty matchbox from Mrs Levine, some of the silver foil that Mama used for covering her cake-boards, and the last of the children's gold glitter.

'It's a frame,' he told her. 'You can put a small photo inside, maybe of somebody you love or somebody you miss.' He didn't want to say her son's name. She had never mentioned him to Benedict, and for Benedict to know would have meant that there was gossip. 'It can fit in your pocket or your hand-bag, then that person is always with you.'

Mrs Patel looked at the frame for a long time before she held it to her chest. 'So much of happiness you are bringing to my heart,' she whispered, and if she hadn't been looking right at Benedict as she said it, he would have thought she was talking to the photograph of Sandeep that wasn't yet inside the frame. He hoped that the happiness his gift was bringing to her heart might help it – even if just a little bit – to unbreak.

'Chilli-bites,' she said, smiling and using the hand that wasn't holding his gift to bring a plateful out from the glass cabinet on one side of the counter. 'Very nice. Fresh today, nè?'

Benedict took one, biting into the warm, spicy ball of fried batter. He chewed and swallowed before he asked his question. 'Did you bring it, Mrs Patel?'

'Yes. Yes.' Her head disappeared behind the counter, and when it popped up again she had let go of his gift and there was an envelope in her hand. With her other hand she passed Benedict a paper serviette. Finishing his treat, he wiped the chilli-bite grease from his fingers before he took the envelope from her.

'Thank you, Mrs Patel. I'll bring it back soon.'

'No, no. Keep. Keep.'

He began to thank her, but Mr Patel came in from the

back with a new load of paper bags and plastic spoons, and Mrs Patel waved Benedict out of the shop with the back of her hand.

Back on the front seat of Baba's red Microbus, Benedict slipped the envelope into Mama's handbag before securing his seatbelt.

'We were just saying,' Mama said from the seat behind, 'how proud of you we are.'

'Yes,' said Baba, easing into the Saturday afternoon traffic. 'That business we just went to, it's there entirely because of you.'

'Mama trained the ladies.'

'But why did she have ladies to train? Because you had an idea. One small idea for a unique selling point, and the result is a business that's thriving, a business that's putting food in hungry stomachs by giving people work. That is the dream of any businessman.'

'Or any businesswoman,' said Mama from behind him.

Baba seemed not to have heard her. *'Eh!* How can I see you as a small boy now that I've seen the business that you built? I'm very proud of you today, Benedict. Very proud indeed.'

'And me, *shujaa wangu,*' said Mama, reaching forward and giving his shoulder a squeeze. 'And me.'

All the way back down the Malagwane Hill, Benedict felt like he really was Mama's hero, and Baba's too. His chest swelled with pride. Baba had compared him with a grown-up businessman! Now that he had started a business, he must surely be big.

Surely he could do it now?

He was certainly ready to try.

Saying that he felt like visiting Auntie Rachel's chickens, he asked Baba to drop him at the beginning of the driveway. Mrs Levine happened to be driving out just as they got there, and as the red Microbus had to stop outside the farm gate for Mrs Levine's pale blue Corolla to pass through first, that was where Benedict got out. Baba drove Mama up the hill, leaving Benedict behind to watch the red Microbus disappearing around the bend beyond the shed.

Now he had to manage, otherwise he would never get home.

He looked at the cattle-grid.

The more he looked at it, the more it began to look like a gate that was lying on the ground, a gate that had been pushed over.

An upright gate said keep out, but lying down it said welcome, come in. It looked a bit like a bridge that wanted to make it safe for him to get from here to there.

The metal bars of the grid were really so close together. Surely he couldn't possibly be small enough to fall through the gaps?

Two of his fingers began to cross, but he stopped them, certain that he didn't need their help.

Holding his breath, he ran quickly across the bars.

Eh!

It was so easy!

He turned round and walked back over them, then danced back across them again. Grinning widely, he began to walk slowly up the long driveway, stopping every few steps to turn and look back at what he had done.

Tomorrow he would walk along the narrow bridge to the

just-in-case pump in the middle of the dam. He knew he was big enough to do that now, he no longer had to stand and look at it from the edge of the dam like one of the little ants that wanted to get to the jar of honey in the middle of the dish of water. He would stand there in the centre of the dam and turn round slowly, slowly, slowly, taking in how all the things he knew from the edge looked from the middle.

Turning again to look back down the hill, he wondered how long it was going to take the cows to understand that the cattle-grid was really just the same as a pushed-over gate. It would mean trouble for Uncle Enock if they ever did, so Benedict would never say.

Because he kept turning back to see how far he'd come, it took him a long time to make his way all the way up to the house. When he got there, Mama was sitting on one of the couches looking at a magazine. His brothers and sisters were down at the other house, and Baba and Titi were both in their bedrooms taking a nap. Benedict decided he would tell Mama that all this time he'd been afraid of falling through the gaps in the cattle-grid, and that now he was too big to be afraid. He went to sit next to her.

She smiled at him. 'Your envelope from Mrs Patel is there,' she said, pointing to the dining table.

'Thank you, Mama.'

'Are you going to tell me what's inside it?'

'Uh-uh. Not yet.'

'Okay.'

'Mama, you know the cattle-grid at the gate?'

But Benedict could say no more to Mama, because a quiet knocking sound began to reach them from the kitchen. Was

309

somebody knocking to come in there? They both went to look, and Mama opened the back door.

Mavis was standing there with a blanket of bright squares draped over her arm and a Cobra floor-polish tin in her hands. 'Sorry to disturb, nè? I want to ask, can I come for ordering a cake? A cake for somebody late?'

While Mama spoke to Mavis on one of the couches, Benedict settled at the dining table to concentrate on the cake for the cleansing ceremony that was about Petros. He had known so little about him, very little more than the story about his treasure. But the cake couldn't say anything about the treasure, on account of the treasure being a secret that nobody was allowed to know.

Inside the envelope from Mrs Patel was a piece of card the size of one of the pictures in Mama's photo album, and on it was a smaller version of the picture of the god called Krishna on Mr Patel's wall. Benedict was going to ask Mama to make a cake that looked like that picture. Okay, Petros wasn't an Indian somebody, and he didn't believe in the Indian people's gods. But Petros and this god both loved cows, and Petros's dog and this god both had the same name, so it seemed a really good choice.

On the couch, Mavis was asking Mama to make a cake decorated like her blanket for the cleansing ceremony that was about her long-ago baby boy. It was the middle part of her blanket that was important.

It was the middle part of Benedict's picture that was important, too. All the trees around the edges didn't matter so much, and they could maybe go around the sides of the cake. Mama could make them look more like the trees that grew on their hill. It was the figure of the god that was important. Mama would need to make some parts simpler, and he wanted her to add a golden dog next to the cow that lay at his feet. She could make the young man's face brown instead of blue, and she could leave out the flute, on account of it being Petros's own voice that had called the cows. The really important part was the gold trouser and matching shirt that the god was wearing. That part was about the secret stone treasure that Petros had valued as much as real gold.

Eh, Mama was going to love doing all the colours and brushing on plenty of her Dusting Powder (Gold).

TWENTY

Mrs LEVINE WAS MAKING A PARTY FOR BENEDICT'S whole family. Baba said she shouldn't, on account of the Tungaraza family not needing a party, but Mama said she should, on account of a party being exactly what the Tungaraza family needed. Mama said they had many things to have a party about, not to mention that they needed the chance to say goodbye to all their new friends.

School had already finished for the year, so Benedict was happy that Mrs Levine's party was going to give him the chance to be with Giveness and Sifiso one last time. The Tungarazas were going to travel home to Tanzania to meet Josephine straight after Christmas, but they didn't yet know where they would go to from there. Baba had some new jobs to choose between but he hadn't chosen yet, it still depended. Anyway, Baba had said he was going to take all of them to the clinic for tests just as soon as they got home. They were all going to have their blood checked and their chests looked at, so they were all going to be fit and healthy and strong enough to go absolutely anywhere at all.

Very early in the morning, Mrs Levine brought Samson to dig a hole in the Tungarazas' garden. Samson said it wasn't right to dig up any of the grass, he should rather dig it at the side of the house, near the lucky-bean tree.

'Please not there, Mrs Levine!'

'*Ag* Bennie, man, don't be bloody difficult. What's wrong with there?'

'It's a holy place, Mrs Levine, King Solomon's queen is buried there!'

Mrs Levine looked at him as if he wasn't right in his head, like people used to look at Petros, but she looked around for somewhere else. 'There,' she said, pointing to the hedge of yesterday, today and tomorrow bushes. 'Just in front of that. The grass isn't good there anyway. Okay, Samson?'

'*Yebo*, Madam.'

When the long hole was ready, Samson filled it with wood and the sheets of newspaper that Benedict and his brothers had scrunched into balls, setting it all alight with Mrs Levine's matches. Then Samson helped Mrs Levine to put up some poles at either end of it for the spit that was going to roast a whole entire lamb. A spit was nothing to do with the kind of spitting Petros used to do. No. It was a long metal stick that could turn meat round and round over a fire so that every side of it got cooked.

Mrs Levine had said it was best to have the party at the Tungarazas' on account of Auntie Rachel not wanting a whole entire animal cooking in her own garden, but Benedict knew it was because Mrs Levine was busy marking her territory. When the Tungarazas left, Mrs Levine was going to live in their house. She had already done a bit of gardening there, like an animal moving onto new territory and putting its own scent everywhere to say this is my place, I live here.

She could charge for her speech therapy now, on account of using some of Mr Levine's money to get a work visa much more quickly than it usually took – though the children she had already started to help for free before her visa, those children still didn't have to pay. She was still going to help children in their homes after school in the afternoons, and on Saturdays she was going to have group classes right here in the house. The TV was going to go into her bedroom and the long lounge and dining room was going to look like a classroom.

The poles for the spit were only just up when Uncle Enock's bakkie pulled in to the garage and he came up to the garden with the skinned lamb slung across his wide shoulders. The lamb's head wasn't joined to its body, it was still in the back of the bakkie. Uncle Enock was going to ask Lungi to put it in the fridge, and Samson could take it when he went home for his Christmas. There was wood in the bakkie, too, and Samson must bring it and place it neat-neat next to the fire.

When the long pole with the wind-up handle on the end had gone right through the lamb and Uncle Enock and Samson had secured it with wire and balanced it across the poles at either end of the fire, Benedict challenged Daniel and Moses to try turning it, while Mrs Levine watched nervously. Neither of them could, it was just too heavy. Benedict pretended that he couldn't either, so they both helped him, and together they managed.

'Now you lot stay away from the fire, hey? I don't want any bloody accidents.'

The lamb was going to need turning every now and so often, and that was Samson's job. It was going to be hours of work in the sun, so the sleeves of Samson's blue overall were rolled up high, and a hat sat on his head. Lungi was doing most of the other cooking at the other house, and when the party started, Mavis was going to come and do cleaning.

Titi wasn't going to do any work that day, it was her party, too. She put on her pretty dress, the new one she had been wearing when the family picked her up in Mwanza after her last Christmas there. The blue, green and pink of it looked even more beautiful with the red and black of her *umcwasho* tassels. Benedict wanted to wear his suit, but he hadn't worn it since the special Easter Sunday service at Mater Dolorosa, and it really didn't fit him any more.

'The trouser is okay,' said Titi, turning him round and looking at him carefully.

'But look how short!'

'No, it's okay. Just wear it with a white socks, it's the fashion here.'

The jacket was much too small, but the waistcoat was okay, as long as he didn't try buttoning it. Baba helped him with his tie.

'You look very smart, my boy. You *are* very smart. Smart outside and in.'

Benedict stood straighter, his chest swelling. But that put a strain on his shirt buttons, so he relaxed again. Baba didn't know about Benedict wanting to help him by finding some gold: Benedict had never said. He knew that if he told Baba now, Baba would squeeze his shoulder and say that his eldest boy had started a business and knew what he wanted to be in his life, and that was richness enough for any man.

Benedict knew that not finding any gold didn't matter at all, not really.

But still.

Mama looked beautiful! She wore her emerald-green silk dress that had shiny jewels around its neckline, her hair was big with large, soft curls, and her lips were shiny and red with lipstick. The girls looked pretty too, and even the boys managed to look neater, a little less scruffy.

By the time the guests began to arrive in the early afternoon, the lamb smelled delicious! In between turning it, Samson sat on a chair in the shade of the lucky-bean tree, with Lungi making sure he didn't get too hot by taking him cans of coke from the sink outside the back door, the cement sink where Titi always washed their clothes, only Mrs Levine had filled it with ice and cans of drink. The front part of the Tungarazas' dining table was bright with bowls and plates of snacks, and underneath the cloth covering the back part were things to eat with the lamb when it was ready: the biggest bowl of lettuce, tomato and cucumber Benedict had ever seen, some potatoes covered in a creamy sauce, freshly cooked beetroot with slices of onion, green beans in spices, grated cabbage with grated carrot, and little cubes of cheese.

Wrapped in silver foil in a bowl on the kitchen counter, onions waited to go into the fire under the lamb, while wrapped in silver foil inside Mama's gas oven, long, thin loaves of bread filled with butter and garlic waited to be heated when it was time. On top of Mama's oven, a huge pot of water waited to be boiled for making *ugali*, and a pot full of Lungi's spicy tomato and onion sauce was ready for re-heating.

The first vehicle to come up the driveway was Mr Simelane's Buffalo Soldiers van. Benedict wanted to run down the steps to say hello, but Mama and Baba said that wouldn't be right. It was Mrs Levine's party, she should be the one to greet guests. Benedict went to find her. She was at the window in Mama and Baba's bedroom with a tape measure and a notebook. She put them down on the windowsill and, picking up her drink, she led the way out of the house and down the steps, the ice cubes clinking in her glass as Benedict followed.

As well as Sifiso, Mr and Mrs Simelane had brought Giveness and his aunt. *Eh*, Benedict was so happy to see them!

'*Eish*, Benedict, you look smart, nè?'

'Thank you, Mr Simelane.' Benedict noticed that Mr Simelane's trouser was also a little short above his own white socks. Titi was right. It really didn't matter.

Giveness's aunt was untangling her shawl from one of the spokes of Giveness's umbrella. 'Something is smelling too nice!'

'There's a whole lamb cooking!' Benedict told her excitedly.

'*Eish!*'

'*Ag*, come up and get something to drink, hey.'

The next people up the steps were the bigger Mazibuko children, followed a few minutes later by the smaller ones with Uncle Enock and Auntie Rachel. Soon after that, some of Baba's work colleagues arrived, together with their families. And by the time the Ubuntu Funerals van brought Zodwa, Mrs Patel and three of the cake ladies, Mavis already had many glasses to wash in Mama's sink.

Mrs Patel looked different. She was dressed for the party in beautiful swirls of orange and yellow, with part of her stomach showing. Maybe part of her stomach showed every day, Benedict didn't know. He had never before seen her without the high counter of Mr Patel's shop in front of her. She had brought with her a big plastic container of warm, spicy samoosas, which Lungi emptied onto a plate and placed with the other snacks on the dining table.

Benedict had invited both Mr and Mrs Patel, though in truth he was just being polite and he only wanted Mrs Patel there. Mr Patel was a little frightening, with his funny hair and his mouth that wouldn't smile. Okay, he was doing good things, keeping drugs away from schoolchildren, but *eh*, it was like sharp pieces were sticking out of him, and Benedict didn't feel like getting close. He had guessed that Mr Patel wouldn't be able to come on account of somebody needing to be in the shop, and he was glad to be right.

He even managed to be a little glad that Jabulani and the rest of the cake ladies weren't able to come on account of being busy with orders. That meant that business was good. The cake ladies who did come brought a box with them. It had a secret inside it, and nobody was allowed to look, not yet. Mrs Levine made Mavis stand on a chair to put it on top of the fridge, where it would sit until it was time.

Together with Giveness and Sifiso, Benedict made a point of going to each of Baba's work colleagues and their wife or their husband, one by one. 'I'm Benedict,' he said to each of them, shaking them by the hand like a grown-up, 'Dr Tungaraza's eldest boy. This is my friend Giveness, and my other friend can introduce himself.'

'I'm Sifiso. Sifiso Simelane.' Each time he said it, all three of them grinned. Every *sss* was perfect.

Together with Lungi, Mrs Levine made sure that nobody was ever left with an empty glass or an empty throw-away cup. First she told the children to get stuck in to the snacks, then she told them to stop or they wouldn't be able to eat any lamb.

'Is there cake?' Sifiso asked Benedict in a whisper, his eyes darting around the table.

Benedict shrugged. 'I don't know. Mama wasn't allowed to do anything, it's all Mrs Levine.' He imagined a cake sitting on the large table in the kitchen of the other house. Auntie Rachel or Lungi would have made it from a box, and all the Tungarazas were going to have to pretend that it was nice.

Leaving Sifiso and Giveness to eat cashew nuts sprinkled with *pilipili*, Benedict went looking for Nomsa. She was in the garden, talking with Vusi.

'So you'll live here, with *Gogo* Levine?' She didn't look happy.

'Uh-uh, I'll still be at home for meals and sleeping. But I'll have my own study-room here, with a desk. I can stay here late as I like with my books.'

'That's nice.' Nomsa didn't look very sure. 'But you'll be with us for meals?'

Vusi nodded. 'I promise, nè?'

'Good.'

It sounded to Benedict like they'd finished talking about that and he wouldn't be interrupting if he spoke now.

'Nomsa, you know my hoopoe?'

'Mm?'

'I don't know what Mrs Levine is planning to do with the garden. Can you help me with siSwati asking Samson never to dig under the tree? It's her grave, he mustn't dig up her casket.'

Vusi made a strange face. 'What are you talking about?'

Benedict told him all about it, and then he showed Vusi and

Nomsa exactly where it was, and together they called Samson over and explained everything to him. A little way into hearing it, Samson took off his hat respectfully, and Benedict knew that he understood and that King Solomon's queen was always going to be safe.

Then Mrs Levine shouted that the lamb was ready, and everybody came to watch and clap as Uncle Enock carved off pieces, putting them on a big tray that Lungi held for him, while Mrs Levine used a long, metal spoon to dig the blackened silver onions out of the hot coals.

Their plates loaded, Benedict, Giveness and Sifiso sat to eat in the shade that the sun was making with the house. They began to talk about what they were going to be, and Benedict told them he was going to be a game ranger.

'*Eish*, with a rifle?' A splodge of garlicky butter rested on Giveness's upper lip.

'Only for just in case,' said Benedict. 'I'm not going to shoot any animals.'

Sifiso said he was starting to think about being a teacher, but Giveness wasn't thinking anything yet.

'You could be a game ranger, too,' suggested Benedict, unwrapping the foil from his onion.

'With *my* skin? Out in the sun all day?'

As Giveness rolled his eyes, Sifiso began to giggle.

'What?'

'Giveness with his umbrella in one hand and a rifle in the other!'

Benedict giggled, too. 'Say a lion comes and Giveness has to shoot it, then he gets confused. He aims his umbrella at the lion—'

'I shoot the sky with my rifle!'

They began to laugh, and giddy with excitement at the amount of food, dizzy with the excitement of no more school and Christmas coming in just three days, they couldn't stop. Benedict knew that if anybody asked him tomorrow, or even tonight, what it was they were laughing about, he wouldn't be able to say. They began laughing at something, and then they went on to laugh at nothing and everything, and they laughed so much that other people came to sit with them to try to find out what was funny. Grace, Faith Innocence, Nomsa, all of them came, and soon all of them were laughing, too. Then Titi came with Mrs Patel, and in no time Titi was reaching into the neckline of her dress for a tissue to wipe her eyes, and Mrs Patel's bare stomach was jiggling and she was throwing back her head and showing the gap where the teeth were missing from her dentures.

Afterwards, after Mavis had cleared away all the plates, Mrs Levine asked Uncle Enock to get down the box from on top of the fridge, the box with the secret inside it. Everybody gathered to look as Uncle Enock put it on the dining table and Zodwa opened it.

Eh! It was a cake, and it was Mama's oven! People looked at the cake, then they went into the kitchen to look at Mama's oven, then they came back again to look at the oven-cake sitting on the dining table.

'*Eish!*'

'Exact-exact, nè?'

'*Ag*, even that silver nut where the knob is missing!'

'Ooh, nè?

The cake ladies beamed and Mama took off her glasses and

wiped her eyes with a tissue, and Zodwa told everybody that Mrs Levine had ordered a cake to remember the family by, and they had chosen the oven because everybody who knew the Tungarazas had tasted cake from that oven. One of Baba's colleagues said that was true, and everybody else agreed and looked around to see that everybody else was nodding.

Benedict had spent a long time worrying how people would ever celebrate Mama with a cake. It would have to be a cake about cake, but how could anybody make a cake about cake without it just looking like a cake? The oven-cake was perfect. And even though it had come out of a box, it wasn't the kind of box that a cake from the other house would have come out of. It was a proper cake, made with proper flour and eggs and butter and sugar. It was almost as delicious as Mama's own cake, but not quite.

After the cake, while Mrs Simelane was still wiping some of it off Sifiso's face, Benedict slipped off to his bedroom and changed from his suit into a T-shirt and a pair of shorts. He had promised Mama that he wouldn't take anybody up to the dam before the meal was over, and that he wouldn't go in his smart suit and spoil it. Okay, the suit was too small for him now, but it was still good, it could still go to another boy.

He gathered Giveness and Sifiso, but he couldn't see Nomsa. He would find her in a moment. Meanwhile, as his two friends stood outside the kitchen door, he sat on the small step there, putting on his old pair of shoes.

'There's a bridge at the dam,' he told them. 'We can walk along it right to the middle.'

Giveness looked excited. 'We can stand in the middle of the water?'

'Mm.'

Sifiso was a little giddy with sugar after too much cake. '*Eish!* Can we shout out our names there?'

Benedict smiled. 'Yes! Let's do that.'

Nomsa came round from the far side of the house as Benedict stood up from the steps. 'We're going to the dam,' he told her. 'Do you want to come? There are still some nests.'

'We're going to stand in the middle and shout our names,' said Giveness.

Nomsa smiled. 'Okay,' she said.

Inside the kitchen, washing up at the sink, Mavis heard the children talking. *Eish,* a name was a very important thing. The remembrance cake for her boy, the cake that Titi's madam had finished making just that morning, was safely inside the wardrobe in the room she shared with Lungi. After church tomorrow morning, Doctor was going to drive her with it to where her mother lived on the far side of Manzini. She would have one week for her Christmas, and then she would come back and Lungi would go for hers. Mavis's sisters were going to be waiting for her with their mother, and together they were going to cleanse themselves of the loss of her baby boy and let him go. The ancestors would know who he was, the ancestors knew everything. But how would her boy know who he was? He had been pulled from her belly already late, and they had never given him a name. They had never spoken about him, what would a name have been for? *Eish!* When she finished here, when everything was clean and nice, she would phone her mother and ask her to speak to the priest. They would give

her boy a name before they let him go. He would have a name
to know himself by. He would have a name to shout into the
world.

Benedict led the way up to the dam, going more slowly than
he usually did on account of Giveness's umbrella catching in
bushes and needing Nomsa to free it, and on account of
Benedict practising at being a game ranger by pointing things
out and stopping to tell his friends about them. There was a
bird's nest high up in a tree near the water-tank, and close by
there was a large spider's nest with a small spider in it. He
didn't know what kind it was, but they all looked at it carefully, and Nomsa said she would look it up in Uncle Enock's
spider book. Benedict couldn't help hoping that his new sister
Josephine was going to be the kind of girl who would know
about looking something up in a spider book.

Giveness was nervous of getting spider-web all over his
umbrella, and Sifiso teased him by pretending there was a big
spider sitting right on top of it. Then they all laughed and said
sss because Sifiso had said spider, and then Benedict and
Nomsa said *shh* because soon they would come out of the trees
onto the plateau and they mustn't make noise that would
scare away birds.

For the last few steps they were as silent as they could be.
Leading them, Benedict broke from the trees first, but quiet as
he was, his movement startled a bird into flight – not from a
tree, but from the ground to the side of the dam. It flew up
and away, then it circled back and flew towards him.

Eh! It was a hoopoe!

As he held his breath and watched it flying directly above him, its beautiful black and white wings seemed to move in slow motion, with every beat almost meeting below its cinnamon body as if it was clapping silently.

Benedict imagined it was the same one he had buried so respectfully. Maybe it had come from Heaven, just to thank him.

Then he caught his breath as a new thought came to him. Imagine if it had come to show him where King Solomon had hidden all his gold!

Eh!

Imagine.

How a statue of the Indian god, Krishna, came to be buried deep in the mountains of Swaziland is a puzzle which will probably never be solved. The head·was unearthed at the entrance to the Mlawula gorge in the Lubombo mountains during the building of the Swaziland-Maputo railway line in the early sixties. There is a body as well, this may have been found with the head, accounts vary.

Although reliably identified as a late 18th or early 19th century statue of Krishna from eastern India, its presence in Swaziland cannot be explained.

The statue was never put in the hands of the Swaziland authorities (there were no relevant authorities in the colonial early sixties).

Its present whereabouts are as mysterious as its past.

A Traveller's Guide to Swaziland
Bob Forrester

POSTSCRIPT

IN AUGUST 2005, KING MSWATI OFFICIALLY ABANDONED the anti-AIDS campaign obliging girls to wear *umcwasho* tassels and to practise abstinence. Only four of its intended five years had passed, during which the king himself had ignored it, his teenage daughters had flouted it, and many girls in urban areas had refused to participate in it.

Swaziland continues to have the highest rate of HIV/AIDS in the world.